MW01402429

HUNDRED to ONE

by

Freya Barker

For Holly
Life won't wait!
Love,
Freya B.

'HUNDRED TO ONE' (Cedar Tree #2)

TABLE OF CONTENTS

TABLE OF CONTENTS	3
HUNDRED TO ONE	5
DEDICATION	7
ACKNOWLEDGEMENTS	8
PROLOGUE	10
CHAPTER ONE	13
CHAPTER TWO	26
CHAPTER THREE	38
CHAPTER FOUR	52
CHAPTER FIVE	65
CHAPTER SIX	75
CHAPTER SEVEN	87
CHAPTER EIGHT	97
CHAPTER NINE	107
CHAPTER TEN	119
CHAPTER ELEVEN	128
CHAPTER TWELVE	137
CHAPTER THIRTEEN	149
CHAPTER FOURTEEN	161
CHAPTER FIFTEEN	171
CHAPTER SIXTEEN	180
CHAPTER SEVENTEEN	191
CHAPTER EIGHTEEN	201
CHAPTER NINETEEN	215
CHAPTER TWENTY	229

CHAPTER TWENTY-ONE	**242**
CHAPTER TWENTY-TWO	**253**
CHAPTER TWENTY - THREE	**263**
CHAPTER TWENTY-FOUR	**278**
CHAPTER TWENTY-FIVE	**291**
CHAPTER TWENTY-SIX	**308**
CHAPTER TWENTY-SEVEN	**319**
CHAPTER TWENTY-EIGHT	**329**
CHAPTER TWENTY-NINE	**342**
CHAPTER THIRTY	**351**
CHAPTER THIRTY-ONE	**362**
CHAPTER THIRTY-TWO	**370**
CHAPTER THIRTY-THREE	**379**
EPILOGUE	**393**
ABOUT THE AUTHOR	**399**

Freya Barker

HUNDRED TO ONE

(Cedar Tree, Book Two)

Copyright © 2014 Margreet Asselbergs as Freya Barker

All rights reserved.

No part of this publication may be reproduced, distributed, or transmitted in any form or by any means, including photocopying, recording, or by other electronic or mechanical methods, without the prior written permission of the author or publisher, except in the case of brief quotations embodied in used critical reviews and certain other non-commercial uses as permitted by copyright law. For permission requests, write to the author, mentioning in the subject line:

"Reproduction Request" at the address below:

freyabarker.writes@gmail.com

This book is a work of fiction and any resemblance to any person or persons, living or dead, any event, occurrence, or incident is purely coincidental. The characters and story lines are created and thought up from the author's imagination or are used fictitiously.

ISBN: 978-0-9938883-1-1

Cover Design:
Rebel Edit & Design

Cover Model:
Steve Gehrke

Photographer:
Ivan Avila

DEDICATION

To the three most important women in my life.
The heroes of my existence:
My mother, my sister Maaike, and my amazing daughter Sanne.

Each in their own way, they have taught me that within each of us lies an endless supply of strength;
a bottomless resource that helps us endure, overcome, and face the world with an open mind and heart.

I love you all so much.

ACKNOWLEDGEMENTS

This time I have to start with my Mark. The man is a virtual Saint, I swear. He puts up with mood and lack of communication for days… No, weeks on end, because I constantly have my eyes glued to one or other screen, my fingers whipping across a keyboard. Admonishing fingers sticking up in the air, warning him not to interrupt my train of thought. A lesser man would have long tossed my behind to the curb. And even if he can't remember the names of my books, let alone know their content, his silent evidence of support shows in the way he makes sure the house is taken care of; the fridge is filled and the occasional meal is cooked. You are exactly what I need.

The unbelievably generous women who have volunteered their time to read and critique my writings; my beta-readers, are an invaluable group. In no specific order: Linda, Deb, Catherine, Bonnie, Sam, Pam, Lena and Sarah.

They make sure that by the time I send a manuscript to my editor, it is as clean as nine people with varied levels of experience can get it! I ask that they are brutally honest with their feedback, and they honor me with their trust when they do nothing less than that. These women also make up part of Freya's Barks & Bites, a group that works hard to help me brainstorm, vent, decide, laugh, ogle, and most of all support. Nancy, Deb, Linda, Pam, Catherine, Kerry-Ann, Aimee, Tracy – you are always ready to pimp and promote whenever an opportunity comes along and I am so very grateful for that.

Then there are many author friends who have taken time out of their own busy writing schedules to help me along; DM Earl, Mel Stringer, Brook Greene, Ava Manello, Elle Raven, Jaci J. and there are many more who should be on this list, which would make it a virtual 'Who's Who' of what is right and beautiful in the world of the Indie writer!!

Deb Blake and Pam Buchanan who have worked very hard behind the scenes to keep my blog, Ripe For Reader going strong, while I have been busy focusing my energies on writing, and all that comes with it. Without these girls I would have had to make choices I am not ready to make at this point.

Linda Funk, my muse for Arlene and my 'twin'. A character so colorful and special, it was impossible not to write a character with her in mind. Besides, she is better than any spellcheck software on offer.

Steve Gehrke and Ivan Avila, whose joint artistry brought my vision for Seb alive, long before his story was completely written down.

And once again I have kept my editor, my partner, and my close friend Dana Hook for last. I have no choice. By the time I get here in my dedication and acknowledgements, I am a blubbering puddle.
Anyone who has had the privilege of working with Dana knows that she doesn't only put all her knowledge and care into her work, but more importantly... her entire heart and soul.
By the time she is done with my books, I know they mean as much to her as they do to me. She digs herself in *that* deep. There simply isn't any way I could leave my stories in anyone else's hands. Dana, from the bottom of my heart... if you ever leave me, I will hunt you down!!

PROLOGUE

I feel strong hands massaging my back, slowly working on the knots in my sore muscles. Thumbs are pressing down right beside my spine, easing their way up to my neck until I can feel myself slowly begin to relax.

I know it's him because I can smell him; a combination of yeast from the bread he insists on baking himself. Bacon fat from this morning's breakfast and always that hint of cloves that hangs around him, which is something I've never quite been able to figure out. I have to fight not to lean back into his body.

Those skillful hands I've observed many times with the colorful tattoos that come down all the way from his shoulders to where they almost reach his fingertips, have made their way to my neck. I can't really help the deep groan that escapes me. It feels so good.

"How's that?"

"Mmmmm. Don't stop."

He chuckles and I can feel him moving closer as the heat from his body spreads over my back. I have no idea why I let him touch me like this; why I let him slide his hands in my hair and move my head forward while he licks and bites at my neck. I just don't have it in me to fight this attraction – this draw – between us anymore. It's been building for months and now I just want his hands and mouth everywhere.

His body is pressing into me and I can feel the hard ridge of his cock against my back when suddenly he grabs a handful of my hair and yanks my head back. My heart stops dead in my chest and I can't make a sound.

I am back in that dirty old bungalow with the dead man on the kitchen floor… All I can see is blood – his blood and mine. Someone is holding me by the hair and my head is being slammed into the floor. Each time my head hits, my eyes close and I can remember another time – another man – before I'm pulled up and slammed down again.

The next thing that I remember is waking up with his body on top of mine as he moves and grunts in pleasure. I thank God as I gratefully pass out again.

CHAPTER ONE

I'm cold and shaking on the floor, but this time it's different. I am in a different place and something feels off. My stomach hurts so bad… Wait! Who is laughing? Oh no, it's him. It's my miserable ex…

"No. Fuck, no. Not again."

"It's ok. Calm down, you're alright." The voice is deceptively calm but it doesn't fit the sight of my ex-husband so I continue to fight with everything I have.

"Arlene! Stop fighting me. Wake up!"

Damn if that woman isn't scraping layers of skin off my arms. I can barely keep my face out of her reach. That must have been one hell of a dream for her to go wild like this.

I was preoccupied with the early dinner prep in the kitchen. I hadn't noticed her slipping into her office but when those soft whimpers and cries started coming out of the little space beside the large industrial fridge Arlene likes to call her 'domain', I knew it was her. Damn. She hasn't been sleeping again. Being stubborn as hell, she won't take anything to help her and she falls all over herself during the day trying to stay awake, sneaking off at times trying to catch a few. Every time I try to say something she bites my head off.

"Wha – Seb? What the hell are you doing in here?"

"Sounded like you were having a nightmare, Arlene. Heard you yelling so I came to check on you."

She looks at me through squinted eyes as if I'm making this shit up so I throw my hands up in surrender and head back into the kitchen; My domain.

"Suit yourself, Arlene. I was just trying to help, and for the record, you're a mess. You don't sleep. You're even crankier than usual, and yesterday you had the new girl, Julie, in tears. You won't allow anyone close enough to help, but dammit… start helping yourself!"

It's probably the most I've ever said in to anyone but I've had it. I care for the woman.

Probably more than I should.

I drop my head on my desk when Seb backs out. Jesus. I know I'm a mess but I sure as hell don't need him to point it out. I've been taking care of myself for a good few years now and the fact that I'm still here shows I can't be too bad at it, or at least that's what I tell myself. I just wish I could get a good night's sleep then maybe these damn nightmares would stop. I'm just so tired.

Deep down I know there is more to it than that, but I'm working hard to convince myself otherwise. I'm just not ready to go there yet. I hate that Seb makes me feel vulnerable, something I particularly do not enjoy given how that has worked for me in the past. Vulnerability gets you hurt.

"Arlene, you in there?" I push myself up to go out there and see what's up. On the other side of the counter is Caleb, a fantastically beautiful and large Native American man who has won a permanent spot in my heart since he and the rest of the GFI team managed to prevent me from being mangled in a car compressor a few months back.

"Hey gorgeous. How've you been?" His bold and stern features soften when he breaks out into a smile.

"I'm alive. How about you? Decided yet whether you are joining GFI permanently and move here?"

"Not yet. Still rounding off some jobs and checking in on Katie. She's been moved into a rehabilitation center."

"Yeah, I heard that. I understand she has to relearn a whole bunch of stuff?"

"Her large motor skills are coming along but the fine muscle control is still a challenge. She still struggles with cognitive functioning, but she's determined to resume her job. She'll have to retake a lot of her certifications after having suffered a brain injury that severe, especially with the loss of function she's had, but she's a hard-headed woman." His eyes are as animated as I've ever seen them when he talks about Katie. Pretty sure there is something brewing under that stone surface somewhere, but I know it's a complicated history.

"Let me get you something to eat and you can tell me what brought you to town this time." When I turn around to pour him a coffee, I can see Seb right by the kitchen island, glaring at me. His normally lush lips are a tight line. What the crap have I done now? With a curt shake of his head he turns around and focuses on the grill. Whatever.

I look over my shoulder at Caleb to get his order and catch him looking pointedly back and forth between Seb and myself. He has a tiny smirk on his face and has obviously noticed the odd exchange but I just shrug my shoulders. I don't have the time or the patience to figure out what everyone else has their panties in a bunch over… I'm having a hard enough time untangling my own.

"What's Seb making for the early dinner menu?" Caleb asks.

"Why don't you ask him yourself?" I have no interest in wading into the storm I saw brewing in Seb's eyes just now. I have enough shit of my own to muddle through and not enough energy to deal with it all.

"No problem. I'll check in with the chef." Caleb says and

slips around the counter into the kitchen.

I busy myself wiping down the counters, refilling condiments and seasonings so Julie can put them back out onto the tables for the dinner crowd as soon as she gets here, which should be shortly… hopefully. She's been late a few times already and I really don't want to have to start looking for help again. There are pretty slim pickings these days and when she is here, she works hard but I have to be able to rely on her.

Every so often I glance into the kitchen where Caleb is comfortably leaning against the workstation next to the grill where Seb is focused on cooking. Caleb appears to be doing all the talking 'cause all I can see from Seb is the odd shake or nod of his head. Finally after ten minutes or so, Caleb comes sauntering back around the counter and sits down on the stool where I'd set his coffee.

"Probably cold now." I tell him, "Let me warm it up for you. I just made a fresh pot."

"Thanks." He says as I freshen it up and watch him add cream and stir it in.

"So you never told me why you're back in Cedar Tree?"

"Finalizing some details on the case against Will Flemming." I can feel his eyes observing me at his mention of that name. I instantly feel bile rise from my stomach and me knees almost buckle.

19

Caleb's hand shoots out and grabs me firmly by the arm.

"Need to sit down there, Arlene?"

Pressing my lips together tightly I shake my head no. Not wanting to let on how much that bastard's name affects me, I pull myself from his grasp, grab the dishcloth and go over the counters again, just to keep my shaking hands busy. Fuck. I thought I was over this.

It has been months since Kara, Emma's daughter, and I were kidnapped as a way to get to Emma. My head injury had healed but the rest of me I wasn't too sure about. I couldn't remember a lot of what happened the night we were held captive. The man who held us turned out to be the brother of Emma's boyfriend Gus, the owner of GFI, the investigative company that was after the crime lord that was hounding Emma.

Will Flemming, Gus' deranged brother was a man hell-bent on getting revenge on his brother for the pivotal role he played in getting Will locked up for years. By taking Kara and I, he lured Gus and Emma into a trap, but he hadn't counted on the shit storm that hit him when Gus' friends showed up to the party, just in time to haul Kara and I out of the already partially flattened vehicle. Caleb had been the one to lead that charge and managed to prevent Will from killing my friends. Of course, the bastard had already done his damage to me.

Caleb was already on a short fuse because he had just spent time in the hospital with Katie, another of GFI's investigators who had sustained a serious head injury in a previous attack – an attack aimed at Emma who Katie was assigned to protect. Luckily, Emma was spared serious injury, but the same couldn't be said for Katie who is still rehabilitating, needing to relearn everything from talking to walking. Caleb is extremely protective of the women around him, but with Katie in particular whom he tries to spend as much time as possible with.

Will Flemming's name still raises goose bumps all over my skin and causes my stomach to heave. *Me*, who doesn't cower for anything… not anymore, but that one night where he had Kara and me separated, he managed to tear away all my carefully constructed layers of protection and left me bleeding out; physically and mentally. Even without remembering all of the precise details, I remember enough to know I don't ever want to explore those hours spent in semi-conscious awareness again.

The next morning in the hospital when they did a rape kit on me and found evidence of sexual assault, I wanted to scream for letting it happen to me. I'm still upset that the doctor insisted the police had to be notified. That was my business and no one else's. No one should know until the trial because that's when all this shit is going to come out and I'm not ready for it. I'll never be ready for it.

Caleb doesn't say much. He simply sits there sipping his

coffee and looking at me calmly.

"Have you talked to anyone yet?"

The dishcloth slips from my hands and I grab onto the counter. "T-talk to someone? What's there to talk about?" But I'm not looking at him. As perceptive as Caleb is, he would likely pick up on my attempt to feign ignorance, but I've obviously underestimated his ability to read people's minds too.

"Arlene." He says firmly. "No shame, do you understand? If not, then it's time you did. There will be more questions and at some point there will most certainly be a trial, and with that comes depositions, questions, witness accounts… It won't get easier."

"I know." It comes out in a whisper, thank God because just then Seb walks up beside me and slides a plate on the counter in front of Caleb.

"Beef Bourguignon, the dinner special." He grumbles before placing a hand on my shoulder. "Ok, Arlene?" His eyes are turned to me, filled with concern and the heat from his hand sears through my shirt onto the skin of my shoulder. All I want to do is curl up in his arms and bawl, but I don't do shit like that. The only thing it would do is give me a headache, and get snot and slobber all over his shirt. That'll teach him to be nice because I can't handle Seb being nice so I muster up a little smile, "I'm alright."

"Can I get you something?"

"Nah, I'll eat when Julie gets here, but thanks."

With one last long look my way and a squeeze on my arm, he saunters back into the kitchen. When he's out of sight I turn to Caleb and hiss, "What do you know?"

"Enough. All I have to do is look at you and see your struggle written all over your face. Does Emma know?"

"No, and I don't want her to because she's been through enough. She doesn't need to worry about me too."

Caleb just shakes his head.

"You're a hard woman, Arlene, or you're really good at playing one. Your problems are not less than others, you know. You're good at taking care of others and love doing it. I know that, but you're making excuses for taking away other people's opportunity to take care of you for once. Think about that. We all care about you, especially Emma. She would actually be hurt to know that you'd keep her from being there for you. And what about Seb?"

Already raw with the direct honesty and dammit all to hell, the truth of what Caleb is saying, I flinch when he mentions Seb.

"What about him?"

"Are you blind? That man cares for you, doll. A lot."

See? Too perceptive. I know there is something that seems to be sparking between Seb and I – some kind of energy – but I try not to think on it too much. Truthfully? I just thought it was my lengthy dry-spell and the fact that he is extremely hot and interesting to look at with his 'just rolled out of bed' look of messy black hair, rumpled shirts and colorful tattoos that seem to cover just about every inch of his body. They don't seem to match his generally laid back and quiet demeanor at all, but they look perfect and sexy on him.

Caleb grabs my head and plants a kiss on top, knocks twice on the counter and waves at Seb and heads out the door, leaving me with my confusing thoughts.

I almost lost it for a minute there. That damn Caleb cozying up with Arlene had my blood boiling. I've been giving her time and space, doing my best not to crowd her and here he comes waltzing in, getting right in there. It pisses me right off and he knows it too. Bastard.

He wasted no time in coming over to lay it all out on the

table for me. Says he's seen it for a while now, how deep my interest in her goes. Yeah, whatever. I'm here to make sure she's looked after. Somebody has to. Then he goes on to say that I need to talk to her because she's hurting. I know she's fuckin' hurting. I know more than he thinks I do and I'm not gonna force myself on Arlene if she doesn't want me there, but I'll be damned if it isn't getting harder to keep my distance. In those unguarded moments I can see the darkness slip over her. There are things she just won't open up about and I've never been a big talker, just more of a listener really.

He did catch my attention when he mentioned that he's in town for the case against that pile of shit, Will Flemming. It's all about to come to a head and when he mentioned that it was likely going to require Arlene's involvement again, I wanted to get to that fuck and beat him with my bare hands. This is gonna stir it all back up for her again and there isn't a damn thing I can do about it.

I've decided I've been patient long enough. When I came to Cedar Tree I only intended to stay for a while, but what I found made me want to stick around. I'm done waiting.

CHAPTER TWO

It's after 10 when I finally have the kitchen back in order for breakfast prep, which unfortunately comes sooner than I care to think about. The days are long ones and the only time Arlene is willing to close up shop is Mondays, which is probably the best day of the week for it. Opening at 7 am on all other days means I'm up and in the kitchen by 6:30am at the latest. Usually we have a few hours a day we shut down before the dinner crowd which is from 4 till 7, and most days those hours are spent prepping the specials.

Before Arlene got hurt we would each take an additional day a week off, but I haven't for months now, and I'm starting to feel it. Starting to show my age, I guess.

Just as I drag my sorry ass up the stairs to my apartment, which is conveniently located above the diner, my damn phone rings. I sit down on the steps to answer it.

"Yeah."

"Sebastian?"

"Oh, hey pumpkin. You're up late. How come?"

"I wasn't feeling too good and I couldn't sleep."

"What happened?"

"Well first I had a nightmare that woke me up and I pushed the button and Janet came, but then I got sick to my stomach and puked all over my bed. Janet said I could call you."

"You know it, sweetie. I'm only a phone call away."

"When are you coming again?"

"I'll try to real soon Faith, ok? Now, if I talk to Janet for a minute, do you think you'll be able to sleep?"

"I think so. I feel better now. I love you, Sebastian."

"Love you too, Pumpkin. Now hand me over to Janet, ok?"

I hear some rustling on the phone and Faith's little girl voice in the background before her favorite night nurse comes on.

"Hi Seb. We had a bit of a rough go of it tonight, but we're doing much better now."

"Yeah? Does she have the flu or something? Stomach bug?"

"No, I don't think so. She had more of a night terror than a simple nightmare so when she woke up, she was still fairly hysterical and it took a while to calm her down. I think it was just her body's reaction to the emotional upheaval."

"Dammit, Janet."

"I know, hun. Don't worry, I'll schedule her for therapy tomorrow and see if she's ready to let anything out. We can't force it – not with her, and you know we take good care of her here, right? We always will until you're ready."

"I know that and you will never know how much that means so thanks. Thanks a lot, Janet."

When I hang up the phone, whatever little reserves I had left are now long gone with the guilt and responsibility that are weighing heavily on my shoulders. Hell, I feel like that's all I've been carrying around most of my forty-two years with more and more piling up every day.

I manage to get myself in the door and on the couch where I gratefully throw myself down and fall asleep within minutes only to be woken up a few hours later by the ringing of my phone.

My immediate thoughts are of Faith as I snatch the phone off the coffee table where I managed to drop it before I crashed.

"Faith?"

"What? No, um... It's Arlene. I..."

A quick glance at the clock shows that it's 3:45am so I know something is wrong. I can hear her panting.

"Arlene, talk to me."

"I'm ok, really. I mean, I'll be fine. I'm sorry I woke you. I don't know why I called."

And fuck if she doesn't just hang up on me. That's it. No more pushing this away.

I'm an idiot. I'm such a fucking idiot. Why on earth did I call him? It's bloody Caleb's fault, with all his talk of letting Seb in and all that shit. I just have a bad case of indigestion or something which is causing me to have these nightmares. That's got to be it, right? Wish I had a something to explain the hang-up phone calls I've been getting these last couple of days. Could be my imagination from lack of sleep. You know, like my mind playing tricks on me? Add to that the Will Flemming case and my private hell is complete, driving me straight into some sort of madness. I hate feeling this shaken up, and now I've gone and crossed a line that I just know can't be uncrossed. Seb might not talk much but once he has his jaws locked on something, you can't beat him off with a stick.

I roll out of my tangled sheets and flip on all the lights on my way to the kitchen to make a pot of coffee, ready to call this night officially over when the front door bursts open and Seb comes flying in.

"Jesus on a broomstick, Seb! What is wrong with you? You almost gave me a heart attack barging in like that." I'm clutching my dinky old nightshirt that has seen one too many washes and is hanging together by a thread to my chest. "What the hell?"

I look at Seb and he isn't moving. He's just standing there in the doorway, breathing heavily with his brows pulled together over his dark eyes, scanning me thoroughly from head to toe and back up again, making me feel a little too exposed to say the least. After all, my comfy nightie doesn't leave a whole lot to the imagination anymore and neither do the spider veins on my legs or the boobs that are enthusiastically giving up their fight on gravity without their customary hammocks. Play it cool, I tell myself before turning around to finish my track to the kitchen to start that highly necessary pot of coffee.

I risk a glance over my shoulder to see he still hasn't moved an inch from his spot by the door. Creepy.

"I'm making some coffee. You coming in or are you just gonna stand there? You're making it a free for all for the bugs in the neighborhood so you could at least close the damn door."

I'm in the kitchen putting the grinds in the coffeemaker when I finally hear the front door close and his heavy boots make their way into the kitchen. Forcing myself not to turn around, I hear him pull out a kitchen chair and sit down at the table. He hasn't said a word yet and I'm starting to feel a little worried he may be pissed off at me for calling him at this hour.

"Look, I'm really sorry – " I begin.

"Jesus, Arlene –" He starts at the same time.

He stops and looks at me to go ahead, so I give him a little smile before I continue, "I shouldn't have called you. I woke you up and there was no reason for it. I'm sorry if I scared you and made you come out here for nothing."

"For nothing?" He looks at me with confusion clear on his face. "Really, for nothing? That's what you think? For months I have

31

been fighting to be able to take care of you, to be there for you to help out when you were recovering. Every fucking cup of coffee or meal I brought you, every damn thing I tried to do for you I had to fight you tooth and nail and finally, Arlene, you call me. You actually call me in the middle of the night, for what I can only assume is my help. And what do you do? You fucking hang up the phone! Without any explanation."

His voice is steadily rising as he strings together more words than I have ever heard him say in one go, to the point where he is practically yelling. Releasing an inarticulate groan, he rubs his hands over his face and through his unruly hair, which really doesn't help matters much.

"Did you honestly think I could go back to sleep after that? Without checking on you? Fuck, Arlene. What do you take me for?"

Honestly? I don't know what to do with myself right now. He's right. I don't know how to respond to it so I turn back to my coffee duties and pull down two mugs. We're both black coffee drinkers so that's all we need. I turn around to hand him his and find his eyes on me.

"I'm sorry... really, I am."

"Don't want to hear you're sorry. I want to know what caused the panic in your voice when you called me tonight." Pulling out the chair next to him, he grabs my hand and pulls me down to sit beside him. "Talk to me."

I want to, I do, but it's so difficult for me to show my my weak spots. It has cost me dearly in the past and I have trained myself hard not to let anyone have that kind of power over me ever again. With his big calloused hand still holding mine as his dark blue eyes stare into mine, I know I owe him this little bit of me.

"I get nightmares... bad ones, but they don't start off that way. In fact, they start off as regular dreams that turn evil, always catching me off guard."

"About that bastard?" Seb bites out.

"Partly. I don't remember much of what happened but it's like during the nightmares, more things try to make themselves clearer. I don't want to remember, but the evil at the end is always my ex."

"Your ex? The not so nice ex?"

If that isn't the understatement of the year.

"The not-so-nice ex, as you put it, was more of an abusive ex. I know I don't seem like the kind of person who would allow herself to be abused, but there you have it."

Suddenly Seb turns to me and takes my face into both his hands, leaning in so close his nose almost touches mine.

"You listen to me. You did not allow yourself to be abused. You carry no responsibility here. The responsibility is all on him, not you… Never on you. Remember that."

Once again, I'm not sure how to respond. Something is happening here and I'm feeling completely out of my depth.

"Yeah. He hurt me really bad the last time and then he disappeared when I ended up in the hospital." I wince when my hand that Seb has grabbed once again is being crushed in his. When I look over, his jaw is clenched and he's staring at the door. I have no choice and squeak out, "That's really starting to hurt."

"God. Sorry, babe." He immediately loosens his grip and pulls my hand to his mouth and kisses my palm as if it's the most natural thing in the world. Once again, I am dumbfounded.

"Go on." He prompts.

"Alright. Long story short, he was charged and picked up, sent to jail and is now serving out his time in Wyoming. I divorced his ass and never looked back, well, except in my nightmares apparently."

"Have you had them all these months? The nightmares I mean?"

"Not as bad as now, and none that involved my ex, oddly enough. That didn't start until a few weeks ago and now with that whole case coming up, I guess shoving it down as deep as I can really doesn't help in the long run." I look sideways at Seb and still find his eyes focused on me, which is mesmerizing and a little unsettling all at once.

"What are you thinking?"

"That I'm glad you're unloading a little. Glad you're allowing me to be the one to unload on and hoping you'll trust me enough to do a bit more of it and more often."

Being the ditz that I am, my mouth, normally so eager to spout off any and all kinds of sarcastic or irrelevant nonsense, decides to go numb. Not good at all with awkward situations, I jump up, grab the mugs and start splashing coffee around. Klutziness is always good for a distraction.

Happy that she finally opened the door a crack, I decide to let her off the hook for now. No need to push her completely out of her comfort zone and by the looks of it, she is plenty uneasy already. Fiddling with the edge of her nightshirt and her eyes looking everywhere but at me, it's clear that she's not quite sure what to make of this change in the atmosphere between us. I'm finally feeling good about something, even if I did miss a full night's sleep. This here was worth it.

I get up, ready to head back to my apartment before the temptation standing before me in her ratty old nightshirt becomes too much to resist. I figure I should have a quick shower before I start my early day in the kitchen when I notice her body stiffens at my movement. Being the idiot that I am, I slowly walk up behind her, reach around and move my mug from the counter to the sink. Damn she smells warm and soft, so unlike the person she likes to put out there. With my mouth already almost touching her ear, I can't resist.

"No more coffee for me. Gonna get cleaned up and get breakfast prep going. You gonna be ok?" I keep my voice low and I can feel a shiver going through her body.

"I'll be fine." She replies a little out of breath. Did I scare her, or am I actually affecting her the way she affects me? For once I apparently haven't pissed her off so I grab the opportunity and press a quick kiss to the spot right behind her ear before turning around and walking out the door. I'm trying hard not to make it too obvious as I adjust my massive hard-on while doing it.

CHAPTER THREE

"Dammit, Julie. What is so hard about coming in on time? This is the third time in the last five days that you've been at least half an hour late? What's going on?"

It's been three days since Seb left me standing in my own kitchen, completely at a loss with my emotions. Three additional days of little to no sleep and three more tardy arrivals of my newest waitress who is standing before me about to burst into tears.

"Aw geeze, girl. Don't start bawling. Just talk to me, will ya? What the blazes is happening with you? I'm just looking for your reasons for all of a sudden having a problem getting here on time. There's gotta be something going on."

Sure enough, one after the other, big tears come rolling over those innocent rosy cheeks. Well hell. Don't I feel like the wicked witch of the west? I hate crying, even though I've secretly done my share recently.

"Come on. You can talk to Arlene." Putting my arm around her I try for my best impersonation of a nurturer as I lead her into my office, or better yet, my glorified broom closet where I sit her down on a stack of napkin boxes when I hear Emma's voice from the front.

"Arlene! Delivery."

"Sit tight. Be right back," I say to Julie before checking out the baked goods Emma has for me today. She faithfully started supplying me with pies and other baked sweets since she came to Cedar Tree sometime in June. That was five months ago. It seems so much longer than that.

Coming around the counter is a short, fiery sparkplug with a mass of auburn curls and an infectious smile whom I am lucky to call my friend.

"Hey woman. Whatcha up to?" She wants to know. It sounds like a loaded question to me, but I just move on.

"Not a lot of good, ya brat. What have you got for me today?" I walk over to the kitchen island where she just dropped the last of the boxes she hauled in on her walker. Stubborn woman gets a little pissy when anyone tries to lend a hand so we've all learned to stand back and let her do her thing.

"Mixed berry pie, apple crumble, peach and almond, and two pumpkins 'cause it's the season." She says with a big smile. "So when are we decorating, Arlene?"

I groan. It's not that I don't like the holidays, it's just that they're a headache and I don't really do anything anyways but work, so it's simply easier to forget all about it and avoid the questions and anything else that go along with them.

"I don't know, Ems. What do you have in mind?" Emma has been bugging me for weeks to go out and get trees for each of our homes, as well as one for the diner. I don't even have enough decorations for the diner and I've never really had anything in my house. There was never a point in it.

"I though maybe next Monday we could all go and make some hot chocolate with a little something to help it go down smoother." She winks at me, the imp, "I could bake something to bring along, too. We could see if Beth and Seb want to come. Maybe Caleb will still be here, so what do you think? Joe could help us get a permit, I'm sure."

"I guess." I give in reluctantly. It's still four days away and I really have no good excuse to postpone any longer.

"By the way, you look like shit, Arlene."

"Okay, I think I just changed my mind about the tree cutting adventure." If anyone else talked to me like that I think they'd be horizontal by now, but I know Ems is concerned. "I'm ok. Just not sleeping too well."

She tilts her head to the side and squints her eyes. "Pain? Or is it something else going on that your best friend should know about?" She says to me in no uncertain terms, but I have no intention of telling her about the things that keep me awake at night. Her load is heavy enough and I'll get over this. I will simply will myself to do so.

"My pain is mostly under control. I've just been restless."

"Talk to someone yet? Kara tells me she finally has and it's making a world of difference. I wish you would quit being so stubborn and go see someone too."

"Ems, I can't even remember most of what happened so what do I have to talk about?" I try to bluff my way out of this conversation but as usual, I underestimate Emma's perceptiveness.

"You can lie to me all you want, Arlene. It doesn't bother me none, but don't you dare lie to yourself. That's just pure stupidity on your part, and I never took you for being stupid." With that Emma swings her walker around and marches right out the diner. Guess I've been put in my place.

Hoping Julie hasn't bailed on me, I head back to my office, only to find the door, which I had left open, now almost closed. When I push it open a little I see Julie sobbing, wrapped in Seb's arms. An unfamiliar but very ugly feeling of jealousy forms in the pit of my stomach. What did I miss? I try to back out quietly, but not quietly enough because Seb's eyes shoot up and catch mine. His are filled with a mix of sadness and anger; a combination I can't quite place. And mine? I'm not sure what mine are showing, but from the look he gives me it probably isn't pretty.

I return to the kitchen to put the pies away, all the while thinking about those strong muscled and intricately decorated arms wrapped around someone else and why that would fill me with such an instant sense of loss.

When the phone rings I barely register it at first. It's only when Seb sticks his head out of the office that it propels me into action as I pick up the kitchen phone.

"Afternoon, Arlene's Diner."

"Hello? Arlene's Diner. Can I help you?" There is nothing but silence on the line. Well, not quite silent but just like all the previous times, I can hear shallow breathing and a distant rustling, but nothing else.

"Who is this please? Can I help you?" I try again but get nothing except for a click; hung up exactly like the other times. I wonder if it constitutes harassment if you don't even know who is doing the harassing? At least Emma's anonymous phone call landed her a good man. I have a feeling my calls are just going to bring me trouble.

I observe Arlene as she picks up the call and see her back stiffen as she listens intently before prompting the caller to identify themselves. I can tell something is off but before I can make my way over to grab the phone from her hands, she lowers the receiver and turns around to face me. She looks to be in a daze and barely reacts when I close the distance to grab the phone and listen, but find nothing but a dial tone.

"Who was it?"

She blinks her eyes a few times at my question before responding.

"I don't know. They hung up again."

"What do you mean – Again?" Her green eyes finally focus in on mine and I can see her gathering herself.

"It's nothing, Seb. Just some prank caller, I'm sure. Nothing to fuss over." Something unidentifiable passes over the way she looks at me, before she glances over my shoulder and resolutely turns around. "Let's get back to work, shall we?"

I've been dismissed, with the added cold shoulder.

"Thanks," I hear Julie's voice behind me. "For listening, I mean."

The poor girl had been in near hysterics when I found her in Arlene's office, afraid she was going to lose her job for coming in late. As it turns out she had a pretty good reason for being late. Her boyfriend had apparently up and left a few weeks ago without even a goodbye, leaving her and their three-year old son behind with a pile of unpaid bills and rent a month overdue. This was when she got the job at the diner. Cedar Tree wasn't exactly convenient for her, living in Cortez, but beggars can't be choosers and she took what was available, but Julie apparently had no one except an elderly aunt nearby to give her a hand with the baby and she was less than enthusiastic about babysitting. Giving her such a hard time when she would drop off her son, it would take her forever to get things calmed down. The kid was stuck between a rock and a hard place and I told her to talk to Arlene, but given Arlene's recent short fuse, maybe I should just do it.

"Anytime. Don't worry, we'll work it out."

With a watery little smile, she hurries to the front end to get the tables ready.

The rest of the afternoon I spend filling food orders. Thursday nights are generally busy, so both Julie and Beth are running tables and Arlene is at the counter filling drink orders and manning the cash. Even with the kitchen officially closing at 7 pm, it usually takes a while to get the place clean and ready for the next day's business so every now and then, in between orders, I try to stay on top of the kitchen as much as possible.

I don't have much of a chance to talk to Arlene, being as she seems to ignore me most of the evening, which is starting to piss me off. Always bristly, it takes time to thaw her out and time is something we don't have a hell of a lot of in this line of work. The woman has frustrated me since day one… frustrated me and turned me on, all at the same time.

I had heard about her, but the first time I saw her she put me flat on my ass. Part of me had expected some vixen-like bimbo, but Arlene is anything but. She's refreshing; like a drink of really cool water on a hot day. She has long limbs with strong lines, softened with age. Short blond hair that doesn't seem to want to submit and is constantly falling in her eyes and incredible green cat eyes that will warm you from the inside out, but can just as easily freeze you the same way. And the cherry on top? Fucking freckles. They kill me. No, she's no vixen, but she's the girl next door – one who can turn my crank by just being in the same room. Her abrasive nature only makes me want her even more. I must be one sick bastard, especially since I still haven't told her the real reason for showing up here eight months ago. It's becoming more difficult by the day and Christ knows I'm getting sucked in more and more.

"Heading out." Arlene's announcement pulls me out of my head.

"Hold up, Arlene. Got something I need to talk about."

"Can it wait? I'm dead on my feet. Julie and Beth are taking care of those last two tables and they'll clean the front."

"Won't take a minute. Your office?"

"Fine." She mumbles reluctantly but leads the way into her space where I sit down on the stack of boxes and let her take the only chair that'll fit.

"I wanna talk about Julie."

Arlene surprises me by throwing her hands up. "Whoa! No need. Whatever you two do, make sure to do it on your own time. I don't need that drama here."

What the fuck? "What the hell are you talking about, woman?"

"I don't want or need to know what is going on with you two, so now if you'll excuse me, I'm ready to get home."

She's already getting up and making her way out the door, but this time I'm not letting her off the hook so easily. In one step I'm right behind her, reaching over her shoulder and slamming the door shut with my hand leaning against it to keep it closed.

"What are you doing, Seb?" She tries to turn around and squirm away but I'm faster and plant my other hand on the other side of her head, caging her back against the door with only a few inches between us. I'll be damned if she's not going to listen to every last word I have to say.

"I swear to God, half the fucking time I don't know how you come up with half the crap inside your head."

"But I thought –" She's trying to interrupt but I'm not gonna let her.

"I don't know what you thought, or assumed, or whatever, Arlene. I found Julie crying in your office. We talked and she told me her boyfriend abandoned her with unpaid bills and a three-year old to care for. And she only has an unwilling aunt to turn to for support. That's why she was late those times, trying to coax her aunt into babysitting."

A flush of indignant anger creeps up her cheeks, something I have come to recognize on Arlene.

"Let me go. I'm gonna..." She starts trying to push her way past me again but I'm not about to let that happen so I lean my body in so she can't move an inch.

"You're not gonna do anything but listen to me, and listen to me good. I tiptoe around you. I give you space and try not to push, but you are fucking driving me insane. You hear me? I'm done being careful and patient with you. It's not working for me anymore."

She's doing her best not to look me in the eye and at my last words, she lets out a loud huff. I take her face in my hands so she has no choice but to look at me.

"I'm interested in you. Been that way since I got here and saw you. Only you." When I lean in I want to imprint myself on her, leaving no doubt of my intentions, but at the same time I want to savor this moment.

I touch her nose with mine first, rubbing gently as I breathe her in and feel her sharp intake of air. I love her plain, clean smell; a combination of soap and maybe a hint of coconut. The rest is all Arlene and to me it's the most delicious smell. I lick her top lip and get a hint of a darker flavor as I slide my lips over the wet track I made and change my focus on her pouty lower lip that I suck into my mouth and rub with my tongue. My cock is ready to burst through my zipper I'm so fucking ready for this. Her breathing has become shallow and the hands that were clasping my wrists before are now making their way up my arms and around my neck. Oh, fuck yeah! I'm not alone here.

Finally I let go of her lip, change the angle of her head slightly and cover her mouth with mine, plunging my tongue between her lips. I have waited so long for this shit. I'm so fucking turned on I swear I just came a little in my fucking jeans. Fuck, if she doesn't stop mewling the way she is, I really am going to shoot my load. It's been too fucking long and she tastes so damn good.

Oh. My. God. I am buzzing with sensory overload. With just his mouth and that wicked, wicked tongue, this man has me losing my ever-loving mind. Five years and I've only ever been aroused in my dreams – and only because they were of Seb. My body is on fire and I feel like I could come from just this kiss! I can't believe my parts are still working after all these years. I thought for sure I had dry rot. I can't stop the sounds coming from my mouth, like a deranged kitten or something. I never would have guessed that he would want me and that confession has completely blown my mind.

When he pulls back and lightly kisses my mouth once more, I can't help the disappointed sigh that escapes. The sparkle in his eye tells me he heard it too. Dammit! There goes my reputation as a certified badass. Once again, I'm struck dumb by Seb, which appears to be a new trend.

"Not rushing this, babe. We work on trust first. Yeah?"

"But…" I look down at his crotch which is showing a very prominent and straining bulge. I really want to help him with that "uncomfortable" situation.

"Don't worry 'bout that. I've had blue balls for almost a year now because of you so I'm sure I can deal with it a bit longer." He says with a wink. He starts backing away and I feel the loss of his weight and heat immediately. Seb just winked. The broody, 'two word maximum' Seb has not only spoken more in the past few days than the entire eight months I've know him, but he actually just winked. Devil best be investing in a winter coat.

CHAPTER FOUR

My mind has been going a mile a minute since Seb accosted me in my office on Thursday night. I'm angry with myself for letting down my guard and allowing that kiss to even happen. Granted, his mouth devouring mine felt better than anything I had imagined. Yesterday his hands were skimming my arms or my back every time we passed each other, giving me goose bumps and keeping my senses on high alert, but the man makes me forget myself. That's something I can't afford to have happen. I will not give up that kind of control to someone ever again. Been there – got the bloody t-shirt. It doesn't even matter that he is nothing like Geoffrey, who looked innocent in comparison. Seb should not be my type at all; dark, broad and dangerous looking, covered in tattoos and wearing a permanent scowl on his face. Geoffrey is a choirboy next to him except I know from experience he is far from that. And Seb, despite his fierce appearance, has never once made me feel unsafe… quite the opposite, actually. He has shown his protective nature time and time again with his actions and not just for me, but for Emma and Beth. Now Julie as well.

I pull into Emma and Gus' driveway where evidence of the new construction is obvious. Since moving in, Gus has managed to buy the property from the old owner and they are building an extension to the little bungalow. By the time they're done, it's not going to be a little bungalow anymore, but a single level ranch house with an office wing and separate entrance to house Gus' investigation and security company, GFI, along with a guest house out back for out-of-towners.

I don't just walk in the house anymore like I used to since catching Gus one morning cooking eggs, butt-ass naked. Nope. Once was enough for me. Emma opens the door before I even knock, probably seeing me drive up.

"Hey you! What are you doing out here so early?" She asks. "Come in, woman. Have a coffee. Gus just made some."

"Sure thing. Oh, hey Gus."

"Mornin', Arlene. Black?"

"Please." I take a moment to appreciate the man's fine backside, currently clad in only jeans and nothing else when Emma slaps me upside the head.

"Eyes off my man."

"Ouch." I say, rubbing the sore spot on my head. Bitch slapped me hard. "What'd ya go and do that for?'

"You need to get your own man to ogle and leave mine alone."

"Why would I wanna do that when I can come here and get all this eye-candy for free? Not worth tying myself down for, Ems."

"Ahhhh, but he's not just pleasing to the eye, smartass. He pleases everywhere." She snickers.

"Kiss my ass, Ems."

"Sorry love. Gonna have to find yourself a man to do that for ya."

"Ladies." Gus puts mugs of coffee on the counter in front of us and puts up his hands in a defensive manner, "I think my ears are bleeding. I'm going to retreat to the bathroom now and make sure I still have all my boy-parts."

After a good chuckle at Gus' expense, I sit down in the living room with Emma and fill her in on my dilemma with Julie. I conveniently leave out any mention of my little interlude with Seb, not quite sure what to make of that myself, so I shove it to the back of the pile.

"So you're saying the bastard just disappeared? Left her with a baby and bills to pay? What a fucking asshole. Can I help? I mean... I know we're in the middle of construction here but for now, the main house will stay intact until the last minute. I could help with the babysitting?"

"That would be awesome. I was actually going to see if you could help, or at least help figure out how to get a support circle together for this girl. You're good at networking and you know me... I just don't have the time or the patience for it."

"Sure thing. I'll ask around locally so she can bring him in to Cedar Tree. It's easier if something happens during her shift to get to him quickly than having to go all the way to Cortez every time. All she would have to do is drop him off before she starts and pick him up when she's done. He's still young enough that it won't matter too much. He'll adjust to her schedule."

"I'll trust your word on that."

Happy I've made a little headway with one of the things weighing on my mind, I stick around for a couple more minutes to catch up before saying my goodbyes.

Walking toward my trusty yellow rust-bucket F150, I can hear Gus calling behind me.

"Arlene. Hold up."

I turn around and watch him jog toward me.

"Did Caleb come by to see you?"

"A few days ago. Why?"

"I just wanted to give you a heads up that most of the interviews are done. They've saved you for last."

Suddenly my happy feeling is gone.

"What about Kara? Do they need to interview her again, or is it just me?"

"Everyone, Arlene. Everyone who had even the smallest part in what happened has to go through it one more time before the prosecutor. Emma and I did ours yesterday."

"She didn't say a thing."

"She didn't want to upset you. She knows there are some tender spots you have about those events and doesn't want to be the one rubbing them."

I do not want to do this again. I don't want to open that barely scabbed over wound. I'm terrified.

Gus pulls me in his arms and I gratefully rest my head on his strong shoulder while he rubs my back.

"You'll be alright, girl. You're tough, but if things get too hard to handle, I know someone you can talk to. She's good too."

I lean back to look him in the eyes and he sees my question so he answers, "Yes, Arlene. I've gotten some help. I had a lot of shit to come to terms with, especially after what my brother put everyone through. I haven't just seen her in the past, but I see her still, and I'm damn glad I do."

"Okay."

"Okay – what?"

"Okay, I'll go see her. Can you text me the number?"

"Sure thing, girl." With that, he kisses me on the forehead and heads back up the ramp to go inside.

I pull myself up in the cab, start my grumpy old truck and head for the diner.

I loved hearing every hitched breath out of Arlene's mouth yesterday when I would purposely pass by her, just to touch her. It's obvious that the kiss from the night before has left an impression with her as well. I've never been good with words, but I let my body do the talking for me. I'm a patient man; I've had to learn to be that way, and building the tension between us seems like a good thing to do. There are things she's holding back and truth be told, I haven't been open and honest with her, either. Knowingly omitting information is as good as lying, but the events from two months ago set me back some on that front. She seems even more resistant to accepting help and protection than she was before and I'm afraid if I come clean, she'll send me packing and there will be no way for me to make sure she's alright. Slow and easy will hopefully do the trick, but I'll be damned if I let up. If need be, I'll throw her over my shoulder.

Arlene is late this morning so when the phone rings a little after 8am, I step behind the counter to answer it. Beth's got her hands full pouring coffees for the breakfast crowd.

"Arlene's Diner."

Nothing.

"Hello? Arlene's Diner." When I hear a distinct click on the other end of the line, I hang up. Beth walks up to the counter and hands me the empty coffee pots.

"Was that another hang up?"

"Yeah, why? Has that happened before?"

"A few times with me in the last week or so, but they hang up quickly when I answer, but not when Arlene answers. I can hear her going off on whoever is calling. I don't think she gets much response, but they sure seem to like listening to her talk."

Doesn't sound to me like some random wrong number or prank call. I really don't like the idea of Arlene aggravating whoever it is on the phone. Looks like she and I need to have a talk about this.

I'm just emptying my recycle bucket in the compost bin I started behind the diner when I hear the familiar rattle of Arlene's truck behind me. Waiting for her by the backdoor, I watch her as she hops down from the cab, genuinely smiling. She is gorgeous when she smiles. I'm a little stunned at the transformation and a nagging thought pops up that she almost looks like she had a *really* good night. That better not be fucking true. A scowl settles on my face the closer she gets to me with her long legs in the black cargo pants and her poncho wrapped around her body to keep the cold out with the sting of winter on its way. She stops right in front of me and tilts her still smiling face to the side.

"What's with the scowl, Cookie?"

"What did you just call me?" I'm sure I misheard her, that is until I look at her face and see her mouth lifted in a big smirk as her eyes dance with mischief.

"Cookie. Like they used to call the cook on the cattle drives, Cookie? It suits you."

All vocabulary has abandoned me. I am left glaring at her and she is very noticeably unimpressed. Even the growl that escapes me just makes her smile bigger.

"What the heck's gotten into you?" I want to know.

"It's a good day. A day for new beginnings."

Well hell. I don't know whether that's a good thing or not.

"Come in the kitchen where it's warm and tell me about those new beginnings."

"Alright."

She precedes me into the kitchen where she pulls the poncho over her head, leaving her short blond hair sticking up all over the place with static, and she doesn't seem to notice or care. She never seems to care much about her appearance and I find her even hotter for it with her gorgeous freckled skin, those penetrating green eyes and impossibly long legs. She's stunning, no matter how hard she tries to hide it.

"I've had a very productive morning. Had some help problem solving and a brilliant man encouraged me to take a leap, so I did."

That does it. I grab her by her hips and back her into the door of the walk-in freezer, where I put my hands on either side of her face, leaning right into her space.

"Who had his hands on you, Arlene." I bite out, barely able to keep my volume down. Her eyes are big as saucers and her mouth is hanging open.

"What are you doing?"

"I want to know who had his hands on you so I can wring his neck."

"You. Are. Insane." Every word she spits out is emphasized by the stab of her finger in my chest. That shit hurts.

"Don't want anyone's hands on you but mine, babe." I growl out between clenched teeth.

"Ha!" She scoffs. "Good luck with that, Cookie." And with a firm knuckle to my sternum that has me flinching, she manages to squirm out from under my arms and into her office, but she doesn't quite manage to close the door before my boot slams in the opening and I force it open, only to shut and lock it behind me. Without a word I pull her in to my body and slam my mouth on hers. Yes, I'm finally claiming what is mine, so so much for slow and easy, but the woman makes me nuts even now as she makes noises of protest that are turning to those mewling sounds again. She drives me fucking insane. I can't get enough of her taste as I leave her lips to explore along her jaw line and down her neck, sucking and biting. I'm feeling completely out of control when she pushes me back and from eyes that are heavy-lidded with anger and need, she glares at me.

"You done pissing all over me?"

I immediately drop my arms, step back and look away. Fuck me. Talk about a bucket of ice water.

"I… " I start, but that's about as far as I get as I'm about to turn and walk out the door when her voice stops me.

"Don't you walk out, Seb. I have words for you."

Shit!. I stop in my tracks but don't turn back to face her fully.

"If you had given me even a moment to explain before your ass went all Neanderthal on me, I could've told you that Emma and Gus were happy to see me this morning."

My eyes flash to her face. One of her eyebrows is waging war with her hairline and one side of her mouth is twitching. Brat.

"Emma is going to help set up a support group for Julie, for babysitting and things like that and Gus, well, Gus was helpful in other ways." That elicits a growl from me.

"Oh chill out. I'll tell you, but only because you are being ridiculous. He gave me the number for a therapist and I actually called and set up an appointment." She suddenly doesn't seem to want to meet my eyes so I walk up to her and lift her chin so she has no choice.

"I'm proud of you and so fucking glad you decided to do it." Resting my forehead against hers, I know I'm not done yet. "Sorry I lost it. I promised myself to take it slow with you and when I thought someone else might have gotten the jump on me... well, you see what that did to me."

Arlene's hands slide up over my chest and come to rest on either side of my face.

"Seb. You're an idiot."

I can't help it. I bust out laughing. She's got me there.

"And I love it when you laugh. You don't do it enough. Stop being such a grouchy ass, ok?"

I have a smirk on my face when I answer.

"I will if you will."

CHAPTER FIVE

So that was kind of hot. I couldn't believe I had the strength to push him back. Oh I'm strong enough, I'm not talking about muscle. I'm talking about will power. Those lips and that mouth are nothing to turn your nose up at, not to mention those strong arms trapping me. WOW! But I promised myself never to let a man walk over me again and even if that man has the ability to melt the panties right off my ass, come hell or high water, I will not let him control me. I will set him straight and *then* he can proceed to divest me of my panties.

I don't know what he wants from me or what it is I'm doing. All I know is that I am sick of being miserable and I want to make it stop. I want this for me, which is why, even though it terrifies me, I am also excited about seeing a therapist. It signifies a cleansing of sorts. Even the interview with the prosecutor, which I'm sure I'll get a call about soon, is a sort of closure for me and if the man who has been the lead in every one of my fantasies is making the moves on me, I am inclined to let him, even if he's not really my type. Oh hell. Who am I lying to. I may look and act like a stiff middle aged spinster, but I have always had a soft spot for the proverbial bad boy. It's why I hired Seb in the first place. Teasing the wildness in me. I'm so tired of being a victim to circumstance. I just want to let go for once without restraint.

After that steaming kiss in my office, the pace in the diner started picking up so we were busy all afternoon. I was happy to see Julie in on time and actually talked to her about getting some dependable babysitting organized for her little one. Of course that brought on a new waterfall of tears. Shit, I really am no good at dealing with criers. I shoved a box of Kleenex her way, walked out of the office and told her I'd give her a minute. I'm such a coward. The thing is, it always gets me choked up when someone else cries and I'm scared once I start, I won't ever be able to stop. Saved up those tears for too many fucking years. I'm bound to drown in 'em.

Beth pops her head in the office.

"We're about cleaned up out front, Arlene. Julie and I are gonna head out."

"Alright, girls. See you tomorrow. Oh wait, let me have a quick chat with Julie."

I find her refilling condiments for tomorrow's breakfast behind the counter.

"So are you going to be okay for tomorrow?" She looks at me a little confused so I add, "I mean the baby. Is he gonna be taken care of tomorrow, or do you need to bring him in to town, 'cause we can figure it out here, you know? If it's a problem, I mean. Call Emma or whatever is all I'm saying." I'm suddenly rambling when I catch Seb leaning on the far side of the counter with a little smirk on his face, Beth standing right behind him looking at me too. I'm fucking trying to be nice here for once but I don't need an audience. "Yeah well…" I say to Julie. "Just try and call if there's a problem, ok? Next week you can sit with Emma and figure all this shit out, but in the meantime I don't wanna have to worry my ass off about you when you're late."

"Sure thing, Arlene. I'll call, but I'm good for tomorrow. Thanks."

With a smile she grabs her purse from the drawer under the counter and walks out the backdoor with Beth.

Seb hasn't moved from his spot and is still looking at me.

"What?" My hands are on my hips and if my chin was

sticking up any higher, my head would roll off my back.

"You were nice." He says with a raised eyebrow.

"So? I can be nice. Just 'cause I haven't had a reason to before doesn't mean I don't know how." And I immediately busy myself wiping down the counters... again.

"Uh huh..." Comes from behind me before I feel his arms sliding around my waist.

"I like you nice." He mumbles with his face buried in my neck, which has my body on high alert and aching.

"Don't get used to it." I manage, but I can't resist leaning back a little, feeling his hard chest against my back. One big hand slides up under my work shirt and his rough fingers skim my stomach. My instant reaction is to suck it in, but he catches me.

"So soft. It's nice."

Just the feeling of a man's hands on me; *this* man's hands on me causes me to moan. It's been so long since I've felt anything other than anger from a man's hand. There is no anger in Seb's touch, just a teasing gentleness that makes my wild side flare up and take notice.

When I feel his callused fingertips brush the underside of my breast then slip under my bra, my breath hitches in anticipation.

Damn I want his hands everywhere on me; his mouth. My nipples are so tight it's almost painful, and when his touch finally finds them I can't hold back anymore.

"Seb..." Reaching behind me I pull his head down and attack his mouth; my tongue eagerly finding entrance and tasting his while my hands tangle in his hair. I can feel his resistance waning and a greedy whimper escapes me.

He breaks the kiss to look at me with eyes that are almost as black as midnight. He turns and lifts me up on the counter, initiating himself between my legs, pulling at my knees so that my wet and aching center is lined up with his mouthwatering erection. Instinctively I wrap my legs around him, pressing him closer to my core as both of his hands find their way under my shirt and work at releasing my bra. He shoves it out of the way along with my shirt and latches on to my breast while plumping the other with his hand. At this point, I have lost all reason.

"So fucking tasty," is all I can hear before he switches to the other side.

Eager to touch him, my hands trace his arms, shoulders and with my fingers, I start pulling up his shirt, needing to touch his skin... The phone rings.

"Fuck!" Seb swears as he leans his head to my sternum, all movements stilled by the insistent ringing. He pulls my shirt down and in a daze, I reach over to grab the receiver off the hook.

"A- ... Arlene's Diner." I manage to get out.

"You think you can get away with that? You're nothing but a fucking whore! I swear, I'll teach you…"

That damn woman almost had me lose all control again. God, the taste herald touch of her alone had me so damn close to coming in my fucking jeans. I'm trying to catch my breath and bite down on my frustration when I glance up to see all the blood drain from Arlene's face. What the fuck? I snatch the phone from her hand.

"Hello? Who is this?" But there is no response except the distinct click of the phone being hung up on the other end.

I turn to Arlene, who is still sitting on the counter looking as if she's just seen a ghost. I put down the phone and grab her hands, willing her to look at me.

"Who was that?"

She shakes her head and suddenly hops off the counter,

rushing from window to window, dropping the half lowered blinds all the way down.

"What the hell, Arlene? What's going on?"

"He can see us." She hisses back at me.

"Who? Talk to me, dammit!"

I have to follow her into her office where she stands with her back against the wall facing the door.

"Arlene? Babe, tell me."

"A man. He… he… he said I couldn't get away with that and he would teach me. He called me whore."

"Away with what?" I'm scrambling to try and make sense of things.

"Kissing you! He saw us, I know he did."

She starts to tremble all over and I walk over to wrap her in my arms.

"I can't breathe, Seb…" Hyperventilating and shaking from head to toe, all I can think of is a panic attack so I force her down in her chair and go on my knees in front of her.

"Look at me. We're gonna breathe together, ok? Keep your eyes on me. In through the nose, out through mouth." I have her face in my hands and force her to look at me while I breathe with her. I have no fucking clue what I'm doing but when her breathing deepens and some of her color returns, I figure it's is working.

I get up to grab her a drink when she stops me.

"Where are you going?"

"Just grabbing you something to drink. Be right back." When she nods I quickly fill a glass of water in the kitchen and bring it to her.

After gulping down half of it, she rubs her hands over her face and says, "I don't know who it was, but it felt like he could see us. I have no idea what this is about?"

"Think this might have something to do with those hang-ups you've been getting?"

"How...? "

"Did I know? We've intercepted a bunch here at the diner, Beth and I. Figured that you might have had some at home, too."

Resigned, she nods.

"Yes, I've been getting those calls for a while, but I honestly thought they were prank calls or something. This is the first time anyone's ever said anything."

"Still should've mentioned something. Call the sheriff… tell Gus. For fuck's sake, tell me."

"So you could do what exactly, Seb? Answer my phone every time it rings? Get real, will ya? I've been managing to take care of myself for years now without any outside help, thank you very much. I don't need you to tell me what I should and shouldn't be doing!"

Well, I've clearly pushed a button but I'm not sit back and let her think she can do everything on her own."

"It's not about telling you what to do. It's about actually trusting people enough to let them in – to let them support and help you when you need it. You are not Super Woman, Arlene."

"I just told you, I don't need anyone!"

That's it. I am not gonna spend energy arguing with this exasperating woman. Grabbing the phone off her desk I dial the sheriff's number.

"What are you doing?"

"We're going to report this and don't bother arguing."

After a frustrating conversation with the sheriff's office where I was told we could come in on Monday to file a report, I find myself thinking about who might be behind this.

I left Arlene fuming in her office and now I'm puttering in the kitchen, coming to the realization that it may be time for me to talk to someone. Maybe Gus. If by any chance the person I'm most concerned about is behind this, then it will only get worse. I need some answers and Gus has the means to find them for me. This is exactly why I placed myself here almost a year ago to look out for Arlene, make sure no harm comes to her but now I can't help but wonder if I should've come clean a long time ago. This is going to blow up in my face, I just know it.

CHAPTER SIX

I'm awake but I don't want to open my eyes yet. I can feel the bright fall sun on my face so I just lie here, soaking it up.

I had been furious last night when Seb unilaterally decided we had to report the calls but I realized that most of that was knee-jerk reaction. To be honest, it felt nice to have a decision made for me by someone who wants to help at least with a decision like that. I'm just determined to stand on my own, although a bossy Seb can be very sexy.

A smile steals over my face thinking about the different side of him I've seen in the last week. From a fairly quiet and unassuming employee to someone who pushes every damn button I have, bad and good, and the good is so very good.

I can smell the coffee before I hear his voice.

"Smiling? You must still be asleep."

I open my eyes to find Seb with a mug of coffee beside my bed and my body reacts to all the possibilities that represents.

"Stop being a smartass so early in the morning." I grumble at him, wiping the sleep from my eyes and groping for my cup, half-blinded by the morning light. I squint up at him to see he has already showered and dressed.

"Up early?"

"The bed in your guestroom sucks."

"You're the one who insisted on not leaving me alone for the night, so suck it up." I tease him.

"As long as you know I'll be testing a different bed next time I'm here."

"Oh yeah? Says who?"

Grabbing the cup from my hand and putting it on my nightstand, he sits on the bed beside me and forces me back into the pillows. I try to push myself up but the bastard grabs my hands and holds them over my head, leaning his elbows beside my head. His clean smell surrounds me and I can't help but stick my nose in his neck to sniff, making him chuckle. He then proceeds to give me a hell of a good-morning kiss that ensures that absolutely every part of my body is fully awake.

"I say, and get your ass out of bed before I decide to keep you here indefinitely. We have a diner to open."

He trails a finger down my nose and lets his eyes roam over my face. "I love these, you know."

"What?" I whisper, lost in the deep blue of his eyes.

"Your freckles… spots that make you unique." And with one last peck on my lips, he disappears from the room.

When I get downstairs about twenty minutes later, showered and dressed, he has French toast waiting for me. I should be irritated by how comfortable he makes himself in my kitchen but I'm not. Thinking back, he spent enough time here baby-sitting me immediately following my injury so I shouldn't be surprised or bothered.

"Eat up. I'll feed you properly at the diner."

"This is plenty. In fact, more than my usual."

"I know, I'm fattening you up."

I almost choke on the piece of toast I just put in my mouth.

"You what?"

"You've lost a lot of weight so I'm making sure you put it back on." He says with a shrug of his shoulders as if it's the most normal thing in the world.

"Okay, hold on for a minute." I'm trying hard not to overreact to that statement because, well, there is the rare occasion I might do that. "I work hard to lose weight, it never just happens. Once I finally start losing some on my own, you want me to put it back on? That makes no sense at all."

He turns to me as calmly says, "You were always fine. I always liked what I saw, always wanted my hands on it. Don't want you to lose all that softness. It feels good against me."

Oh good Lord. For lack of any sensible thing to say, I cut another piece off my French toast and stuff it in my mouth. When I look up and meet Seb's eyes, they twinkle. Cocky bastard.

Sundays at the diner are always a family affair. People we don't see all week long come in for a breakfast or lunch, and usually with the entire household. The parking lot is overflowing and between Beth, Julie and I, we are scrambling to keep up with the tables. Seb usually has one of us giving him a hand in the kitchen when need be, but mostly we try to stay out of his way. With both grills on and an oversized electrical skillet for pancakes on the counter, he's able to manage feeding half the town. Every now and then when one of us appear in his line of vision, he'll holler for more eggs or potatoes and we'll grab it for him so he can keep his eyes on the food. Good thing we close after lunch on Sundays because all of us are worn to the bone from the long week by then.

I'm just cashing out some customers when I hear my name yelled out from the kitchen. Quickly finishing up at the register, I wash my hands and I'm wiping them on my apron when I walk into the kitchen.

"What can I get you?" I ask Seb, watching him turn from the grill and give me a long lingering scan up and down my body, sending prickles of awareness everywhere.

"Can you see if we have any more Swiss cheese in the cold storage? Those Swiss and mushroom burgers are flying out of here today."

"It's because you put it on the special with the red roasted pepper soup. You know when the weather gets colder everyone goes after your soups, whatever they come with," I remind him. "I'll go check."

We have a freezer the size of a decent broom closet, but next to it is the cold storage. This room is like a walk-in closet, with shelves on both sides and the far end. It's kept at a cool temperature, between 35 and 38 degrees Fahrenheit and I love going in there on busy days like this. It's quiet and refreshing when you've been out in the constant chaos and on your feet all day.

When I pull open the door and kick the wedge in place so the door doesn't close on me, I stop and let the cold envelop me, just for a minute. All of a sudden, I'm shoved in causing me to stumble further inside. I swing around to see Seb standing with his arms resting on the shelves, blocking the exit with the tiniest of tilts to his mouth.

"What are you doing?"

"This." He says as he leans forward and teases my mouth with his lips, testing me for a response. When I relax into his body he releases one hand to grab me by the back of my head and the mood of the kiss changes instantly from easy to voraciously hungry. A groan escapes him as he takes long sweeps with his tongue and I can feel heat collecting just under my skin. Not even the frigid temperature of the space can cool me down – from cold to blistering hot in an instant. I forget everything; food, diner, and customers. All I know is the mouth that's possessing mine, the hand twisting in my short hair and the racing heartbeat in the hard chest I press myself up against.

When Beth's voice filters in through the crack in the door looking for Seb, he pulls back slowly, tucks my head in his neck and kisses my hair.

"I'd better get out there before I set the kitchen on fire."

"You almost did that in here." I point out, making him smile. Damn. He is beautiful when he smiles but it's rare, and when he does, it makes my heart stutter a little.

"Good to know. Thanks, I needed that." Then he disappears back into the kitchen.

"What was that all about?"

"Don't know what you're talking about. What was what all about?"

Beth had her hawk-eyes on me the moment I was back behind the counter. I managed to avoid her by keeping busy, but that wasn't working so well anymore with the crowds thinning out.

"I'm not blind, Arlene. I know you and Seb were both in the

cool storage room. Not only that, don't think I haven't noticed how you two have been circling each other over the last half year. I may not be the sharpest knife in the block, but I can still see just fine." Hands perched on her hips, she stares me down, waiting for and answer.

"Fine. We've had some... run-ins, but it's nothing."

"Uh huh. Nothing? I'm calling bullshit, sister. I've never seen you blush but I gotta say, red's a pretty color on ya." Beth turns her back and makes her way to clear off her section, cackling like an old hen. She passes by Emma and Gus who just walk in the door, giving her an odd look. Sidling up to the counter, Emma immediately turns her attention to me.

"So what is Beth all on about?"

"Oh nothing. She's being a pain in my ass." But that doesn't deter Emma. With a tilt of her head and her eyes squinted to slits, she silently observes me.

"If it's nothing then how come you look like you're overheating when it is almost below freezing outside? You're beet red, woman."

"Geeze Ems. It's been busy, okay? We've been busy running around is all." A loud snort from behind me tells me Beth has returned to overhear my excuse and she feels it necessary to blow my excuse out of the water.

"Right, but only two here have been busy enough to make steam come out of the cold storage, and I can tell you that Julie and I were nowhere near it." I whip around to pin her with my death glare only to watch her walk off throwing me a big smirk over her shoulder.

"I'm still your boss, Beth." I bite off, knowing it's already too late to put the cat back in the bag.

"Oh. I'm intrigued." Emma coos. "Pray tell, Arlene. We're dying here."

"Shut up." Is the best I can do, especially after seeing the self-satisfied smirks on both Emma and Gus' faces. Just then I feel an arm snake around my waist from behind and a familiar dark voice speaks so close to my ear I can feel the breath from his lips. Damn the man.

"You in for lunch?" Seb wants to know.

Frozen in place, I notice the lack of surprise when Gus answers. Probably means Seb has been standing behind me for a bit. Lovely.

"Yes." Gus says. "Just a quick one before I take Emma into Cortez for some shopping."

Eager to change the subject, I jump on that. "Shopping? What are you shopping for, Ems?"

"Christmas decorations. I left most of mine behind in Boston when I moved out here and I want to set up the tree tomorrow night when we get back from our tree-cutting expedition. You guys still coming?"

Shit. I totally forgot. I never even mentioned it to Seb.

"Yeah, sure."

Without hesitation, Seb adds from behind me, as if he had known all along. "What time are we leaving?"

"Why don't you guys come over for breakfast to our place for a change at about nine and we'll take it from there?" Emma waves Beth and Julie over as well. "You girls up to going tree-cutting tomorrow?"

Both of them are staring at Seb who still has his arm firmly around me and with his chin almost on my shoulder. Beth with a big grin on her smug face and Julie just looks surprised.

"I'm game." Beth turns to Julie. "I can come pick you and the little guy up if you want, Julie."

"Uh... no. Tomorrow isn't a good day for me. I'm gonna have to pass." She says turning back to her tables.

Beth and I exchange a questioning look. I can leave it to Beth to figure out what that was about.

"Well now that we have that sorted, I'll get on your lunch. Gus, do you have a minute?" Seb squeezes my side and walks into the kitchen with Gus close behind.

The instant they're out of sight, Emma turns to me. "Spill."

Beth laughs and says, "Busted," before turning to Emma. "Arlene and Seb were nowhere to be found, the door to the cold storage was open a crack and steam was coming out."

"Buzz off, old woman." I tell her, waving her off. Knowing when I'm beat, I tell Emma the entire story, minus one or two details I'd rather keep to myself, including the middle of the night appearance by Seb in my doorway which has her laughing out loud.

"Finally. Now don't mess it up," is the only response I get before Gus is back and helps Emma to their favorite booth.

What the hell is that supposed to mean?

CHAPTER SEVEN

It's 8:45 am when I pull up to Arlene's front door. Her house is an older, small two-story log home on the outskirts of town on a quiet street with five other houses. Her neighbors are a few retired folks that frequent the diner for meals, but other than that you don't often see them out and about. Of course I'm mostly stuck at the diner so I'm not out and about much myself, either.

A good frost settled in overnight and the morning sun is trying to burn off the white residue that remains visible on every surface. It's gonna be a cold trek in the mountains today. Good thing I dressed in layers, I'm looking forward to some outdoor time. It's been too long.

Yesterday afternoon, after we closed the diner for the day,

Arlene had tried to find out what I had needed to discuss with Gus but that's not something I intend to share with her for now. Knowing how pissed she can get when she feels someone is crowding in on her independence, and not quite prepared to share my personal knowledge with her yet, those confessions will have to wait for a better time. She was ticked enough that I had quite obviously staked a claim in front of everyone in the diner when I put my arm around her which almost had me laughing out loud when I felt her freeze under my touch, but now that I've snuck in, I'm not about to back away. I'm not gonna force myself on her, which is why I only followed her home last night to make sure her house was secure and she was locked in and safe. She didn't ask me to stay and I didn't push the issue, but if she thinks I've been scared off, she is in for a big surprise. She better get used to having me in her space. Besides, I first wanted to get a better handle on what we might be dealing with. Gus had seemed pretty disturbed when he heard about the phone calls and I told him a bit about her background. Emma had known a little and shared with him, but apparently not all. Arlene liked to play things close to her chest. Only thing I haven't told him yet is my connection with her ex. The middle of the kitchen at the diner with Arlene just steps away was not a good place for that. I'm thinking that conversation might end up being a bit of a challenge.

I'm hoping to catch Gus out in the open today, but as for Arlene, letting her know the full story is going to have to wait until I'm sure she's getting herself some support. Right now it looks like I might be the only one who has a foot in the door and although I have a suspicion there's a lot more that she isn't telling me, I don't want to risk losing that edge, especially if there's no one else she can fall back on. Stubborn woman.

Just then she comes out the door and sees me waiting by my truck.

"What are you doing here?"

"Picking you up."

"Why? I was just gonna drive myself."

"No need. Hop in. We're both going to the same place."

With a dirty look and muttering under her breath she apparently decides it isn't worth arguing about. Big surprise.

The drive over to Emma's place is silent. I'm not a huge talker and prefer actions to words, but I guess Arlene is stewing inside her own head 'cause all I hear every now and then is huffing. Stubborn woman doesn't realize that attitude of hers only makes me want her more.

"Before you know it we'll have snow." Gus says as we're trudging up a trail, looking for trees to cut. We followed a logging trail as deep as we could by car into the woods and set up a little base camp where we could build a contained fire. Beth and Arlene opted to hang out with Emma, whose mobility issues prevented her from going too far up any trails. They were gathering pine cones and cutting branches for decoration while Gus and I went off in search for trees.

"I hear up near Telluride already has some. They're predicting a stiff winter. Better get snow tires on the trucks."

"Trucks?" Gus wants to know.

"Mine and Arlene's."

"So it's like that, huh?" I can feel him glaring at me.

"Yeah, it's like that." I say, deciding now's as good a time as ever. "Arlene doesn't know this yet, but with everything going on you should probably know that when I was in prison, I…"

"You were cellmates with her ex? Found that out last night, Seb. What the hell?" Gus stops in the middle of the trail and turns to me. "Had Neil pull up some background on that dick last night and I was about to pay you a visit when I found out that tidbit of information. Care to explain?"

Fuck me. Not how I wanted this to go down.

"Yes. He was my cellmate for a few months. Nasty piece of shit, that one. Always spouting off about an ex who got him in there and the revenge he was planning when he got out. Not something I deal with well, abusers. Reason I ended up in jail for assault in the first place. Had a neighbor with loose hands who thought it was okay to use his wife as punching bag. I snapped."

"Knew about that, too. Never bothered checking before, want you to know that. I have pretty good instincts and no flags ever went up around you, but when things went down two months ago, I had Neil pull your record. Standard procedure at that point given the circumstances."

"Hey, I get that."

"What it doesn't explain is why did you come here? Why not simply make Arlene aware, or the authorities for that matter? Why insert yourself into her life, and under false pretenses?"

Ah shit. I run my hands through my hair, stalling. These are answers I don't really have 'cause I'm damned if I even know why.

"Honestly? I don't know. Thought about it. He had this

picture he kept waving around, and sure, she was attractive but that wasn't all. All the things he was so angry about; the fact that he thought he had her beaten down and yet she managed to turn on him from a hospital bed and land him in jail. The fact that she was strong enough to rebuild her life all by herself and make a go of it at a point in her life when things should've already been smooth sailing made me want to know her, and most of all that she did that not only after living with the hell he put her through, but also dealing with a chronic illness she never talks about. From what I can tell, very few people know about."

"Arlene? She doesn't look like there's anything wrong with her. I know Emma once mentioned they met on a website for pain patients or something like that, but it never really sunk in. What does she have?"

"Fibromyalgia. I looked it up myself, had no idea what it was. Turns out it's not that uncommon, but difficult to treat. Basically chronic pain that can travel through the body, pretty random shit, too. Comes with a lot of side conditions; poor sleep, central-nervous system dysfunctions, problems with cognitive functioning and a shit load of pain. Anyway, the woman sounded like she fought an uphill battle her entire life and deserved a break. I didn't even know if he was just blowing smoke or if his threats were serious. I still don't, but with those phone calls I'm not so sure. Did you find out anything about his whereabouts?"

Gus shakes his head. "He's still incarcerated as we speak. Neil is checking to see if he can get a hold of the outgoing telephone records for the jail he's being held in but that might be a tall order. Then again, Neil is just about the best there is, so if anyone can, it's him."

For a while we hike along the trail without speaking, each lost in our own thoughts until Gus stops again.

"Look. Arlene means a lot to Emma, and to me. Don't fuck around with her if you don't mean it. I suggest you come clean with her about knowing her ex before it blows up in your face."

I'm pissed that my motivations are being questioned but I get it, so I try to stay calm. "Not fucking around, Gus. And let me deal with Arlene."

"Fair enough… for now."

By the time we make our way back to the fire where the girls are hanging out, we're dragging two trees each and my fucking arms are about to fall off. Emma wants them all upright so they can figure out which one goes best where. Whatever. I'm just glad to be off my feet for a bit with a mug of hot chocolate and rum to warm my hands. Damn, it's colder than a witch's tit out here! Arlene looks to have cheered up some; an outdoor flush on her cheeks and her eyes sparkling. She doesn't even give me the evil eye this time when she sits down beside me on a log and I pull her close for a quick kiss. She just flicks her eyes over at the others who aren't even paying attention. She'll get used to it.

We sit by the fire, drinking for another hour or so until the cold starts to cut even the heat from the flames. We get the trees in the bed of my truck and tied down. Beth rides with Gus again in the SUV, along with the branches and bags of pinecones and we head down the mountain in a convoy style. First it's Beth's house where Gus and I quickly put the tree in a stand for her. Then we drop a tree off at Emma and Gus' before heading to the diner. The plan is to set up the tree there after the breakfast rush with the girls so they can have fun doing it. I find myself thinking of Faith and how much I miss her at this time of year and the pleasure she gets from decorating. Hopefully next year I'll have her close and we can celebrate together. It's been too many fucking years.

I pull the truck up outside Arlene's house when Arlene suddenly grabs my arm.

"What is that?" She points at a basket sitting on the front step.

"Don't know. You expecting something?" I look at her pale face as she shakes her head no. Something has her spooked for sure. "Sit tight and I'll check it out."

Walking from the truck to the door, I scan my surroundings but don't see anything out of place and I'm not quite sure what has Arlene so freaked out. It's a picnic basket with a handle. Lifting the thing up I'm surprised at the weight. I balance it on the planter and flip up one of the lids and I'm met with the cloyingly thick smell of decay. Holy fucking hell! What sick bastard… Dropping the lid, I immediately put the basket down and turn away to pull out my phone, dialing Gus when I see Arlene getting out of the truck from the corner of my eye.

"Stay there, Arlene. Stay put!"

"What the fuck, Seb. What is it?" Damn stubborn woman. Before I have a chance to intercept her she has lifted the lid on the basket and drops it immediately, slapping her hands over her mouth and whipping around to throw up in the bushes. Just then Gus answers and it takes me half a minute to tell him what we've found.

CHAPTER EIGHT

It only takes a few minutes for Gus to get here, but it feels like a lifetime. I'm surprised to see Emma is with him. After I puked up my guts all over the burning bush in front of my house, Seb hustled me inside and got me a washcloth and a glass of water, telling me to sit my 'stubborn ass' down. He wasn't too happy I hadn't listened to him and to be honest, I wasn't too happy with myself either but dammit, ordering me to do something is like waving a red flag. He should know that by now.

Seb goes outside to intercept Gus and Emma walks in and plops next to me on the couch.

"What the hell happened? Gus just said you'd had a scare and I should come because you might need a friend."

"Fuck, Ems. It freaked me out. We come home and there's a basket by the front door. Seb tells me to stay in the truck and goes to check it out but when I saw his reaction, I had to see for myself." A shiver runs down my spine when I recall the sight and smell of the contents. "I didn't look too closely, but it looked like a dead cat with its belly cut open. Stank to high heaven and it was in a fucking picnic basket. I knew it was bad when I saw the damn thing sitting in front of my door. I just knew there was something off."

"Jesus, woman. That would freak me out, too. Who would do such a thing? That's sick!" She cuddles up beside me on the couch, hanging on to my arm and putting her head on my shoulder.

"Dunno, but what I glimpsed from the cat in the few seconds I saw it, it looked like Mrs. Evans' cat and she was pregnant… I don't even wanna think about what I was looking at, I'll puke all over again."

Gus comes in and walks right over to me, pulling me up and into a big bear hug.

"Hey, girl. Bad scare, huh? That's some sick shit." Right. Trust Gus not to waste words.

I look behind him for Seb. "Where did Seb go?"

"I asked him to give Joe a call while I talk to you about some stuff." He looks at me with penetrating eyes and I'm starting to feel

93

like a bug on a slide, highly scrutinized and decidedly uncomfortable.

"Ok. What?"

"Anything you need to tell me, Arlene? Is this the first strange or threatening thing that's happened to you?"

He knows. Fucking Seb. I know he must have told him about the phone calls. My face goes tight with anger at the sense of betrayal but Gus catches it and calls me on it. "Don't you get pissed, Arlene. If anyone should be pissed, it's me. We are your friends, your family. Why the hell wouldn't you tell us about the shit you've been dealing with, huh? You didn't think it was important enough for us to know?" As Gus' voice starts rising, Seb comes in and slides in between us.

"You wanna keep it down a little, friend?" He points out to Gus. "I get you may be frustrated but yelling won't make anyone feel any better. Besides, I don't particularly appreciate you being in Arlene's face."

I'm just as stunned with Gus' unexpected outburst as I am with Seb's interference, so while the two of them are staring each other down, Emma gets up, shifting her eyes from one to the other and holding up a hand.

"I seem to be the only one without a clue here so may I

suggest you all sit the hell down and one of you tell me right this minute what the blazes is going on with my best friend. Or maybe my best friend would like to do the honors?" With that she turns her fierce glare at me. Oh shit. Kind and gentle Emma doesn't look so kind and gentle right now with her red curls flying about her head and fire shooting out of her eyes.

We all comply and sit our asses down, Seb pulling me close with his arm around my shoulder and Gus still looking irritated as a poked bear.

"I've been getting hang up phone calls for a while now. Whoever it is calls, I answer, and I don't hear a thing until I hear the click of a hang up. A few nights ago there was another call, and that time he said something." I'm uncomfortable going into what lead up to the phone call so I stop right there, but Seb takes over.

"We were in the diner after closing - kissing. The phone rang, Arlene answered and the guy called her a whore. Some of the things he said made it sound like he could see what we were up to. By the time I got the phone from Arlene he had already hung up. All the blinds were up on the windows so it was easy for anyone to see in."

Uncomfortable with the exposure of the conversation and still shaken by the experience from earlier, I get up to make a pot of coffee, needing the time to settle myself and wanting to keep my hands busy. I can hear Emma following me into the kitchen. Slipping her arm around my shoulder she leans in to me.

"You okay, honey?" She says softly and suddenly it's all a bit too much. This was supposed to be a fun day. I had been determined this morning I wouldn't let anything sour it. I try to keep my face averted from Emma so she can't see the stray tears that seem to have escaped my eyes, but the damn woman is too observant.

"I wish you'd talk to me, Arlene. I know you're used to keeping things closed off, but so much has happened in the last few months and now this; I'm afraid you're gonna implode with it all if you don't talk."

It is so tempting to tell her everything - to start all the way back to the beginning and lay it all on the table without skimming over the bad parts like I always do. I can hear the heavy rumble of voices from the living room, indicating that Seb and Gus are deep in conversation as well so we would be safe from prying ears.

I tell her. "I'd love to. You have no idea how much. To just let it all go, but honey - I'm afraid if I do, I'll come apart at the seams."

"Oh, Arlene." Emma wraps her arms around me and I just turn to mush, breaking open and bawling. Still unfamiliar with the kind of warmth she gives freely, I would normally bristle at the show of emotion, but I am so ready for it; craving the temporary safety it gives me to let down my walls. When I feel a second pair of arms, bigger and stronger, take over for Emma's gentle and soft ones in holding me together I look up to find Seb's dark blue eyes. Gus, who

I apparently also treated to a first row seat on my little breakdown, is leading Emma out of the kitchen, leaving Seb and I alone. He cups the back of my head, pushes it into his neck and settles back against the counter, forcing me to lean into him and I do with all my weight. I lean in and let it lodge in my soul.

With the slow firm strokes of his hand on my back, time has disappeared and I'm startled when Gus peeks his head in to inform us that Joe just pulled up, but that he'll give him the rundown outside to give us a few more minutes. Seb moves me back a little and I instantly feel cold and a little lost, but his hands quickly frame my face and he leans his forehead against mine.

"When we are done with Joe, we are going to decorate the tree. After that, I'm going to cook us something and then we'll talk. Okay?"

I just nod my head lightly, not wanting to lose the connection with his hands on my face.

Joe and Gus come in the front door as we come out of the kitchen and Joe walks right over to me, enveloping me in a bear hug.

"Heya, girl. How ya doing?"

"Mmm-Okay" I mumble, my face pressed in his down parka. Ironically, of all the people here, I know Joe the least but he knows most about me, being privy to all official information related to the kidnapping and assault two months ago. He and I had a very uncomfortable conversation in which he made it clear he would respect my privacy and wouldn't discuss some of the information that had come to light during the course of my medical assessment after the attack. It felt odd and almost like a betrayal to my close friends who I know truly love me, but had been left mostly in the dark about the full extent of my injuries. Something I realize now has become a real barrier in my relationships with them. I have some soul searching to do, especially if my suspicions are correct because it means I might need all the friends I can get.

"I'll grab us some coffee." Seb says and heads back into the kitchen. I have a feeling he might not be happy with the way I let Joe keep his arm around me as we move into the living room.

Sitting down beside me, Joe asks me to tell him about the phone calls, which Gus apparently already has informed him about. It's easier this time around and by the time Seb comes back in, Joe is already going back over my story with some pointed questions, but when he asks me if I have any idea who might be behind this, I hesitate.

"With everyone being called back for interviews on the

Flemming case, I initially assumed Will might be behind it, trying to scare me off. I'm sure his lawyers are aware that my memory was sketchy from that night and I wondered if he might be worried I remember something more, or he is trying to keep me off balance so they can use my head injury against me to draw my testimony into question, but now I'm not so sure. I mean, I'm sure he could manage an anonymous phone call, but he's still in custody so who would get pissed at me kissing Seb? Or why kill a cat. That's what puzzles me."

"What about your ex?" Seb offers, surprising me.

"As far as I know he's still locked up too. Besides, what would he want with me? Why now?" I have to admit the thought had occurred to me, but I had quickly waved it off, figuring that if he had wanted to piss me off, he would have likely done so a long time ago when he was first convicted, but apparently Joe was of a different mind.

"Won't be long before he is up for parole. He might be out before you know it." Ok, that's enough to send a shiver down my spine as Joe continues, "For now, I don't want you to be alone at any time, Arlene. It's just a safety precaution, but when we go from silent phone calls to an abusive one, to leaving you a dead cat in a relatively short period of time, it tells me whoever is behind it is losing his cool."

"I'll have Caleb stick around town and keep an eye out, and she can stay with us." Gus suggests.

"Absolutely not. I'll not be chased out of my house or my diner. Fuck him. Not gonna do that." I assert myself, realizing that if I let them, these three guys, plus my bossy best friend will try to plow right over me. "I'm staying right here."

"Of course you are." Seb says. "And so am I. I happen to agree with Joe *and* with you. Don't show a reaction, but also don't be stupid about it and go without some extra insurance."

Well then. He makes it sound very reasonable, yet I still feel I'm being played somehow. When Joe nods and Gus agrees to the plan and offers to have Caleb patrol the surroundings from time to time, I know I've been had, but I have to admit, it makes me feel better. Still, I'd rather swallow my own tongue than admit that any time soon.

When Joe has all he wants from us and reminds me to expect a call from the prosecutor's office for my final interview, he heads off, taking the remains of poor Mrs. Evans' cat with him. He promises to stop by her house to see if it really is hers and will call us when he finds out anything more.

Gus and Ems leave shortly thereafter, after ensuring I'm fine and will call them if anything happens or I need them. That leaves Seb and I, and while he clears away the coffee paraphernalia, I try to process everything that's transpired, coming to the conclusion that I'm very fortunate to have the friends I do. I'd be a fool to jeopardize those friendships so I have to try and open up a little more…if I can.

CHAPTER NINE

"You hungry?" I ask Seb.

We've hauled whatever decorations I have plus the tree stand out of the detached garage on the side of the house. The tree is standing in the dining room that I mostly use as an office space since I eat at the diner or at the kitchen table. I've pulled out some of the decorations, but a lot of them are broken or falling apart.

I'm just standing at the table, surveying what there is to work with when Seb asks me.

"I'm getting there. You?"

"I could eat. I'll whip up something. Maybe after that we can head into Cortez and pick up some new lights for here and the diner and decide if we need any more stuff."

"Stuff?"

"Balls or garland or whatever the hell shit you want to have on the tree," Making me laugh. He's been quiet all afternoon and really hasn't touched me since the melt down in the kitchen. We've just been working side by side quietly, something we always do well at the diner, but it's nice to know that it's not limited to only there. My laughing triggers a little tilt of his mouth and some crinkling by his eyes, indicating he's amused. What a pair we make, neither very well equipped in vocalizing what we think or feel. It'll be interesting.

Walking past me, he tags me by my arm, pulls me close and plants a quick kiss on my lips.

"Figure out what you need, I'll be in the kitchen." I hear as he leaves me standing there, slightly dumfounded as he seems to manage each time he puts his lips on me.

We're lucky Walgreens still has some plain white lights because all Walmart had left was those garish multi-colored twinkling things which are enough to give a person a Grand Mal seizure. I prefer my lights understated, thank you very much, just like my decorations which I intend to make with the bag of pinecones I collected this morning for the house. All I need for that is a bit of wire which is sitting in my cart. I still have some old decorations that had belonged to my grandmother that remind me of a time when Christmas was an exciting time for me. I haven't had those up in ages, but I'm ready to see them up this year. Don't ask me why, but something tells me Christmas might be looking up.

For the diner I want simple silver and red. I don't particularly care what kind of decoration, just as long as they aren't too gaudy or flashy.

"I've never seen a woman shop as fast as you do." Seb observes as I line up at the cash register after less than ten minutes in the store.

"I hate shopping, so you won't see me lingering in any stores. I go in, grab what I need and bee-line it out of there. I avoid it like the plague. In fact, I think I might prefer the plague." He bursts out laughing at that.

"You're not like any woman I've ever known."

"Huh. Not quite sure what to make of that, Seb. A man says something like that, you can take it either way."

This makes him laugh harder.

"S'all good, Spot." That's it. That's all he gives me, although I have to admit, the little nickname *Spot* is making me a little tingly. I guess it should make me feel like a dog, but it only makes me feel special. When he tries to pay for my purchases at the register though, I almost throw a full-fledged fit. No one pays for me. I can make my own money, I can spend my own money - end of story.

"I'll let this one go, Arlene... For now." Accompanied by a stern look is enough of a warning to know that any future with us in it will need to involve a ton of compromise.

We say little on the ride home but I can feel the tension rising. Seb had been very clear he expected us to do some talking at some point and I am second guessing my decision to open up a little with him. Other than the very disturbing find when we got back from picking our trees, I have had the best day I've had in a long time, and a large part of the reason is because Seb was there. What I know of him I like, but I realize I don't really know that much, so how do I know how he'll react to what I have to say? With the little I told him before, he completely tensed up. What if I send him running?

"Deep thoughts? I can see the steam coming out of your ears." I simply shrug my shoulders 'cause I don't really know what to say to that and I don't want to lie. Seb grabs my hand and puts it on his thigh with his covering mine.

"Don't fret. It'll be fine," is all he says.

Once home, we have all the stuff tucked away quickly, leaving decorations for the diner in his truck. Not in the mood right then to tackle the tree, I set out to make a cup of tea, hoping to get the inevitable out of the way rather than drag it out any longer. When I get inside, he's sitting on the couch with his feet on the table, arm on the backrest. I choose to sit in the chair opposite him. I feel I need the distance but Seb apparently doesn't agree. Shaking his head no he stands up, leans over and tugs on my hand, yanking me up and half over the coffee table to where I'm dumped onto the couch where he manages to sit back down, right in time to catch me.

"Seb, I think I need the distance." I try.

"Don't think so."

"But it'll be easier to talk when I'm over there." I plead.

"Nope. It'll be easier to keep the walls up when you're over there. I want you here, where you're real. That's all I'm interested in. No tough act, no disconnect, no struggle and no walls. All I want is you, without pretense and as honest as you can be with yourself, I want you to be that with me. You grant me that – I'll grant you the same thing." With his arm firmly around my shoulders, he tucks me to his side and plops his feet back on the table.

Fuck me sideways. Already I have a lump the size of the Sleeping Ute Mountain in my throat and I haven't even started sharing yet.

"Why don't you try telling me about the nightmares first?" Seb encourages and I'm thinking that's probably as good a place as any to start.

"Okay, well... Usually they put me back in that cottage with Will Flemming, or sometimes in the crusher, seeing the ceiling coming down and not being able to get out. Hearing Kara scream and knowing Emma will be heartbroken if something happens to her daughter makes them all the more worse. The feelings of helplessness really suck and not so much for myself in those ones, but for not being able to do something for Kara. I'm mostly angry. I actually *was* mostly angry and antagonizing him while he had us, trying to keep his focus away from Kara and on me, but I'm thinking I may have taken it a bit too far." This is where I am very uncomfortable going on with my story and I'm fidgeting, which Seb notices right away. Covering my hands with his, he immediately steers me back to the dreams.

"What about the ones in the cottage?"

"That's the hard part. See, I could hardly remember any of it initially except for flashes, but after I got better, larger chunks of time came back. I didn't want to remember, I *don't* want to remember, and the more I push it away, the darker and more frequent the nightmares become. Then when the phone calls started up, they got out of control and I'm almost afraid to close my eyes."

Seb shifts in his seat and moves me forward to slide one leg behind me on the couch and pulls me so my back is against his front and his arms completely surround me.

"Feel me at your back?" His gruff voice sounds right by my ear.

"Yeah." I manage to get out.

"You feel safe here, with my arms around you?"

"I do. But I'm afraid if I let it out, I can't reel it back in. If I allow myself to remember, I'm gonna fall apart."

"Not possible." His arms tighten and he kisses my hair. "You are a rock, and you might slide or threaten to be washed away, but wherever you'd end up, you would still be a rock. And I'm holding on so you'll never get far, and I won't allow you to fall apart."

Taking a few deep breaths, I give him what I know.

"I remember lying on the floor with my head turned to the side and there was blood all around me. At first I thought I must be dead because there seemed to be so much of it, but I realized later some of it was from someone who was lying just inside the kitchen and wasn't moving. Our blood had pooled so close together it looked like one big puddle. I can recall some ripping sounds that I couldn't quite place at first, but later realized what they were. Next time I was on my stomach but facing the wall now and I was in a lot of pain and tried screaming, but there was a hand around my mouth. I tried to bite him but he hissed in my ear that he liked it when they fight, so I stopped."

I feel Seb freeze behind me when he realizes what I am describing to him, so I grab his hands and pull them tighter around me. "You promised to be my safe place." Immediately he makes an effort to relax.

"At some point I passed out again until I woke up to his face in my face, calling me names. Every time I tried to turn my head away he would slap me so my ears would ring. I hardly felt anything after the first few times, but I made him mad when he grabbed another condom - he had unwrapped a bunch of them and lined them up beside me for easy access - and couldn't roll it on 'cause his dick was too soft. I made a remark and he got so mad he rolled me again, managing to violate me again that way, except he also damaged me."

"H-how" Seb breathes out behind me, almost soundless.

"I needed stitches."

"Jesus."

I don't know what to say so I say nothing, but the tears are now rolling down my cheeks as I stare at the wall, waiting for him to get up and say he can't deal. Instead I find myself flat on my back on the couch with Seb looming over me, using his hands and his lips to clear the tears from my face. I'm afraid to breathe.

"More than ever, I wish I had killed him."

I simply nod.

"Seb..."

"Yes, Spot."

"It's in my medical records and the police know. I found out when I was brought to the hospital but I didn't remember at that time. I've told no one since. Joe knows because of the investigation and doesn't talk about it, and for some reason, Caleb has guessed something more happened than I will say. Emma suspects there are after-effects that I'm not dealing with very well, but she doesn't even know any of this. It came back in bits and pieces and I'm still missing parts, but the nightmares are vivid and very real."

"Not gonna talk, Arlene. That's yours to tell. Also not going anywhere, if that's what you were expecting."

"I don't know what I was expecting. Actually – that's a lie." I confess. "It wasn't anything good. Sorry." He's not letting me turn my head away when I try to avoid his eyes. I don't see any judgment or blame, no pity either. I only see warmth and concern. Perhaps a bit of anger on my behalf, but I am convinced now it's not at me. Strange how even telling one person can make you feel a little lighter.

Slowly becoming aware of Seb's solid body resting on mine with his hips wedged between my legs, I can feel my heart rate pick up. Without much conscious effort, my hands that were loosely holding on to the sides of his shirt start making their way around his back, following every curve of his muscles. I spread my fingers wide, trying to keep maximum contact as I slide them up to grab his shoulders and attempt to pull him further down on to me. I don't want to break eye contact, but I suddenly want his mouth on mine desperately. With a deep growl he tilts his head to the side and slams his mouth on mine with a hunger that leaves no doubt he wants me just as bad. One elbow rests beside me in the pillows of the couch, keeping some of his weight off me while the other starts a slow but firm perusal of my neck, shoulder and down to my breast, where he encounters a nipple peaked so tight it's almost painful. With another loud groan that our fused lips drown, his hand changes position and starts at my waist, sliding up under my shirt impatiently. Pushing my utilitarian bra out of the way, he rubs the palm of his hand over the hard tip of my breast, almost causing me to jump off the couch the sensation is so electric.

"Oh God, Seb…" Escapes my lips as I tear away from his mouth, overwhelmed by all these foreign sensations.

"Easy, babe. I've got you." He says, shifting his attention and his nimble tongue to my now exposed breast.

I arch my back off the couch, trying to force him to suck more of me into his mouth, getting frustrated with any distance remaining. A blind need is making me wiggle my hips against his, trying to relieve some of this pressure.

"Am I gonna find you wet, Spot? If I put my fingers inside of you, are you gonna be wet for me?" With his dark eyes fixed on mine, he's willing me to answer, but all I can do is nod. The sounds I'm emitting are breathy and mostly incoherent. Fuck. I've never been this needy – this eager.

Seb eases his hand in the front of my jeans that have become too big on me lately, finding me slick as promised.

"Fuck me. You're drenched."

I have nothing to say 'cause when his thick callused fingers find that little bundle of nerves begging for attention, my synapses fires off all over, blanking my brain instantly.

CHAPTER TEN

Goddamn.

So fucking responsive. She went off like a rocket with a single touch and I barely contained myself from coming like a schoolboy, save for the single session that I paid for when I just got out, I had five years, plus another eight months of my own hand for company, all because I've craved the taste of a woman, *this* woman.

Slowly pulling my hand out of her jeans, I wait until her eyes open and her heavy lidded gaze finds mine. I lift the fingers that were just inside her to my mouth and slide them inside. The combination of the smell and taste of her arousal, combined with the now wide open heated gaze she fixes on me floods my senses. I want nothing more than to rip off her clothes and take all of her in, but a slight flicker of insecurity that skims over her face as my eyes devour her calls me to an instant halt.

Crap. I can't do this. I can't jump her after all she told me tonight. No way in hell is that alright, but when I start lifting myself up off her, she clamps on to my shoulders.

"Hey. Where are you going?"

"No need to rush things." I say, bending down to brush my lips over hers.

"But you…" She motions at the obvious strain behind my zipper where the rock hard evidence of my own arousal is causing quite a bit of discomfort.

"That can wait. What I couldn't wait for was tasting you. Fuckin' delicious." Kissing her again, I stand up and look at her splayed out on the couch. Something stirs in my chest and I know I still have some clearing of the air to do myself, but I'm thinking we've done enough for tonight. Arlene doesn't say anything, but from the way she is straightening her shirt, I'm thinking at least part of her is relieved for the temporary reprieve.

By the time the phone rings, we've made some decent headway with the tree; lights are up and only a few decorations are left to be hung. I haven't touched the subject of her ex or the phone calls yet, choosing to enjoy the comfortable silence and occasional touch as we work.

"Hey Joe, what's up?" I can hear Arlene say before listening for a response from the other end. "Let me check with Seb, but that should be ok. Julie is coming in for the lunch shift so provided she is on time, I can make it for one. Is this for the trial?"

Keeping an eye on her from the corner of my eye, I can see her twisting the cord around her fingers. Shit. We can't both go during the lunch hour and I don't like the idea of her having to go alone. Walking over, I hold out my hand for the phone, but all I get is a raised eyebrow.

"Can I talk to Joe for a sec?"

"Why?"

"Need to ask something." Damn stubborn woman. Reluctantly she hands over the phone.

"Joe, Seb here. Can you hang on one sec? Thanks." Holding the handset against my stomach I pull a stormy-faced Arlene toward me with one hand behind her neck until our noses touch.

"Listen, I'm gonna ask for later in the afternoon. I don't like the idea of you doing this alone." The moment I see her trying to protest I cut her off. "Hear me out, Spot. You trusted me tonight. I think you realize I'm pretty serious about you so give me this play. I want to be there for you when you come out." When no answer is forthcoming, I drop down a little and look into her eyes that she has been stubbornly aiming at my chin. "Please?"

Blinking, her face softens a little and she shrugs her shoulders. I'll take it as a yes.

"Joe - Sorry about that. Listen, is it possible to make it an hour later? That way we're sure the lunch rush is done and we have a chance to get Beth to come in as well. I'm driving her to Cortez. That okay?" I never break eye contact during my conversation with Joe until he drops a bit of a bomb, then they fly toward the window. "Uh huh. I see… You want to ask now? Can't it wait until tomorrow? Fine, but you do realize it's 9:30 at night, right?"

Arlene is trying to grab the phone out of my hand, having caught on to the fact that we're talking about her.

What? She's mouthing at me with big eyes. I hand over the phone but am not happy about it, especially not when I see her face lose all color and her eyes blinking furiously, yet she completely surprises me when I hear her say, "Can't think of anything right now but if I do, I will let you know."

"What the fuck was that, Arlene? You blowing smoke up his ass?"

"Don't know what you're talking about." She waves her hand as if I'm some dumb pesky fly as she turns around and goes straight up the stairs, leaving me to stare after her, trying to figure out what the hell just happened.

Joe mentioned the vet had a quick peek at the cat we found this afternoon and had concluded the cat had been pregnant and close to delivery when it was killed. The kittens were killed in the womb. He had wanted to know whether that would have any significance for Arlene and although her response to Joe denied it, her body language told me the complete opposite. That was absolutely something significant to her!

I'm jumping up the stairs two at a time and I march over to her bedroom, but it's empty, although I hear noises from the bathroom. Standing right outside the door I can hear water running, but just underneath that there is the distinct sound of retching.

"Arlene, open the door!"

"I'm fine. Be right out."

"You're not fine and if you don't open up, I'm coming in by force if I have to. Arlene?"

"Hold on! You frickin' bully... can't a person have some peace in her own house!" I can hear her sputter as she unlocks the door.

"I call bullshit."

From her red splotchy face, the watery eyes and the distinct sour odor in the bathroom, I can guess dinner ended up in the toilet. I walk over and wrap her in my arms tightly, putting my cheek on her head, ignoring the struggling woman in my arms.

"Be still."

"Let me go. I smell!"

"Don't care. Something's wrong. Something made you upset enough to cause you to be sick and I need to hold you, so stop struggling for a minute, will you?" Slowly I can feel her reluctance making place for some semblance of relaxation when I refuse to budge. Once a little shivery sigh leaves her lips, I take a step back, kiss her forehead and look around for a washcloth to clean up her face a little. When I notice she's managed to get some on herself and apparently also on me, my decision is made. Leaning into the tub. I turn on the shower and start peeling off my shirt.

"What are you doing?"

"We're cleaning up." I say matter-of-factly as I kick off my boots and drop my jeans.

"Are you nuts?" She's getting a full head of steam worked up now. I can see it.

"No, but you were upset enough to puke on yourself. You'll feel better when you have a shower, and so will I. Besides, I'm not about to leave you alone." Grabbing her face in my hands I lean in. "I am *not* going to take advantage of you. I'm simply going to be with you, that's all. Now let me help you."

Then just like that, all the fight is gone from her. Her face is still white as a sheet and not looking at me, she allows me to help her out of her clothes. I'm doing my best not salivate over every inch of her delicate skin that's revealed. Her body is so fucking soft and dusted with freckles everywhere. I try to keep my eyes above her shoulders but it isn't easy when I'm peeling down her jeans and panties. My cock isn't listening either, but there isn't a damn thing I can do about that except hope she realizes my response to her is a compliment to her gorgeous body and not because I can't control myself. Arlene isn't noticing much of anything right now though. She willingly allows me to guide her into the shower while I shed my socks and my boxers before joining her under the spray.

Determined to keep this as non-sexual as I can, I make quick work of washing her hair and by the time I've done my own, she's going through the motions of washing herself. A quick rinse off and I'm out and ready for her with a towel. Both dry, she doesn't even complain when I slide into bed with her and scoop her up and tuck her against me with her head on my shoulder. Neither of us say another word, although I'm hoping she'll eventually say something, sooner rather than later, I hope.

He's telling me he can still control me – still does control me so now I know it's him. He's the only person who has a reason to send a message like that. The one person who knows the kind of horrible memories that would bring out of me, but how? I don't get it.

Seb is so kind, taking care of me and trying to watch out for me, but I'm afraid what could happen to him. I'm frankly scared of what he would do if he found out. He has his own dark history he's been working hard to make a clean break from, and I don't want to be responsible for pulling him back there. Why now? Just when I'm ready to let go of some of the anger I carry around, something else has to happen to me?

The devil always shits on the same heap…

CHAPTER ELEVEN

At some point I must have fallen asleep wrapped in the comfort of Seb's arms, but the ringing of a phone somewhere wakes me up.

I can feel Seb sliding out of bed, leaving me cold but with a perfect view of the colorful ink that covers almost every exposed part of his skin - legs included. I don't get a good look 'cause my eyes won't open all the way yet and I'm quite distracted by the flex of his ass as he disappears into the bathroom where he left his jeans earlier. Must be his phone. Turning over, I try to snuggle back under the covers and close my eyes but it isn't the same without him. Sleep won't come and after a frustrating ten minutes or so of shifting around, I need to get up to pee. I check the bathroom which is empty, meaning he must have taken the call somewhere else. I do my business and check my watch on the counter. Already 4:30 am. Might as well get up, throw something on and try to get an early start.

There is no sign of Seb when I get to the kitchen and I start my morning routine of getting coffee going and pulling a few slices of bread out of the freezer for toast. I sit at the kitchen table waiting for my coffee, thinking about my appointment with the DA at the County Sheriff's Office in the afternoon. I wonder who will be conducting the interview? Part of me hopes the details around my assault won't come up, but I know I'm kidding myself. After today that will all likely be public record.

Suddenly feeling a need to have Seb close by, I go looking and find him on the deck with his back toward me, still on the phone.

"I know, Faith, I miss you too."

I am about to turn back in the house when I hear him say that and I freeze on the spot, unable to move or breathe.

"Can't wait to see you either, Pumpkin. Love you."

When I hear those words in his deep rumble directed at someone else, something snaps in me and I haul ass. In my ratty old sweatpants, old college t-shirt and bare feet, I hoof through the house, snatching up my keys from the kitchen table and run out the front door, never looking back once. I can hear Seb calling out for me but I'm not willing to hear him or stop. Once in my truck, I peel out of the drive and down the road, my first instinct to head for the diner but I know that's the first place he'll look. All I know is I need to get away. I have tears running down my face and I can feel the hysteria building, but when I slow down for the turn at the end of the road, a truck cuts in front of me and forces me to steer into the curb. When my engine sputters and dies, I fall apart completely and hang onto the steering wheel, sobbing uncontrollably. The knocking on my driver's side window barely registers and not even when the door is ripped open do I move. I feel as if I'm being ripped open, as if the tight control that has held me together for so long has disintegrated in an instant and my insides are pouring out. This was the drop that overflowed my bucket.

I have no energy for anything other than the purging of misery and when strong arms pick me up and pull me out of my truck, I don't even care anymore. I'm just too damn tired to fight, and way too broken to save.

When I hear the sharp intake of breath behind me just as I'm saying goodbye to Faith, who had had another one of her nightmares, I realize instantly I should have told Arlene about her a long time ago, but it's too late now because after all that woman has been through, I have just added to her pain. Fuck me!

I can't catch up with her before she gets to her truck and she is not stopping, but I box her in at the end of the road. What I see when I get to the cab of her truck concerns me. Draped over her steering wheel, it seems to be the only thing holding her up. An agonizing wailing filters through the windows and her whole body seems to be shaking. Unable to get her attention with knocking, I open the door, but when she still doesn't respond to my voice or any sound for that matter, I reach in and pull her out. She falls into my arms without any resistance and I carry her to my truck where I buckle her in. Without thinking, I make the decision to take her straight to the ER in Cortez. When she calms down, she'll likely be furious, but I have never seen someone go off the deep end like this and knowing what I now know about the shit she's experienced and the stress that still puts her under, I'm not taking any chances. I don't give a fuck that neither of us are wearing shoes and I have no shirt on.

Thank God the first face I see when I carry Arlene through the sliding doors of the emergency room is that of Naomi Waters, ER physician and a recent friend of Emma and Arlene's. She rushes over when she sees me carrying Arlene and calls for a clear bed over her shoulder.

"Tell me what happened?" She wants to know and as briefly as possible, I outline the stress she's been under and the finding of the dead cat yesterday afternoon on her porch, followed by a misunderstood phone call she overheard.

"She took off and I had to race after her. When I stopped her, her truck stalled and I found her much like this, slumped over in her truck. I came straight here, thinking she's finally reached her limit."

"Put her down here on the bed, Seb. Check with the nurse at the station outside for some scrubs and booties so you don't catch anything. You have cuts on your feet. Once I've had a chance to look her over, I'll come check those out. Sit tight."

Knowing the drill after the last few months, I do as she tells me. Once dressed and with my feet covered, I sit down in the waiting area and call Gus' cell phone. He answers right away, despite the fact it's 5 am.

"Talk to me."

"Arlene had a bit of a breakdown so I brought her to the hospital. Naomi is checking on her now. We left the house in a hurry and I didn't lock anything or turn anything off. Could you check?"

"We'll do that on our way in."

"Actually... I'm thinking maybe hold off on coming in. If there is something serious to report, I'll call."

125

A grunt from the other end makes it clear Gus is not in line with my thinking.

"You've met my woman, right Seb? That is not something that will go over well. That is her best friend you are talking about." A bit of a scuffle later I have Emma on the phone. "Who are you to tell me I can't see her?"

"Whoa, slow down, Ems. I want to give her some breathing room. She's opened up to me a little the last few days and I'm not about to have her shut the door again because she feels crowded. Too much crap is happening to her at once and I'm scared it's going to break her if we push her too much."

"I'm trusting you to call me the minute you know something, buddy!" A very pissed off Emma slams the phone down, still not happy with my request but obviously on board - for now.

I lean my head back, close my eyes and try to let the tension go from my shoulders. What a cluster fuck.

It is almost noon on Tuesday by the time we are on our way

to Arlene's house. When Dr. Waters insisted she avoid work for at least the next 48 hours to rest up or face hospitalization for a few days, Arlene stopped arguing long enough to get in the truck where she begins to start in on me; wanting to know why I took her to the ER in the first place when she'd only had a small crying fit. Right. I am not responding to her tantrum and it just seems to infuriate her more.

"I can't believe you had Beth and Julie open the diner for lunch! There's no cook - Hello! Don't know why the hell you think you need to stay with me and hold my hand. You should have just opened yourself. They'll never be able to manage like this."

I sigh, having been through this argument at least once before. The medication they gave her was supposed to level her mood, but it seems to me it only brings out the stubborn and contrary side of her. Have to admit though, I like seeing this side of her better than the broken, whimpering shell of a woman I was holding in my arms earlier. That shit tore me up, especially since I feel responsible for her breakdown, or I was the straw that finally broke the camel's back. I've called Joe and asked him to postpone the appointment with the Prosecutor's Office to a date later in the week and plan to keep things calm and quiet for today as best I can, but there is one thing that has to be cleared up right away. I can't have her thinking there is someone else.

As for the rest, after today I can't postpone this anymore. No more distractions and evasions. Things are too damn volatile and shaky and she needs to hear the whole truth from me before something else happens. I'll just have to deal with the consequences.

Putting my hand on Arlene's leg as we take the turn off to Cedar Tree, I try to reassure her once again.

"Emma will help with the cooking and she roped Caleb into helping as well. Stop worrying and let it go. It'll be fine."

With a derisive snort, she folds her arms and pointedly looks out the side window. The way her breasts squeeze together and lift has my cock stirring awake after the shock of seeing Arlene come undone left it virtually useless. Not the right time, but thank God for that sign of life! Shouldn't be surprised, though. I figure this woman could get any kind of rise out of me, alive or dead.

True to his word, Gus had been by and turned off the coffee pot and lights, and even managed to get Arlene's truck we had left half on the curb down the road back into the driveway. Still pouting, Arlene makes her way into her bedroom and I let her go, giving her some room while I figure out how to broach the issue of my past and how it is connected with hers.

CHAPTER TWELVE

I wake up with a warm body wrapped around me and have a sense of déjà vu. This time it isn't the ringing of a phone that wakes me up though, but the gentle nipping of lips and teeth at my neck and shoulder while a large hand simply holds one of my breasts cupped in his hand.

"Almost three o'clock, Spot. You slept a hole in the afternoon." The sound of Seb's voice rumbles against my ear and I let the full-body experience of him settle under my skin. This feels so damn good. I don't have it in me to stay difficult when this man makes me feel so languid and safe with his sound, his smell, and his touch.

Turning around to face him, I run my hand through his hair

that always seems to look disheveled.

"Who is she?"

From the pained look in his eyes, I realize this might not be an easy question, or answer, for either of us.

He drops his eyes when he starts talking, as if he's afraid to see my reaction.

"Her name is Faith and she's my sister. My little sister." The tight band around my chest relaxes a little when I hear him say that, but the anguish in his eyes I find myself looking into when he lifts his gaze cuts me to the core. "Our childhood wasn't great. Dad drank and took it out on our mother and later on me. When I got too big for him to overpower easily, he tried to go after Faith, but I made sure I was always around, except one day I wasn't and he managed to beat her half to death in a drunken rage. She was only eight and I did nothing." He turns away from the hand I stretch out to him, and rolls into a sitting position on the edge of the bed.

"How old were you?" I ask him gently, knowing he couldn't have been more than a child himself.

"Old enough to know I should've gone to the police, but I didn't. I trusted my mother who promised to take care of Faith and get us out. She never did."

"How old, Seb?"

"Twelve. Twelve fucking years old. Four years older and I had promised to take care of her, make sure he wouldn't touch her. I promised her I'd take her with me when I found a job so we could leave. I promised her that and now, she will never have a normal life. No husband, no kids, no dancing. All she has is nightmares that have her wake up in terror almost nightly."

I crawl through the bed and mold myself around his back. Not saying anything, I just wrap my legs and arms around him, trying to anchor him… or something. He shivers before grabbing hold of one of my hands and bringing it to his lips. The kiss he presses to my palm sends tingles up my arm and buzzes my body into a different kind of awareness. I wrestle my way under his arm, trying to climb onto his lap to face him, but I've obviously forgotten I'm not as limber as I used to be. As I'm sliding my ass around, trying to hang onto his shoulders for purchase, I slip and my cranky old body hits the floor before Seb has a chance to grab hold of me.

"Jesus, woman!" He blurts out, shocked. All I can do is laugh. My ass is gonna be bruised and so is my ego, and that leaves only one thing to do - laugh. Seb looks at me as if I've finally taken that last step around the bend, and that makes me laugh even harder as tears run down my face now and my stomach starts to ache.

"S-so much f-for my seduction technique… Did I turn you on, Seb?" Overtaken by a new fit of hilarity, I roll back onto the floor and curl up, holding my stomach as I laugh and cry even harder.

"You're a nut." Seb's eyes appear in my line of blurry vision as he lays down on the floor beside me, humor shining in them. He strokes the stray hairs off my face and wipes at the tears coursing down my cheeks. The instant he touches me I calm down until all that is left is a smile on my face. I take in his gorgeous dark eyes and see to my satisfaction that the pain that was there before has been replaced with warm amusement and something hotter.

"I wanted to make you feel better. Hell, maybe even myself, but this wasn't exactly the way I had it planned." I admit, seeing the lines by his eyes deepen but he doesn't say anything, so I decide to push a little.

"I want to feel better. No. I *need* to feel better, Seb. Please?" Sitting up I lift my shirt over my head and drop it on the floor beside me. Seb's eyes follow every move I make, but still he doesn't move from his spot on the floor. I reach behind me and undo my ugly-ass bra and when that slides down my arms and exposes my somewhat pendulous breasts, I can see I have a reaction. I feel horribly exposed and unsure, but I don't doubt that Seb cares and by the look of his darkening eyes and the flare of his nostrils, he doesn't mind the losing battle with gravity and the bit of extra flab one bit. In a flash he's up, has me off the floor and on my back on the bed, hovering over me, looking me up and down before locking on my eyes.

"Fucking shivers. The smallest things you do turn me on, but seeing you like this - Shivers." Bending his head he kisses my mouth, over my cheek to my jaw and down my neck where he opens his mouth and allows his tongue to drag over my skin. All along my upper chest from clavicle to clavicle leaving a wet trail, never allowing his mouth to leave my skin, mapping every inch with his lips and tongue. Slowly tracing his way up and down the slope of my breasts to the tight peaks where he latches on and sucks me deep into the recesses of his hot mouth. Such a drawn out delicious torture. My body is squirming restlessly and I can feel the arousal seeping from my pussy.

Where does he find the patience? My hands are frantically running along the muscles right under his skin and I can feel the rippling tension so tightly controlled in him. Realizing he is being careful for my sake, I am determined to take this to the next level. I manage to wiggle out of my panties and get to work on his jeans, only to find him commando underneath. One less thing to worry about. Pulling him free he grabs hold of my hand around his cock.

"Slow down, Spot. No rush." His words say one thing, but his eyes are boiling, so making use of the fact he has less leverage with only one hand holding him down, I push off with both legs and manage to flip him on his back. Quickly straddling him, I run my hands under his shirt and pull it up.

"My turn… Up." With a tiny smirk on his face, Seb complies and raises his arms, allowing me to take off his shirt. Then I move down his chest, tracing the gorgeous artwork laid out in front of me. I can't resist putting my teeth into his pecs to test for firmness and from the growl I receive, he doesn't mind that at all. A bit of turnabout play with his nipples and I am sliding down his body, making sure his rock hard erection is caught between my tits as I squeeze them together with my arms. Pressing my forehead down on his abdomen, I can just catch the tip of his cock with my tongue and I get my first taste of Seb's rich flavor.

"Fucking hell. Stop, Arlene. I'm gonna come if you don't stop." His fingers clench in my hair and I stop, only because I want him inside of me. I want to feel him deep when he comes.

Sitting up, I slide my wet core over his straining dick and ease myself down. When I find his eyes, they are burning with heat and his hands are flexing on my hips, telling of the restraint he is putting on himself. I lean toward his mouth, never losing eye contact and kiss him with all the feelings I have bubbling inside of me before dropping myself down the last inch or so.

"Ohh…" The feeling is indescribable. I am in total control. I am filled and stretched by a kind and beautiful man who moves me, and I chose to be here. I chose to be naked, I chose to take him inside my body. When I look at Seb, I can see the understanding in his eyes and it makes me tear up. Slowly his hands start stroking up my back in gentle motions, setting a rhythm for me to follow without forcing my body. I put my hands on his chest and tentatively set my moves to the tempo as he strokes. It doesn't take long for my body to start bucking in a disconnected race for some grand finale. Eyes closed in my strain to reach that elusive peak, I can hear Seb's breathing grow more erratic beneath me - struggling not to take over. Frustrated with myself and needing him to be more assertive, I know I have to ask.

"Please... I can't... Take over. Take me there. Please, Seb."

Seb sits up. "Wrap your legs around my waist, Spot." When I do as he says, he pulls himself up on his knees, still inside me, and while he stays sitting on his knees, he lowers me down on my back. He pulls my legs loose behind him and pulls my ass up as he rises up on his knees, keeping himself embedded inside of me.

"You okay like this, babe?"

I nod and grabbing me firmly by my hips, he slowly starts moving in and out of me. I can see it. I can see his cock sliding in and out and he's watching as well, and watching me. This is so fucking hot. As the tempo picks up I can't help but push my body onto his as hard as I can each time he enters me. I want it harder.

"Fuck me. Seb. Harder...fuck me harder, please."

One look at me and one hand leaves my hips to grab my shoulder and hold me in place as Seb starts pounding into me. I spread my legs as wide as I can so every slam of his pelvis against mine hits my clit and along with the slap of his balls against my ass I can feel the oncoming rush of an orgasm.

When it hits, I can feel the pulse going through my entire body like an electric current. My mind blanks as I scream out my release just as I feel Seb's body giving in to its own release. He groans and jerks inside my body and lays himself over me with his face buried in my neck. We stay like that for endless moments after, wrapped around each other and softly touching, the odd aftershock sending us both into shivers.

"Holy shit." Is the first thing out of my mouth once the lingering spasms have left my body and my dick finally softens and slides out of Arlene. Barely having caught my breath, it seems my brain is still not functioning on all cylinders. Mind-blowing is an accurate description of the release I just experienced. Months of pent up need to touch and taste her.

I push myself up and look in her slightly flushed face. "The anticipation was sweet. The reality? Un-fucking-believable. You amaze me."

She turns her head away slightly, not saying anything, but a small tilt of her lips tells me hearing that pleases her.

"Be right back." With a kiss to her forehead I slide out of bed and head into the bathroom for a quick cleanup, returning with a wet washcloth. Sitting on the side of the bed, I pull down the sheet Arlene has pulled over herself and gently spread her legs so I can wash myself off her. It has occurred to me we haven't used any protection and although it oddly doesn't bother me in the least, I realize it is something that should be addressed. Arlene may feel quite differently.

"No one has ever done that for me before." She tells me when I slip back in the bed with her after tossing the washcloth in the sink.

"Clean you up?" I shrug my shoulders. "I like doing that for you. I've never done it before, but I wanted to."

Snuggling against my side, she kisses my chest. "Thanks. And don't worry, I can't get pregnant and I'm clean. I got tested twice after… well, you know, in the last couple of months."

"I'm sorry, but it wouldn't have made a difference, and by the way, I'm clean too. Was tested shortly after I got out." I can see her eyebrows go up at my thoughts on pregnancy.

"You want children?" Her voice is muffled as her face is turned into my chest.

That makes me think. I never had time for kids, always been too busy looking after Faith and it simply hasn't come up, but I wouldn't have been against children with someone I cared about, like Arlene, so I try to explain. "Kids have never been on my radar, but I wouldn't mind them with the right person. I like children, so if a kid had been the result of us being together, I wouldn't regret that ever."

I look down when I notice Arlene has gone rigid against me. I can't see her face so I try to roll her to her back, but she is determined to keep her face pressed against me.

"What did I say? Babe?"

When she finally lifts her face it is wet with tears. "I hate crying, you know." She says with a sad smile.

"Yeah, I get that."

I don't say anything more, just stroke her back and let her be. She doesn't need to tell me not being able to have kids hurts her. It's pretty obvious and I'm also thinking whoever left that damn cat on the doorstep is aware of that. Picking a pregnant cat and killing the kittens inside was a message to Arlene, and she received it loud and clear, going by her reaction. A few things were clicking into place for me. Most importantly that this was information Joe needed. There would only be so many people with that knowledge.

Arlene is still in bed, snoozing. If it weren't for hunger setting in, I would've stayed right there with her, but we both had to eat, so I'm out on the deck, grilling a few chicken breasts I found in the freezer and some peppers. Slipping my cell phone from my back pocket I dial Joe's number.

"Joe, it's Seb."

"Seb, what's up?"

"Hey, listen. Did you know Arlene can't have kids?"

"Eh...no? I'm not sure - "

"Bear with me, ok? When you asked if the condition of the dead cat had any significance for her, you didn't see her reaction. She said no, but I was there and her body language screamed yes."

"Damn! He knows her, and knows her well."

"That's what I figure. I don't think this is common knowledge, Joe, and another thing. I think it isn't for medical reasons she isn't able to have kids."

"That sick fuck! He cut that cat, killed those kittens inside... You know I have to talk to her, Seb."

"Yeah. She's gonna be pissed, I'm warning you. I'll talk to her and get back to you."

After I hang up, I check on the grill. Just a few more minutes and it'll be done. It's time to get Arlene up, fed and up to speed. Preferably in that order.

CHAPTER THIRTEEN

"Why would you tell him?"

I feel sick to my stomach when Seb tells me he called Joe to let him know about my inability to have kids. What the hell? I'm so stupid for spilling my guts in a moment of weakness. Typical. Just like a man, the first chance he gets he fucking blows through that trust like it's nothing.

When he tries to hold me by the shoulders to look me in the eye, I try to twist out of his grasp but he won't have it.

"Arlene! Listen to me. I never would have said a thing if I didn't think it was crucial to your safety. Just hear me out." Reluctantly and with my lips pressed together to show it, I raise my eyes. Only concern meets me when I find his dark blue ones staring into mine.

"The person who has been harassing you… who left the dead cat, has to be someone you know, and, Arlene? I think you know that." His now stern expression has me lowering my gaze because he's right. I do know that, I just don't want to deal with it. It means opening up about a wretched time in my past when I am still raw from a more recent assault and I just don't think I can keep it together once I dig it up. I'll fly apart. I know I will.

"You don't understand… I *can't* go there. I just can't." I plead with him.

Working his hips between my legs, he pulls my body to the edge of the stool and folds me in his strong arms, tucking my head under his chin. "You can, Spot. You've got to. It will help us get a better grip on what is going on here and why. Please. I'll be right here, I promise."

A sudden wave of anger flares through me as I push Seb away from me and get up. "I am sick of this shit! So tired of struggling every goddamn day! Tired of being weak, always in pain, terrified and terrorized! What the hell did I ever do to deserve this crap, huh? Tell me!" By now I am screaming in frustration. I seriously would like nothing more than to curl up in a ball in a corner somewhere and disappear. I've had enough. Seb just stands there, hands in his pockets, not saying anything. Just as quickly as it came, the anger leaves me like a balloon deflating, a numb resolve left in its place.

"Fine. You win, but I'm only telling once and I need you with me."

In two steps Seb reaches me and takes my face in his hands placing a kiss on my lips. "Wouldn't be anywhere else, love." My chest tightens a little when the endearment falls from his mouth so easily, but I am willing myself not to make too much of it. No use setting myself up for more pain.

Joe is still at his office when Seb calls and asks if we can come there; he'd prefer to make a recording of what I have to say. I agree, if only to prevent having to open up that dreaded chapter of my life more than once.

I'm nervous driving into Cortez. My carefully controlled life is effectively coming apart at the seams. The capable and badass Arlene Bowers is going to be exposed for the whimpering fool that she is, and for the whole world to see. Fuck me. There goes my reputation. I've never talked about my divorce a whole lot, never feeling the need to rehash old hurts. Emma may be the only one who knows about the violence, but even from her I've kept some details.

"You okay there, Spot?" Seb rubs his big hand up and down my leg, throwing me a glance. I manage to squeeze out a tight smile.

"Yeah. Just stick by me."

"Of course." His eyes are warm and the side of his mouth lifts up as he looks at me. For a minute I forget everything but the man sitting beside me. A warm feeling starts spreading, loosening the tight fist that's been squeezing my chest. *'Of course.'* Could it really be that simple? Just trust someone to have your back without question?

Joe is waiting at the front desk when we get to the Sheriff's Office. Getting out of the truck, Seb grabs my hand and laces his fingers through mine, giving me a reassuring squeeze and holding tight. Glad for the silent show of support, I hang on.

"Arlene. Seb." Joe nods at us. "Let's find a place to sit." Turning, he leads us behind the front desk into the first room on the right. Prepared for some kind of interrogation room, I am surprised to see he has brought us into his office. He obviously picks up on my expression. "Thought we might be more comfortable in here. Have a seat. Seb, if you'd like, you can wait out in the hallway."

I grab our joint hands with my free one and shake my head. "Seb stays. I need him here."

His eyes traveling from our clasped hands to our faces, Joe smiles. "Sure thing. Have a seat, Seb." He gestures to the second chair this side of his desk.

"I have a feeling this is not going to be easy for you so I will tell you what I know and I will leave it to you to fill in the blanks. I will try to leave the questions to a minimum. You need to take a break, you tell me. Okay?"

I nod. I've been trying to keep my mind void of the dark memories as long as possible, but sitting here, knowing I'm going to have to relive the most painful event of my life once again has me breaking out in a sweat.

"Turning on a recorder now, Arlene. Is that okay with you? That I record our interview?"

"Sure, I'd rather not have to repeat myself if I don't have to," I tell Joe.

"Here is what I know," he starts, "you have been receiving anonymous phone calls for weeks. No identification, no voice, just dead air and a hang up both at home and at work until last week when you and Seb were in the diner after closing. This time there was an angry male voice on the line, one you didn't recognize. At that point Seb became aware and talked to Gus. Am I correct so far?"

I nod, but Seb speaks up.

"Actually, I had noticed something about those calls earlier at the diner and when that last call came in, we called your office."

Joe's head shot up. "What do you mean, my office?"

"Immediately following the threatening phone call, I called the Sheriff's Office and was told to come in on Monday to file a report. That was it. We never had a chance to because we found the little surprise on Arlene's doorstep on Monday and you ended up over there anyway."

Joe's face had gone tight. "Remember who took your original call?"

"Sorry, no. I never asked. Is there a problem?"

"There was no record made of your call. I'll deal with it. Let's move on."

I've been quietly listening, waiting for the inevitable. When Joe looks at me, I know it's time.

"It's Monday and you find a picnic basket on your doorstep. In it is a cat belonging to your neighbor. Like I told you, the cat was pregnant and her kittens were killed in the womb."

I can't help flinching at the matter-of-fact description Joe gives. Seb strokes my knuckles with his thumb, sensing this is not easy for me.

"When I called you to give you that news, you indicated that fact had no significance. As I understand it, there might be something you would like to add or change to that. Take your time." His kind eyes focus on me as I feel all the moisture drain from my mouth, making it impossible to speak.

Seb leans in and whispers in my ear. "You've got this, babe. And I've got you."

"Okay." I whisper back. With my eyes downcast I begin. "My marriage wasn't always violent. Verbally abusive, probably, but not violent until the last few years. It kinda snuck up, I guess. Rough treatment at first where initially I would think it was an accident to where I realized he liked seeing bruises on me. Then came the slaps and punches. Again, pretty harmless initially, or at least it seemed that way to me at the time. My butt, my legs, my back. Then my face. I didn't like that at all, but I had already numbed myself to so much at that point that letting one more thing slide for the sake of keeping the dream of my marriage, the hope of my future alive, didn't seem like a big step. It was my life, you know? I knew nothing else."

Seb grabs a handful of tissues and wipes my face. I hadn't even realized I was crying. My voice monotone, I force myself to get through this part of my sordid story all at once with a minimum of emotion. Enough tears have been shed.

"I got pregnant at thirty-nine years old. Geoff had wanted kids, but when I didn't get pregnant quickly he became surly. When tests showed it was his low sperm count that was the issue, he became furious and of course, took it out on me. For years he was determined to make our lack of children my fault. My unexpected pregnancy at such a late stage surprised me… surprised us. He beat me bad the first time I told him. I thought he would be happy. He was convinced the baby wasn't his. Nothing I could say or do would change his mind. I was hospitalized twice during the first four months of my pregnancy with a variety of broken bones. Doctors suspected I'm sure, but the pregnancy gave me the excuse of clumsiness. Don't ask me why I didn't leave then. I ask myself that question every day and don't know. I wish I had."

"You need a break, Arlene?" Joe's kind voice interrupts. I shake my head. I want to get this over with now.

"He was finally successful at the end of month five. He broke one arm and dislocated the shoulder on the other so I wasn't able to protect my belly. He kept kicking until blood started flowing. Then he ran."

"Jesus…" I hear Joe mutter and Seb says nothing but he stands, lifts me and sits back down with me on his lap. His arms tight as a vice around me, nose buried in my neck. I'm surprised to find my eyes dry.

"A neighbor found me and I ended up in the hospital. My baby had died. I almost did from a ruptured uterus, which they had to remove. My shoulder was popped back in, the other arm was set and I finally filed charges for abuse and for a divorce, but too little, too late." I look up to meet Joe's eyes. "Somehow he's behind this. I know he is."

"I will ask to have his calls and outside contact monitored. I will find out who is doing this, doll, if it's the last thing I do." Joe says as he gets up from behind his desk and walks over to where I am still sitting on Seb's lap. Seb reluctantly lets me up but keeps his body right behind mine, his hand on my hips.

"Gonna let you guys get out of here. Get some rest. There are no words, Arlene, to express what I'm feeling right now, and I'm sorry just doesn't seem to cut it." Joe wraps me in a strong comforting hug, but Seb never lets go of my hips. Despite everything, that makes me smile.

I can't speak. The entire drive back home I'm hanging on to Arlene's hand, but I'm afraid to say a word. I can feel her eyes on me from time to time, trying to gauge where my mind is at, but my anger is bubbling so close to the surface, I'm afraid to open my mouth for fear of what will come out. To think I had that fucking miserable excuse for a human being in my reach for all that time... It makes my blood boil. I would have gladly ended him. Hell, I get my hands on him, I *will* end him.

When we pull into Arlene's driveway I turn off the engine and finally let go of her hand to get out. By the time I get to the passenger side she is already standing beside the truck staring at the ground in front of her.

When I put my arm around her and start walking to the front door I notice she is stiff as a board. Once inside I flick a few lights on and take her along to the couch where I sit down and pull her on my lap. Lifting her chin I notice she is fighting back tears.

"Don't cry." I manage, my voice cracking. "You hate crying, remember? I'm sorry you had to live that and that I forced you to share it. I'm angry with that sick bastard. So fucking angry I'm shaking with it, and I'm frustrated I can't make it right; that it's too late for me to protect you from that. All those things run through my head and I -"

"Shhh. I get it now. It's okay." She winds her arms around my neck and leans her cheek against mine. "You were my rock today. I couldn't have done that without you."

Fuck me sideways. My eyes are burning now and I have to swallow a big lump from my throat. Next I'll be growing a pair of damn ovaries. Seeing hard assed Arlene undone and hearing honest and humble gratitude in her voice is enough to bring me to my knees.

"You want something to drink or are you ready for an early night?"

"Both. Glass of water and bed. I'm exhausted."

I shift her off my lap with a kiss. "Why don't you head on up. I'll make sure we're locked in and be up with your water shortly."

With a tap on her luscious butt as she passes me on the way upstairs, I head off to do the rounds and turn off the lights.

By the time I get upstairs with her water, Arlene is curled on her side in bed. I make a quick bathroom stop before dropping all my clothes and sliding under the covers with her. Immediately she turns and wraps herself around me and snuggles in. I'm a bit calmer now that I can feel her skin to mine and hear her soft breathing slowing down as she slides into sleep. I love my sister with all my heart, but this woman owns me heart and soul. I have a feeling there won't be much sleep for me tonight.

CHAPTER FOURTEEN

The diner is busy when we walk in the door at a little past eight the next morning. To my surprise I had fallen asleep at some point during the night after all and didn't wake up until the smell of fresh-brewed coffee reached me. Arlene was up before me and planning to go in to work today. She didn't appreciate my reminder that she was supposed to stay home a full forty-eight hours and today was only day two. Of course that resulted in Arlene trying to get her way and me putting my foot down. That did not go over too well until I suggested we go to the diner for breakfast so she could check in, provided she didn't interfere with the goings on and would come home with me after, without any fuss. She promised, so we'll see.

Caleb is the first person we encounter. The big Native-American is standing behind the counter, looking ridiculous in a cook's apron and sporting a cocky smile when he spots us.

"See you weren't able to keep the boss lady at home, were you?"

"Fuck off, Caleb."

"Should've tied her to the bed, my friend. Always works for me." He says with a shoulder shrug.

"Hey. You two Neanderthals, I'm. Right here." Arlene bites off. "And for the record, Caleb. That was way too much information. I could've lived a long and happy life without that knowledge, I'll have you know."

Caleb throws his head back and laughs. First time I've ever heard that. Throwing a kitchen towel over his shoulder, he leans on the counter.

"What can I get you folks? I assume you are here for breakfast, or did you just come in to harass your underlings?"

"Bite me, buddy." Arlene's retort is delivered with a smirk on her face. "If you can manage, I'll have a mushroom omelet with home fries."

"Three eggs scrambled, bacon and rye toast for me, thanks." I add.

"Sure thing. Coming right up. Have a seat and Beth will be

right with you." When he disappears into the kitchen I try to lead Arlene to a seat, but she tries to follow Caleb into the kitchen.

"Hey. Where are you going?" I stop her.

"I just wanna go have a look."

"No, you're not. We're gonna sit down and have breakfast. Look around you. All these people look well taken care of. The place is clean and no one is running, screaming for the exit. It's under control. Let's sit." I firmly take her by the arm and march her to an empty booth.

"Must you manhandle me?" She challenges and part of me is happy to see her fighting spirit back. This is the woman I know.

"If you're not gonna listen and follow through on what we agreed on, then yes. I must."

With a derisive snort, Arlene starts rearranging the cutlery on the table before she checks the levels of the condiments. I smile.

"What's so funny?"

"You are. You can't help yourself. You don't want to believe everything is running as it should, even when you're not here."

"That's not true." She frowns as she seems to ponder that.

"No?" I raise my eyebrows questioningly holding her gaze.

After a silent power struggle, where neither of us seem to budge, Arlene finally lowers her eyes.

"Whatever."

My smile only gets bigger. Damn scrapper, fighting for every inch even when she knows she's in the wrong. Leaning my elbows on the table I take her face in my hands and kiss her full on the lips, startling the breath out of her.

"What'd you do that for!" She hisses at me. "We're in the middle of the diner. Everyone can see."

"Yup," says Beth, who appears at the booth with a pot of coffee. Arlene drops her face in her hands while I flip up the cups on the table.

"Morning, Beth. How's things?"

"Everything is running smoothly. Hard to believe, isn't it? Without the sergeant-major here to keep us in line." She winks at me and earns Arlene's dirty look from between her fingers. It doesn't seem to have an effect on Beth, who has been working here since long before Arlene owned the joint, and seemed immune to her bark.

"Emma will be in for lunch and Caleb will be back for the early dinner shift." She fills us in.

"Where is Julie?" Arlene wants to know.

Beth fidgets a bit and I have a feeling she'd rather not get into that right now, but Arlene is not likely to let up.

"Uhm… I actually haven't been able to get a hold of her. Last time we spoke was yesterday morning when she said she was on her way in. She never showed. I called her phone a few times but was sent to voicemail right away. Emma hasn't heard from her, either. She had made arrangements for Liam, Julie's little boy, for this week."

For some reason I don't have a good feeling about this. When Julie begged off Christmas tree cutting with the rest of us, I was getting some odd vibes off her, but I was too focused on Arlene to look into it further. Dammit. I regret not pulling her aside at the time. One thing for her to be in late from time to time, but unusual not to hear from her, or be able to get a hold of her.

"Anyone know how to get in touch with her aunt?" Arlene is one step ahead of me and asks the question that is brewing in my mind.

Beth shakes her head. "Emma talked to Gus and he is looking into that already. Sorry we didn't say anything but we figured you wouldn't be able to do more than we were already doing, and you sounded like you could use a bit of a break. You mad?" Beth eyes Arlene tentatively.

"You know what? I'm surprised I'm not. I'm worried about her, but you're right. Nothing would've changed had I found out earlier. S'okay, Beth. Really."

Relieved, Beth heads off to get our order leaving us looking at each other.

"You want to check it out, don't you?" She asks me and she's right. I do, but I won't leave her side, not for a second. Not without knowing who is out there playing sick games with my woman.

"I'm happy that Gus is looking into it. Truth be told, he is the better man for the job anyway. Let him do the investigating. I'll take care of protecting what's mine."

Her smile does me a world of good after the shit days we've had. "Yours, huh?"

"No two ways about it. Staked my claim in public, didn't I?" I tease her, making her snicker.

"Ape."

"You betcha. With some mean opposable thumb action, if you recall." At that she bursts out laughing, causing half the diner to turn their heads in our direction with stunned expressions on their faces. I guess laughing is another luxury Arlene hasn't afforded herself a lot. That is going to change, for both of us.

It's Caleb who shows up with our plates a minute later. "You heard about Julie?" When both of us nod, he says; "Beth just mentioned it. I'm heading into Cortez as soon as Emma gets in to see what I can find out. Thought I'd let you know."

"Thanks. Keep us in the loop."

"No problem. Enjoy your meal." With a wink for Arlene and a chin lift for me, he disappears into the kitchen.

"Damn, he's good. You may have some competition, Cookie." I shoot Arlene a glare at her use of that ridiculous nickname.

"What are you talking about?"

"His omelet? It's frickin' fantastic."

"It's a bunch of eggs, Arlene. Not that hard, you know." I'm getting a little irritated. Seriously. You'd have to be an idiot to mess up eggs. I know she likes Caleb, but *'frickin' fantastic'* for a simple omelet is a bit over the top. Not like it's a soufflé.

"You jealous, Seb?" I can hear the smile in her voice and when I look up, I see the mischief in her eyes.

No shit. Not a feeling I'm familiar with, but the thought of another man feeding her has me pissed off. I am so fucked. Not only that, her smart mouth and teasing has me hard as a rock and I'm glad I'm sitting in a booth so I can shift slightly to hide the obvious boner she gives me with her taunting. Witch. It's all I can do not to yank her over the table and have a taste of her alongside my breakfast. Plunge inside her, balls deep, and feel her wet heat suck me in. Christ! She turns me inside out. I have to press my hand on my erection to ease the pressure some.

"You yanking my chain, woman?" I growl at her, which only turns her smile wider.

"Maybe..."

Leaning over the table, I grab the back of her neck and pull her face closer. "I have no compunction about turning that juicy ass of yours red, you know."

Instantly a flush creeps up her cheeks and her breath hitches. There. *Serves you right*. That takes care of that smart mouth, at least for now.

The rest of the meal is eaten in silence, only accompanied by an occasional heated glance across our plates. When Beth comes around with fresh coffee again, both of us decline and I get up to pay the bill while Arlene slips into the ladies room. At the cash register, Caleb is waiting for me.

"She tell you yet?" Immediately the hair on my neck stands

on end.

"The fuck are you talking about?" I bite off, not liking the intimate way he talks about Arlene.

"Relax. She never told me anything. I guessed. I just figured if she told anyone, it would be you."

Okay. That takes me aback a bit.

"She's told me several things." I am careful with what I say, not about to share anything Arlene has confided in me, but I'm curious to know where Caleb is going with this.

Caleb runs a hand over his face and seems a bit at a loss.

"I know she was hurt, I can sense it. Don't ask me how, I just did. It's deep, this pain. Don't think this is something she can get over on her own."

"What are you saying?"

"You two together are a good thing. You're good for each other, but unless she gets some professional help, the trauma will always be part of your relationship. Honesty and professional help."

As effective as a cold shower, Caleb's words cooled the heated blood in my veins. How does that man know so much? I know what I have to do and I fucking hate it. I have to add more hurt to the woman I have come to love. I have. Haven't told her, don't know if I'll have the chance any time soon and don't think the time is ripe for confessions of that kind, but the fact remains. I've waited too long already. The truth has to come out.

"If she turns me away, will you make sure she's alright?" Fuck. I hate asking that, especially of him.

"Don't think it'll be necessary, but you have my word without question."

With that, Caleb leaves me to wait for Arlene who comes out of the ladies' room just seconds later.

CHAPTER FIFTEEN

"Anything planned today?"

The first words from Seb since we left the diner. I thought it was pretty clear what the plans had been up until it was time to leave, then he turned cold all of a sudden. Attentive enough, opening the door and shit, but the heat from earlier is gone.

"Nope." I answer. "Just twiddling my thumbs at home until you can peel me off the walls. Any bright ideas? Want to go look for Julie?" A firm shake of his head tells me that plan can go out the window. Damn. No bite.

"Not getting in Gus' way. Maybe we can drive into Durango this afternoon if you feel like it. We can see."

I haven't been in Durango for fun in donkey years. Every time I've gone has been for a pick up or drop off, or to visit the dang hospital. I might actually enjoy the pretty drive this time, but first I want to find out what is going on in that head of his. Something has turned his mood and I'm not about to let that slide.

"I wouldn't mind going... later."

Once home I head for the kitchen. "I'm making another pot of coffee. You want more?" I ask Seb over my shoulder.

"Yeah, I'll have another cup." He responds before slipping up the stairs. I'm not going after him, no matter how much it kills me to be patient. I keep myself busy pulling mugs down and scrounging around the pantry for some cookies or something, chocolate wouldn't hurt either, but it appears I have ransacked my stash at some earlier date. There isn't a damn thing left in any of my hiding spots. Something is making me nervous. Why else would I be craving sugar after just downing a sizeable omelet?

By the time the coffee is done I have conjured up so many different scenarios in my head - most of which having a pretty dire outlook for me, so by now my stomach is rolling. This is what not working does to me. It allows me to drive myself crazy, and that damn Naomi Waters thought she was being helpful. I'll tell her when we have our next girl's night out. Idle hands put this chick in a straightjacket!

I wish it were warmer so we could sit out on the deck, but it's been pretty overcast this morning. Normally it's nice, even in the early winter when the sun is out to sit out there with a coat on and something warm to drink. Not so nice today, so living room it is. I holler upstairs to let him know coffee is ready because I haven't seen him yet, but I did hear the shower a bit ago. I hear his boots on the stairs and sit down on one side of the couch, my hands wringing in my lap. *Jesus, Arlene! Get a grip.* He leans over the back of the couch and tilts my head back.

"What are you doing, Spot?" Fixing his eyes on mine he strokes the line of my jaw, but doesn't let me turn away.

"Waiting for you." I squeak out. He runs a finger down my nose and over my lips to my chin, holding me firmly before he kisses me.

"You seem nervous. How come?" Walking around the other side of the couch, he sits down and pulls me into him. I straighten up a little and consider him.

"If I'm nervous, it's only because your mood flipped like a flapjack and I've been trying to figure out why."

A tad pissed, I resist at first when he wraps me in his arms and tries to pull me onto his lap, then he mumbles *'sorry'* in my ear and I easily give in, snaking my arms around his neck.

"I realized there is still a lot for us to deal with, to talk about. It's so damn easy to get distracted with you. All I think about is being inside you, having my mouth on you, but I want it without any secrets."

I still can't quite fathom having this effect on anyone and am reveling in that knowledge when it suddenly hits me. "Secrets? But you know all there is to know about me, and you've told me about yourself, about Faith. Well, not a lot about Faith and I'd like to know a lot more, but I figure you'd get around to telling me. Who has more secrets?" The nervous feeling in my stomach from earlier is turning into a pinch when I see guilt in Seb's eyes.

"You may not want to hold me after you hear what I have to say."

Despite the niggle of doubt in the pit of my stomach, I stay firmly attached to him as he takes a deep breath.

"I explained to you how my sister got hurt. Well, Faith ended up brain damaged and stopped developing mentally and emotionally. Physically she is unable to look after herself and needs full time care. She was placed in a facility and I waited until I was twenty-one when I was able to get custody of her. We moved to Montana to get a fresh start together. I ended up working as a sous-chef at a small restaurant and Faith was looked after by a neighbor while I was gone. We did okay." Standing up, he leaves me no choice but to let him go from my grasp. He turns to me and sinks down on his knees in front of me, placing his big hands on either side of my face. "This is the part where I need you to look in my eyes so you can see the truth, and please hear me out. All of it, Arlene."

Okay, that little niggle? Turning into a big fucking hurricane in my stomach now. I do not have a very good feeling about this. Still, I nod at him. "Okay."

"We had new neighbors who fought a lot. It got out of hand one night and I walked into the man beating his wife and I snapped. I beat him badly. They arrested me for assault since the wife never filed charges against him. She ended up testifying against me. I received five years and got out early for good behavior. During most of my time inside, I had one cell mate."

And suddenly I felt like throwing up as small connective pieces of information started forming a vague pattern in my mind. The timeline, the location, his appearance in Cedar Tree, the phone calls? Some of this didn't make sense…but before I can question him about my suspicions, he carries on.

"I don't handle abuse well, Arlene. It pulls at me. I failed someone once at great cost, and I may have failed another, if you count my neighbor. I didn't know who you were, but when that son of a bitch started spouting off about how he would beat you to try and break you, I wanted to kill him. I wish I had, but I had Faith waiting in a nursing facility. Waiting for her big brother to come and get her and I couldn't risk leaving her to face life alone. Had I known then what I know now, I wouldn't have stopped to think. He'd be dead."

With one hand stretched out in front of me to ward him off, I pull myself into a corner of the couch. Wrapping my arms around my legs, I try to get some control over the whirlwind of emotions rushing through me all at once.

"When I was released I needed a job and a place to make a new start with Faith. I figured Cedar Tree was as good a place as any and it would give me a chance to keep an eye on you. That bastard talked often about revenge on you for putting him behind bars. I couldn't let that happen. I *can't* let that happen."

I hear the words and I understand their meaning, but for some reason all I feel is a deep sadness. The one thing that filled me with hope and a taste of happiness, a new step to a possible future, a new me - turns out to be a big lie. At the very best it was a tainted connection, darkened by the fucked up shadows of our pasts.

When Seb tries to get close to me, I ward him off with my hand and a shake of my head. I seem to be unable to form words.

"Okay, Spot. I'll give you time, but hear this. What I just told you has *nothing* to do with what has happened between us, or how I feel about you. Look at me, Love."

Reluctantly I give him my eyes.

"I care for you so much, and you know it. Whatever you tell yourself, it isn't because of some misguided hero-complex, because you are the furthest from a victim I can imagine. So fucking strong and resilient and annoyingly independent, it makes me want to spank your ass red, but what you are not - is a victim."

When he bends down to kiss my forehead, I can't help but flinch and I see it hurts him, then he's out the door. He hasn't even had a sip of his coffee.

I'm not sure how much time has passed when Emma comes in and scoots on the couch beside me, putting both her arms around me and hugging me close. Only then do I dare let the full gamut of emotion wash over me and I cry while my soul sister strokes my hair.

I fucking wrecked her. I could see it in her eyes. The slow

realization of what I was saying and then the disbelief, the shock and ultimately the pain. I sit in her driveway in my truck and dial Caleb, who answers right away.

"Told her man. I hurt her bad, I have to give her some space. Can you come take over? I have the diner - It'll keep me busy."

"Give her time. You did the right thing. Emma just walked in so I'm gonna bring her along. I'll stand guard outside."

"Thanks, Caleb."

It takes them less than ten minutes to get to the house. Emma is out of the SUV before Caleb even has a chance to open his door. I run over to give her a hand, but of course she waves off my help. She is just as stubborn as her friend. Two peas in a pod, those two.

"Thanks for coming, Emma."

"Of course. That's my best friend in there." She shoots me a stern look, but when I start to turn away, she holds me back and puts her hand on my face. "I'm angry my friend is hurting in there, but I am not blaming you. I'm blaming fucked up circumstances. Yes, you probably should have told her, but I know Arlene too and I can make a pretty decent guess as to why you didn't. I can't say I wouldn't have done the same. You're a good man, Seb. It'll be alright. She loves you." A peck on my cheek and she is moving into the house.

I look at Caleb, who is back in his SUV on the phone and I lift my hand as I turn to get in my truck and head for the diner. *She loves you…* God I hope so.

CHAPTER SIXTEEN

I've been working non-stop since getting here. Beth has been collecting orders and doing her best keeping customers waiting with complimentary breadbaskets and drinks, but I had to hustle to fill the pile of waiting slips. Luckily Caleb had done a decent job at prepping this morning because I find a hearty leek and potato soup hot, fresh hamburgers made and apparently someone had made a run into Cortez to the organic bakery because we have a good selection of breads and buns. As soon as I work away much of the backlog, I start chopping some bacon, onions and peppers and toss them on the grill. I add cut up leftover home fries and ham from the breakfast rush and quickly heat those along. Adding some cumin seed, Hungarian paprika, hot chili flakes, I finish it off with some black pepper and salt before scooping the whole thing into a large greased oven dish. A dozen or so eggs in a bowl with a few good hands full of grated sharp cheddar mixed in, thrown over top, and the whole thing can go in the oven. A quick King Edward Skillet to add to the menu. It'll only take fifteen minutes in the convection oven and it's the easiest thing to make, but it always goes over well. Especially with a bowl of soup and a slice of fresh bread.

With the kitchen a little bit more under control, I venture out to the front, where I am immediately cornered by Beth.

"What happened? Why did Caleb and Emma have to rush out of here? Is Arlene alright?"

I throw my hands up at the barrage of questions and don't really feel like getting into it with Beth in the middle of the diner, so I opt to stay a bit vague.

"Arlene is a bit upset about something and she needed to talk to Emma. Caleb is taking over for me for a bit looking out for them at the house and I'm giving him a break in the kitchen here, while Emma stays with Arlene." From the suspicious look she sends my way, I can deduct she doesn't believe a word I say, but that's too bad. It's all she's getting out of me. "Everything okay out here?" I purposely change the subject.

"Fine. A bit hectic before you got here, but it isn't really busy yet so we're good. Emma mentioned Gus might be in at some point lending a hand at dinner if she isn't back yet."

I'm relieved when a customer calls her over and gives me the opportunity to disappear back into the kitchen.

By the time the dinner crowd is thinning out that night, Beth can barely stand on her feet. Poor woman has been working almost non-stop since morning, same as yesterday.

"Go home, Beth. You're beat. I'll finish up here with Gus." Gus had shown up around four, mentioning Emma was still holed up with Arlene and like a good sport, he picked up a rag and started cleaning off tables and pouring coffee right away.

"What about tomorrow?" Beth wanted to know.

"I'll be here, and likely Arlene will too. Regardless, I'll make sure you have some help. And maybe we'll know more about Julie."

With a nod, she grabs her bag and goes to head out the door, but Gus stops her.

"Wait up, Beth. No walking outside in the dark alone, remember? Dark early this time of year. Let me walk you to your car."

I berate myself for missing that. I have been on eggshells all day, trying not to think of Arlene or the bombshell I dropped on her this morning. Not to think about the damage I may have done to our relationship, which was pretty damn shaky to begin with. Not to think about Julie's mysterious disappearance or all the fucking unknowns we were dealing with. They all come rushing at me now. All these things I have no control over almost knock me on my ass. Instead I slam both fists on the counter in frustration. A sharp intake of breath has me snapping up my eyes, to find Mrs. Evans standing on the other side of the counter, obviously waiting to cash out. Great. I scared the woman half to death.

"Sorry Mrs. Evans. Didn't mean to startle you, it just got away from me. You know what, dinner's on me tonight."

"Tough day, Sebastian?" I crack a smile at the use of my full name. Only my little sister and little old ladies can get away with that.

"Couple of tough days, more like. I'm sorry about your cat, Mrs. Evans."

She just nods, crooking her finger for me to come closer. When I lean down, she puts a hand on my face.

"You're a good boy, Sebastian. You shouldn't be so hard on yourself." And turns to walk right out the door, which Gus is holding open with a smirk on his face.

"What?"

"Seems like sound advice to me," is all he says, picking up dishes from the table Mrs. Evans just vacated. I turn and head back into the kitchen starting my clean up there.

When I close the door on the last customer and turn the lock, it has just turned 7 pm. Gus is putting away the last glasses behind the counter when I approach.

"What's going on at Arlene's?" Is the first thing out of my mouth.

"Nothing right now. Emma convinced Arlene to come to our house for the night and Caleb drove them over earlier." His eyes on me are sympathetic. "Look man, give her the time. You know neither Emma nor I will let her hide away."

I sit down on a stool at the counter and rest my head in my hands. I just wanna fucking puke, I feel so miserable.

"There was just no good way, Gus. It was a rock and a hard place, that was it. Fucked up from the get go. Just so much more complicated now."

"No shit."

Needing to stay busy, I get up to close the blinds. "Anything

175

on Julie yet? Or her aunt?"

"Found the aunt, but she says she hasn't seen Julie or the boy since the weekend. Doesn't know where they are and doesn't care. Piece of work she is."

"No wonder she needs help. You can't choose your family."

"Ain't that the sorry truth. She did mention a friend who works at Koko's on Main Street. Something to follow up on."

Closing up the rest in silence, I pull the door shut to the diner. Gus slaps me on the shoulder before climbing in his truck and pulling out of the parking lot. I just watch him drive off, to where his woman… and mine, are waiting. Then I walk around the building to take the stairs to my apartment, preparing myself for a long lonely evening.

I sink back into the large comfy couch that takes up most of Emma's living room. The rest of the house is a bit in shambles with the renovations ongoing, but that hasn't stopped them from putting up the tree we cut down on Monday. The house has a distinct

Christmassy feel to it, and as always, it smells like fresh baking in here.

After spending the better part of the day bawling all over my friend, she finally convinced me to pack a bag and come to her place for a change of scenery. Gus scurried out of the house as soon as he saw us walk up the porch, with Caleb in tow. I barely noticed the little man-to-man those two had out there. All I know is that Gus disappeared and Caleb retreated to the kitchen to 'whip up something to eat'. Food. I can't bear to think of eating right now. My stomach is still revolting with all the conflicting emotions tumbling around. Part of me feels betrayed, but there is another part that finds the single-minded focus Seb obviously had in keeping me safe endearing. I even understand why it was difficult for him to come clean about his reasons for coming to Cedar Tree and staying, especially after Emma played Devil's advocate with me, something she is frustratingly adept at, and allowed me to see a bigger picture, but it doesn't take away my confusion.

Emma walks in and sits down next to me. She's changed into her signature yoga pants and oversized shirt.

"I put some water on for tea, unless you want something stronger?"

"Better not. I've been skirting the edges of a full-blown flare up and took some medication. I drink alcohol now, and I'll be flying high."

Emma giggles. "Might not be such a bad thing."

I turn my head to face her. "God. Don't tempt me. I'd give anything for a joint right now."

"I may have something for you after we eat. Something to help you sleep."

My eyes bug out. "No shit? You? Life in Colorado is really agreeing with you, isn't it." I have to laugh at the sheepish look on Emma's face. I've been known to use pot occasionally in one form or another, as a means to take the edge off pain that is otherwise difficult to treat. But Emma rarely indulged, and if she did, only from whatever I had available. Times certainly have changed if she has a stash of her own.

"Caleb actually picks some things up for me at the dispensary in Durango when he comes to visit."

"A bona fide supplier. That's me." Caleb walks in with three mugs of steaming tea. "Had I known you use it for pain control, I would have offered to pick some up for you as well, Arlene. Next time let me know."

"Thanks. By the way, with you two here, who is at the diner?"

Emma and Caleb exchange glances, but it is Caleb who answers me. "Seb is in the kitchen. He left straight there from your house. It's his way of still looking after you while giving you space."

That brings a lump to my throat and I take a sip of my tea to mask it.

"Gus went to help for the dinner rush when we got here."

I nod. "You guys really have been amazing, helping out the way you have. Everything seems a little unreal at this point. I mean, there haven't been any more calls - not since the cat - but with Julie gone missing now, I just feel like I'm missing the plot somewhere. I can't wait to get back to work tomorrow and try to get some normal routine back."

"What about Seb?" Emma wants to know. "How will you deal with seeing him all day?"

"Honestly? I don't know. Look, I don't hate him. It isn't as simple as that. He is obviously a very decent man and his intentions are good, I just don't know if I can trust what is between us. I mean, I barely trust what I'm feeling. How am I expected to trust what he thinks he feels? You have no idea what kind of risks I've already taken. I don't know if I have it in me to completely let go of the edge and just jump."

The next few minutes are silent, as if we are each considering my dilemma until Caleb interrupts the silence. "I think it isn't so much the circumstances as it is you that is holding you back. There is a big step you keep forgetting to take."

I can't help but bristle a little at his words, but he grabs my hands and forces me to hear him out.

"You know what I mean. Everything that is going on around you right now is distracting as hell, but the fact remains, you owe it to yourself to process and deal with some of the shit you were handed."

"I know that, Caleb, but I've had other things on my mind." I snap at him, but as usual, Caleb is unflappable and just looks at me patiently.

"You do realize that the sooner you get a handle on your past, the better equipped you are to deal with your present and your future?"

Oh fuck. Why the hell does he have to make such sense? From the look in his eyes I see he recognizes that the message has finally reached me. Resigned I drop my head, but not before I catch Emma mouthing *'Well done'* at Caleb. Bloody conspirators!

I am in luck. I manage to get a hold of Dr. Mora, the therapist Gus referred me to, just as she is leaving the office. My original appointment had been for December 2nd, but when I explain my current circumstances briefly, she agrees to see me before her first scheduled appointment tomorrow. Now I'm nervous, never having had any kind of therapy before, I don't know what the hell to expect. Emma assures me to just be myself and keep an open mind. I can do that. At least, I think I can.

Two hours later, with some food in my stomach and the taste of a very special pot-laced chocolate truffle still lingering on my taste-buds, my frickin' mind is as open as the sky… and as empty. Blissfully so.

CHAPTER SEVENTEEN

The crowd at Koko's is pretty thin. Still pretty early on a Wednesday night. Broncos aren't playing until tomorrow night and the Avalanche are out on a road trip until next week. Most of the TV screens are tuned into various other hockey games currently playing in the league, but things wouldn't really start heating up until after the Christmas break. It had taken me an hour or so of rambling around my apartment after trying to distract myself for a bit with a phone call to Faith. But in the end, the need to do something won out.

When I take a seat at the bar, a tatted up dark-haired woman in her thirties wearing a shirt with the bar's name stretched over her ample tits, struts over.

"Hey gorgeous. What can I get ya?" Her voice is raspy with probably too many years of smoking, drinking and hard living, but that doesn't stop her from trying to seduce me with it. There might have been a time, years ago, when this would have been just the hook up I was looking for. Rough, gritty, a bit dirty and lewd, but most of all forgettable. There wasn't a single twitch of interest in me now. I have to chuckle. Fuck me. Arlene owns me. Unfortunately, my chuckle seems to have given off the wrong vibe 'cause the dark haired chick is now leaning her tits on the bar and scraping her nails over my forearm. I sit back and pull my arms to my sides.

"Just a beer." I turn my back on her, watching one of the bigger screens where an Eastern Division game is ending in a shoot-out.

"Here you go, handsome. My name is Tanya. What brings you here?"

I have no choice but to abandon the game and try to focus on the reason I came here tonight. Information.

"Just checking the place out. Girl I work with mentioned it. Said a friend of hers worked here and it was a good place to grab a drink."

Interest sparks in Tanya's eyes. "Yeah? What's her name...

the girl you work with?"

"Julie." At the mention of Julie's name I see recognition flit over her face, before she hides it behind a flirty smile.

"Could be a friend of Connie's. She's not scheduled tonight."

"Too bad. Although I was kinda hoping to bump into Julie. I know she lives in Cortez. Figured since she recommended the place, she might come here regularly herself."

"Not many female regulars here, honey." Tanya says with what likely is supposed to be a seductive pout. Definitely not a good look on her. "Not on my shifts anyway. More likely to find the guys hanging at the bar." She leans in and semi-whispers, "You ask me, it's my ink that turns them on." She proudly sticks out her arms, displaying the full sleeves of colorful tattoos.

"Beautiful work." I admit.

"You're welcome to see the rest of it." She flirts with me blatantly. "Maybe give me a chance to look yours over as well?"

I'm sure the intent was to get a rise out of me, instead I feel my balls shrivel up in my jeans. There is something slimy and calculated about this chick. I need to keep my focus though. Tanya knows more than she is letting on.

"So do you own this joint, Tanya?" I ask, hoping to move the conversation into safer waters.

"Ha! No, my bro... my boss does. He's in the back." She catches herself.

"Think he might know Julie?" I try, but it appears I've pushed my luck, because all the attempt at seduction is instantly gone from Tanya's face and replaced with a scowl.

"No. He doesn't know any Julie and I think you've overstayed your welcome." She plants her hands on her hips and stares me down. Not itching for a confrontation, I down my beer, slap the glass on the bar and walk out the door.

Gotcha! Tanya lies for shit. Her boss, or if my guess is correct, her brother, might well be the 'friend' at Koko's. Not a girlfriend, like I had assumed, but a guy, and one who obviously does not want his connection with Julie known. That is something for Gus to figure out, although he is likely going to give me shit for coming here tonight.

Flipping up the collar of my leather jacket against the cold wind, I walk around the side of pub to where I parked my truck. It isn't until I turn the key to unlock my door that I notice the street light about 20 feet away that had been on when I got here is no longer burning. The hair on my neck stands up and just as I'm about to turn around my face is slammed into the side of my truck. I can hear a distinct crack and my vision instantly blurs. All I hear is the rushing of my blood as the adrenaline kicks in and I start fighting my attacker. Or attackers, at this point, I have no clue. My face is smashed into the driver's side door and someone is pounding the piss out of my kidneys and ribs. I'll be pissing blood tomorrow. A well-aimed kick to the back of my knee, drops me like a rock and I can't hold back the howl that escapes me. Fucking hell. Not ready to concede so easily, but still half blind, I roll and use my good leg to aim a kick in the general direction of the bastard who is turning me into mincemeat. By the flurry of expletives and insults, I'm gathering I made some kind of contact and I'm squinting to try and make out who the hell is standing over me.

"What the hell? Matt! What the fuck are you doing?" The screeching is coming from the direction of the bar and if I'm not mistaken, it is the grating voice of the Koko's barmaid, Tanya.

"Fuck off, you idiot!" The big guy has his big ass boot on my throat now, and it is all I can do to keep him from crushing my neck.

"You're gonna kill him!" Tanya is obviously not inclined to 'fuck off' just yet and seems intent on saving my sorry ass.

"Fucking hell, woman, would you shut your dumb trap and get back inside."

Grateful for the distraction Tanya provided, I manage to slam a fist clenched around my car keys on the knee of the leg that is holding me down. Stupid fucker should've taken care of my arms too. When his knee buckles with a howl, I slip from under his boot and keep rolling until I find myself under my truck. My body feels like a giant aching wound. Blood from somewhere on my head is running into my eyes and mouth and I'm having trouble breathing. In the distance I can hear sirens. I can only hope Tanya's hollering drew more attention than they bargained for. I don't have a lot of fight left in me.

"Fuck!" I hear Matt spit out from the back of my truck, and there is no mistaking the glint of the gun when I see a figure bend down to look under the chassis. "One word, you cocksucker. One word, one move, I end her and that little brat of hers. You hear me?"

I can't even answer, I'm gasping for air by now and I can feel darkness creeping in. Last thing I see is are his boots, limping away.

I'm giggling my ass off. Don't ask me why, but everything is frickin' hilarious. All I have to do is look at Emma who is sitting on the couch, looking like some goddamn Buddha, looking all serene and shit and I about wet myself laughing. Emma, whose little compact body usually is charged with energy, is sitting there like she's grown roots. I burst out laughing again. I think I'm supposed to rub the Buddha's belly aren't I?

"Hey Caleb! Where are ya?"

Walking in from the new extension out back, Caleb takes one look at us and shakes his head, grinning.

"Christ, you two. You're high as kites."

"Caleb, aren't you supposed to rub Buddha's belly? For good luck or something?"

"That's what some folk believe yeah. Why?"

"See, I told you." I say to Emma who sits there and simply smiles at me. I'm a little worried, so I wave my hands in front of her face. "Emma, I gotta rub Buddha's belly for good luck. I really need some good luck."

Since she just keeps smiling, I pull up the edge of her oversized shirt. "Here, hold this up, will ya?"

Emma doesn't question me at all, she just pulls up her shirt as high as she can. Just as I rub my hands over her belly, tears of laughter running down my face, the front door opens and Gus comes in.

"What. The. Fuck."

Uh oh. I don't think Gus is happy.

"Hi honey." Emma smiles, her shirt still up under her chin and my hands are still on her belly. I can hear Caleb snickering behind me.

"Emma, why do you have your shirt up."

I feel I need to explain this, so I raise my hand. "Uhm. It's for good luck. I need it."

From the puzzled look on Gus' face, I see my explanation fell short somewhere, but apparently it was funny 'cause Caleb is now laughing out loud so I join him. Christ, I feel happy.

"Caleb. Wanna explain why my woman is exposing herself? And why the girls are baked out of their brains?"

Caleb is trying to keep a straight face but he seems to have a hard time with it every time he looks over at Emma and me. I'm still rubbing her belly 'cause I need all the luck I can get.

"Sorry, Boss. The girls had one of Emma's truffles for dessert. I thought they were sharing one, but I have a sneaky suspicion they each had a whole one. Arlene thinks Emma looks like Buddha and wants to rub her belly for luck." Not able to hold back any longer, he bursts out laughing.

"Fucking brilliant." Gus runs his hand through his hair and mutters under his voice, but he can't stop the smile teasing the corner of his mouth. He walks over to us, kisses me on the head and Emma on the lips and gently tugs her shirt down. "Enough rubbing, Arlene. You're gonna wear out a spot."

That has me rolling on the couch again and this time I have to hold on to my own stomach, which is starting to hurt from all the laughing. "Where is Seb?" I want to know. I want Seb, but when I look at Gus I see a concerned look on his face.

"He's home. You'll see him tomorrow at the diner. Let's get you girls to bed. You can shack up in our big bed. I'll sleep on the couch."

I'm a little sad, but I am so tired that I'm happy to crawl into bed. Before I doze off, I can hear Gus telling Caleb something about their lead in Cortez. I hear nothing after that.

CHAPTER EIGHTEEN

"Shit!"

The voice startles me. I've been laying here, I don't know how long, floating in and out, barely aware of my surroundings. I try cracking my eyes open but it's like they've been glued shut and every time I move a muscle on my face it hurts. I gingerly use my fingers to try and pry my eyelids apart. Just then, a narrow beam of light hits my face, sending a hot poker of pain straight into my brain. "Fuck!"

"Seb, buddy. The fuck happened to you?" I recognize Caleb's voice. "Let's get you out from under here."

With some shifting and pulling on Caleb's part and a fair amount of swearing and groaning on mine, I find myself staring up at a dark sky instead of the underside of my truck.

"Jesus. You've been worked over good. Let's get you to the hospital."

"No. No hospital!" I manage, grabbing hold of Caleb's arm. "Just take me home."

"Listen, your face is a bloody mess, your speech is slurry. You need to see a doctor. Don't know what other injuries you have."

"Get me home, then I'll explain." I bite out, teeth gritted against the pain.

Caleb's brute strength, my one good leg and more colorful swearing gets me situated in the passenger side of his SUV, where he has reclined the seat all the way.

"How'd you find me?" I want to know, once we are on the move.

"Checking out a lead on Julie's disappearance, and you can imagine my surprise when I saw your truck in the dark parking lot of Koko's; the place I was supposed to be checking out and appears to be shut down tight. You decide to do some snooping of your own?" He throws me a questioning look. "Why don't you give me a short version of what happened while we drive. I'll get you home and have a look at the damage."

"Fine. The bartender's name is Tanya. She denied knowing Julie but was lying about it. Found out her brother runs the joint. When I asked if he would know Julie, she asked me to leave, which I did. It told me enough. I was getting in my truck to head home when I was taken down from behind. I managed to get a few swipes in, but most of the damage had been done. I did pick up the brother's name is Matt and he made sure to let me know that neither Julie nor her little boy would make it if I spilled."

Caleb slams his hand on the steering wheel. "Fucking hell!"

"That is why no hospital. Besides, I remember every spot he got. Probably a concussion, nose and maybe cheekbone, a rib or two, knee and he gave my kidneys a good work-over. As long as I don't cough up blood, I'm good. I've had worse."

"You know Arlene is gonna kill you for not getting medical help, right?" The smirk on Caleb's face should piss me off, but oddly it doesn't. Feels more like brotherly ribbing now, and I find myself kinda liking it.

"Not sure Arlene's gonna care much at this point. She's pretty upset with me."

"She cares, buddy. Make no mistake, she cares a whole lot."

Oh good lord, I feel like crap. A dull ache lives behind my eyes and when I try to move my body it's like I'm dragging my limbs through molasses. Great way to start back at the diner.

When I look beside me, I see Emma has gotten an early start. Typical. She's probably in the kitchen whipping up something brilliant, which is fine as long as I get to eat it. I am *starving*. A quick shower clears some of the cotton-wool from my head and when I get to the kitchen, I find Gus and Caleb sitting on stools and Emma pouring coffees.

"Seriously? I am the last one up? I can't believe you all beat me to it." Grumbling, I pull up another stool and plop down next to Caleb as Emma slides over a coffee for me. I spot a plate of muffins and snatch one. Still warm… bliss. I close my eyes and enjoy my little moment. When I notice the silence, I crack an eye to find three grinning faces staring at me. "What? What are you all looking at?"

"Morning sunshine." Emma says, laughing out loud now, the others following her lead. "How is your luck holding out this morning?"

"Ah dammit. Y'all can kiss my ass!" I say as I pick up my

mug for a sip of coffee, hiding my smile as I drink.

"Tell me again why we are all heading into the diner this early?" I want to know when a virtual convoy leaves Emma's house. Fine, there were two vehicles, but still.

"We aren't. Caleb is. We are driving you to your appointment, or had you forgotten?"

"Crap. Yes I had. I'm not in the mood right now."

Gus chuckles in the front seat. "Not something there is an appropriate mood for, Arlene. All that's required is that you show up. And we're making sure of that."

"You are pains in my ass. You know that?"

Emma and Gus look at each other in the front seat and burst out laughing. Whatever.

When we get to Cortez, I'm curious. "So what are you going

to do while I see this therapist?"

"We're going out for breakfast." Emma says with a smile.

"You can have breakfast at my diner."

"Actually, this is a breakfast we planned on having months ago, but never got around to. I kind of got run over. Remember? We figure we'd follow through on those plans now and Mr. Happy is just around the corner from your therapist's office."

"You do realize you guys are weird, right? Normal people would avoid any memory of an event like that and you two go and highlight it with a celebratory breakfast. Weird."

"Sure Arlene, and yet who has an appointment with the shrink?" Emma chuckles.

"Oh for Christ's sake! Kiss my ass!" I yell at her, hopping out of the car as soon as it rolls to a stop in the parking lot, leaving the two of them to laugh at my expense. Asswipes. But I love 'em anyway.

Forty-five minutes later they are standing in the same spot, waiting for me, smirks still on their faces as if they had never been gone.

"So how was it?" Nosy Emma wants to know.

"Like I'm gonna tell you."

"I don't want to know what you said, you dipstick. I want to know whether you think it will be helpful."

I can't help the small smile that escapes. It actually had been helpful. Oh, don't get me wrong, I have a long road ahead of me, but it had helped laying everything out, including the debacle with Seb's confession and talking about how and why I respond the way I do. It at least gave me some more insight into myself and that is a start.

"Yes, it will be helpful. Now, can you drop me off at the diner please? Or at home so I can pick up my truck?"

"We are coming to the diner with you."

"Why would you do that? We're gonna only be short Julie so we should be able to manage fine."

"The boys have something to discuss and they wanna stick close, and I want to do some baking, which I haven't had a chance to do yet this week. I can do it just as easily at the diner. Gives me a chance to run the counter at the same time. Now, would you quit questioning everything and just go with the flow for once?"

My most appropriate response is to stick out my tongue at her, which makes Gus snicker.

"Good to have you back, Arlene."

"Don't push your luck, Mister." Which only makes him laugh harder.

No respect.

Getting there I'm surprised to find only Caleb in the kitchen doing prep. When I ask where Seb is, he offers to go check upstairs. Of course I head for the big coffee machine first. That is a necessity. Mindlessly moving through my morning routine, it takes me a while to clue in that Seb is still not here. Instead, the 'three musketeers' are in the friggin' kitchen doing the breakfast prep, whispering among themselves.

"Ok, folks. What the fuck is going on? Where is my cook?"

The schooled blank look on the guys' faces and the one of guilt on Emma's tells me something is up.

"Come on guys. Spill."

Caleb is the one to speak first. "He had a rough night. Letting him sleep it off. Best you do the same."

As I look from Caleb, to Gus, to Emma and back to Caleb, I know they're holding back on me.

"Like hell." I say, marching past them out the backdoor and up the stairs to Seb's apartment. Half expecting to find him half-drunk in bed with some floozie, I burst in ready to kick some ass but when I open his bedroom door, what I see almost brings me to my knees.

Last night Caleb managed to get me up the stairs to my apartment, clean me up and look me over. Already starting to turn all shades of black and blue, he said there was hardly any flesh tone left on my already colorful skin. He was painfully thorough in his exploration of every possible damaged bone, but by his uneducated guess, I had no broken bones save for a couple of ribs and a badly swollen knee. A cut above my eye was taken care of with some butterfly bandages and the hand I fisted around my car keys to pound on that cock sucker's knee was pretty torn up. I likely have a concussion so he spent the night on my couch after giving Gus a call and a brief report.

This morning I wake up feeling like a truck ran me over and backed up on me just for good measure. The urge to piss forces me to haul my ass out of bed. That maneuver is just as painful as I imagine. Fuck me. Relief at seeing no blood in my urine, I shuffle into the living room where I find Caleb already gone. On the kitchen counter is a glass of water and a hand-full of pills. Figuring they're for me, I don't question, just pop them all back and wash them down. Just then Caleb walks in the door.

"Hey, you're up. Good. Not gonna ask how you feel, I figure the answer will be 'shit'."

"Good guess." I say, leaning on the counter.

"So you know the gang is all here. Downstairs, that is. Arlene is bound to start questioning where you are soon enough."

"Don't want her coming up here. She has enough shit going on. She sees me like this it's just gonna add to her stress."

"Not sure if that's possible. We're talking Arlene here."

"Just give me until lunch and I'll be down. Taking a shower and giving the meds a chance to work."

Caleb taps his knuckles on the counter and leaves without a word. Damn.

The hot spray of the shower goes a long way in relieving some of the stiffness and aches this morning. I'm sure the painkiller helped some as well. As I'm drying off, I catch a glimpse of myself in the mirror. *Jesus.* My face is swollen almost beyond recognition and two dark rings are forming around my eyes, likely from the hit my nose and cheekbone took against the truck door. The rest of my body doesn't look much better. Bruising is wrapping around the side from my back distorting the intricate ink patterns on my torso. Makes me wonder what it looks like back there, that's where I took the full brunt.

Walking into the bedroom I rifle through my dresser to grab a clean shirt when I hear the door open behind me followed by an audible gasp. Shit.

"Oh my God, Seb. What happened to you?"

Arlene. Figures. When I turn around to face her, her hands cover her mouth and her eyes instantly fill with tears.

"Ah geeze, woman. Don't cry. Looks worse than it is." She's killing me with big tears now rolling down her cheeks. "Come here." I hold my arms open but she just stands there crying and shaking her head. "Spot, I'm ok. Come here."

Finally moving, she closes the gap, presses her face in my chest and wraps her arms around my waist, squeezing hard.

"Babe. Arlene. Gentle." I groan, almost crying myself now, my ribs yelling in protest.

"Oh. Sorry." She mumbles, loosening her grip and stepping back. I reluctantly let her go.

"What happened to you? Who did this?"

"I asked a few too many questions about Julie in Cortez. Apparently asked the right people."

"Wait. You went looking last night?"

"Needed something to do, Arlene. I was going nuts, sitting at home thinking about you. Worrying about us."

Not wanting to wait for her rejection, I turn back to my dresser for a shirt. It stays quiet behind me while I try to get dressed, but it isn't easy or painless. When I sit down on the bed to pull on socks and boots, I'm still not looking at Arlene. Bending over to reach my feet I hiss at the stab of pain, courtesy of my battered ribcage. Cool hands grab the socks I'm holding from my hand and push on my shoulder.

"Sit back. Let me."

Arlene sinks down on her knees in front of me and takes my foot, sliding my sock on and doing the same with the other. She then manages to get my boots on and ties the laces. Not been able to say a word, I'm overwhelmed at the sight of her. When she sits back on her heels, I carefully stroke her cheek and she tilts her face into my hand. My heart jumps in my chest. For a while we just sit there, Arlene at my feet, her face in my hand. Just feeling. Being in the moment and I am so full.

Then the slam of a car door outside breaks through our little bubble and Arlene gets up, my hand falling away from her face.

"I better get downstairs. Sounds like customers."

"Okay. I'll be down in a bit." I am a bit deflated, I get the feeling something significant just happened, but I have no idea what.

"You sure you are up to that? We'll manage, you know."

"I'll be fine. I'll take it easy."

Arlene just nods and starts walking toward the door. Then she stops, turns and walks right up to me putting her hands on my cheeks.

"We'll talk later, yeah?"

All I can do is nod, and I am surprised to find my eyes wet. Must be allergic to something.

Arlene presses her lips to mine briefly and leaves. When I feel something tickle my cheek I realize it's a tear. Yup. Allergies for sure.

CHAPTER NINETEEN

I've stuck to the kitchen most of the morning. After the shock I gave Arlene, Emma, and Beth, I had no desire to send our customers running or answer any questions, but by two o'clock, my ass is toast.

Emma and the guys left shortly after I got down this morning so it's been the regular crew today. Well, minus Julie. Gus and Caleb are looking into that further.

There hasn't been an opportunity to talk with Arlene, not yet at least, but I am eager to get that out of the way.

The diner is empty except for one customer lingering over a cup of coffee in the far corner when I walk into the dining room.

Both Beth and Arlene are behind the counter looking outside. All morning the sky has had the dark threat of an impending storm and with the temperature waffling around the freezing mark, it's hard to tell whether we'll be faced with snow or just a nasty north wind, but something is coming for sure.

Beth turns around when she hears me approach and gasps again when she sees me.

"Good lord, Seb. You're not looking any better, my friend. Underneath all the black and blue you are turning a distinct shade of grey."

Arlene studies me carefully as well. "You alright? Maybe you should go lie down for a bit. It's quiet now. Beth and I can whip something up for a special tonight, although I don't think we'll have to worry about a crowd, judging by the weather."

Reluctant to leave the women alone, but virtually swaying on my feet I agree. "Maybe I will, but I'm gonna let Gus know first. Don't want you two alone."

"You go. I'll call and I'll come and check on you in an hour or so. Try and get some sleep, but keep your cell phone with you in case you need me." Ignoring Beth and the one remaining customer, she walks up, puts her hand on my chest and gives me a sweet kiss. "Go on."

With Beth watching on, smug grin on her face, I snag Arlene behind her neck and haul her in for another kiss, one that I pour all my feelings into and leaves her blinking her eyes and speechless by the time I release her. "Call him now," is all I say before heading out the kitchen door, not even waiting for her acknowledgement.

"Holy spontaneous combustion!" Beth blurts out, after Seb lays one on me and exits through the side door. I'm still a little dazed by that display of raw emotion exercised by lips and tongue. *Dayum*. If I had any reservations left about whether his feelings for me where the genuine thing, I think this kiss just may have cleared up any remaining doubts. I felt that in my toes and I instantly crave all of him; instantly turned on as if someone threw a switch. Apparently I'm that easy, at least when it comes to Seb. It's almost funny when you think about the times in the past years that I wondered whether I might be frigid, like I was told for so long. I'm thinking… not. Seb makes me want to strip out of my skin and go wild. He makes me want to feel with every nerve ending. He also makes me care, so very, very much.

A chuckle beside me has me turn my head.

"That good, huh?" Beth is wearing a cheeky smile. I plant my elbow in her ribs.

"Back to work, wench." Sending her cackling into the kitchen while I quickly dial Gus.

By the time the last customer is gone and we have thrown together a big pot of bubbling chili, it's 3 o'clock and it's not looking good outside. Aside from the high winds, snow is starting to come down and I haven't seen any traffic come by in the past ten minutes. We could hear the front door when Caleb came in about ten minutes after I called Gus and is working on a laptop in a booth. I don't have any Internet, but apparently he has some do-hickey he can hook up to it for reception. Whatever. Computers are not my thing, I leave that shit to Emma. I still do my books by hand and she converts it to some program on the computer for me. I am what you call 'unkeyboardinated', even texting is a challenge. The cash register is as far as my talents go, and even when the paper runs out I have to call someone else to change it.

Beth walks up behind me.

"Damn that looks nasty. We'll be lucky to get anyone in."

I agree, and I come to a decision. "Go home. Get home while it is still somewhat passable. Won't get any better with time. I'm going to close the joint."

"But what about the chili?"

"I'm gonna stick around upstairs with Seb. Keep an eye on him. We'll let it cool down and I'll pop it in the cooler. It'll be fine for tomorrow."

"And what about cleanup, washrooms and all that? Shouldn't we quickly get that done?"

"Tomorrow morning. Let's get out of here."

"Sure?"

"Yeah. It's no use. Hey Caleb!" He lifts his gaze from the screen.

"I'm closing up. Look at the weather, we're not gonna draw a crowd and I'm sending Beth home."

He throws a glance outside, then stands up, closing his laptop and gathering his things.

"Let me drive you girls home."

"I'm not going." I say. "I'm staying with Seb. But I'd feel better if you dropped Beth off at home."

Ignoring Beth's sputtering, I grab her bag and coat, push it in her hands and shove her in the direction of the door. "Go. Caleb's truck is much safer on the roads than your ratty old car. Don't fight me on this."

"Oh, alright." She gives in, grumbling.

Caleb stops in front of me, tucking a stray hair behind my ear. "You going to be alright?"

"Yeah. Going to lock up, close the blinds and head up. I'll check in with you later, okay?"

"Call me if you need me, Doll."

"I will."

As soon as they leave, I lock and flip the 'closed' sign on the front door and go to lower the blinds. In the kitchen I pull the pot of chili off the burner onto the counter to cool and shut off the gas. I quickly fill up a container with enough chili for two, grab some bread and toss it in a bag. Grabbing my purse and my coat from the office, I set it all on the kitchen counter. The light switches are all located on one panel beside the passage from the kitchen to the dining room. Standing in the door opening, I start flicking them off one by one so I can make sure I get them all. When I hit the last one, the inside of the diner is cast in gloomy shadows, despite the relatively early hour. Sure, it gets dark early nowadays, but not at three in the afternoon. Donning my coat and with my purse and the bag of food in hand, I go to step out when I hear something. I freeze in my spot, trying to place the sound. A shuffling or slight scratching sound. Letting go of the door, I walk back into the diner, my head cocked to one side trying to pick up any sounds. I stop in the doorway to the diner and let my gaze wander around. There isn't a thing out of place and now I can't hear a thing. Must have been the sleet or something. I turn around to go back outside when a loud bang has me drop everything in my hands and freeze with my heart up in my throat. It takes me a minute to identify the sounds of movement that follow as coming from above, and relief floods me. Seb. With the unsettling feeling still leaving goosebumps on my skin, I step outside, lock the door and make my way up to Seb's apartment.

"Hi, Honey." I softly whisper against his back.

The living room is empty when I come in. I dump the bag of food on the counter and find him sleeping in the bedroom. Pretty wiped myself, I crawl into bed behind him, snuggle up and promptly fall asleep.

The brief nap has done me good and when I wake up I find myself in exactly the same position, curled around Seb's back, feeling a little hungry.

Seb stirs at the sound of my voice and slowly rolls onto his back.

"Nice surprise." His voice is gruff with sleep. "You said 'honey'." He smiles, but immediately winces when it hurts his face. "Ouch."

"Serves you right, pointing out my slip of the tongue." I tease him.

"Ahhh babe. You trying to kill me? I find you wrapped around me in my bed and you start talking about slipping and tongue in the same sentence." His hand starts exploring my face and slipping lower to discover I only have on a camisole. "Damn, girl." His finger strokes my skin from my shoulder down to my hand and finds my waist, where his hand slips under my top and over my skin.

I force myself not to think about my soft stomach resting on the bed as I'm resting on my side.

"So soft. I could touch and taste you all day."

"I want to touch you, but I'm afraid to hurt you." I tell him, holding myself back for fear of jarring or bumping him.

"Well… there are some places that are definitely not sore. In fact, right now, they feel pretty damn good."

I try to look stern, but I can't keep a straight face. Especially not when I see the mischievous sparkle in his eyes. A sparkle and heat. Yes, most definitely heat.

"Is that so? Where would those be, those places?" I play along, rubbing my fingers along his lips. "Here maybe?"

"Meh. They're ok, but not what I'm talking about."

"Hmmmm. What about here?" With my tongue I trace the shell of his ear, earning a shiver.

"Not bad, but no."

Shifting down his body a little, my mouth and tongue play over his chest, tracing his ink until I find his nipple and I tug it in my mouth. A deep groan is his response.

"Getting better, Spot. Don't stop."

I trail openmouthed over his abs, feeling every bump and valley and slide my tongue into his belly button. Seb's stomach contracts and he hisses out his breath.

"Am I getting warm?"

"Woman, you don't get to the point, I'll blow just with what you're doing."

"Such a charmer, Honey." I chuckle, carefully climbing between his legs, spreading them carefully apart. When I look at his face he has a smile on his face but there is no denying the lust I see in his eyes.

"Let me see you, Arlene."

I only allow myself a second's hesitation before I grab the edge of my top and pull it over my head, leaving me only in bra and panties. Serviceable, not pretty - just like me. I undo the front closure on my bra and let the straps slide off my shoulders, never losing eye contact with Seb. Slowly he lowers his gaze from my face, over my chest to my breasts and after a moment down to my stomach and back up to my face again.

"I love your body. The feel of it, the taste of it, the smell of it and the sight of it."

Damn that man for trying to melt my insides. I lean over and kiss his stomach, my hands finding the edge of his briefs that I carefully slide down his hips. His erection jumps free and I love the feel of it against my skin. With one hand I rub the length of him between my breasts as I lick and suck his stomach. When my mouth finally finds his cock I revel in the raw taste of him and lick my way around the flange of the tip, making sure to tease the slit that cuts across. Seb's muscles jerk at that and one of his hands finds its way to the top of my head and tangles in my short hair. There is no way I can handle the full girth of him, but with one hand for balance and the other firmly wrapped around his base, I start fucking him with my mouth, taking him deeper and deeper until my lips meet my hand. I squeeze him between my tongue and the roof of my mouth, and suck him hard as I slowly pull back. When I look up from under my eyelashes, I can see Seb's head is laying back on the pillows and his mouth has fallen open, low grunting sounds escaping him. Seeing this man undone for me, does more for my self-esteem than any pretty clothes or piles of make-up could. Even with his eyes closed, he makes me feel beautiful.

As wet and turned on as I am myself, all I care about is bringing him to release and the next time I take his cock, I force myself to swallow around its tip as my hand finds his balls and lightly tugs. Seb's hand in my hair is now fisted and his hips jerk under my body, reaching for his release. With my eyes on his face, my mouth and hand work in tandem, I feel him swell in my mouth. His head shoots up and looking me straight in the eyes, he shouts my name as he shoots strings of his come down my throat. It takes a while for his body to still, but his eyes never leave mine. When he finally talks, his voice is hoarse.

"Come up here, love."

Crawling up the bed, Seb pulls me to his side, his arm tugging me close.

"Kiss me."

Unusually compliant for me, I tilt my head and slide my lips over his. Sweet and tender is his kiss, and full of an emotion I am afraid to identify.

"No words. What just happened? You giving me everything? All of you? There are no words to do it justice."

I haven't said a word. I'm just laying in Seb's arms thinking how amazing it is he knew the importance of what I was giving him, and beyond that, he didn't minimize it by offering to 'get me off' simply to reciprocate. Letting him back in was hands down the right decision. There is no doubt he sees me, not simply a victim. I'm almost afraid to let myself feel happy, but I am. And almost lighthearted.

When our stomachs start rumbling simultaneously we both burst out laughing.

"What time is it anyway?"

Seb looks at the alarm clock beside him. "Almost six-thirty."

"Holy crap. I didn't realize it was that late. Let me heat up some chili Beth and I had made before we shut down the diner." I get out of bed and walk over to the window to check the weather. Other than the signage lights on the diner, it is pretty dark out and I can see it is still coming down. There is a spot of the white stuff here and there but most of it is drifting with the wind. Every surface appears to be glistening.

I turn around and find Seb looking at me from the bed, a smile on his face.

"What are you smiling at?"

"You." He says. When I raise my eyebrows he elaborates. "I love the way you move around, at ease in your luscious body. It makes me happy."

It's true. I hadn't even thought about being virtually naked and walking around Seb's apartment like this. Huh.

Walking over to the bed, I lean over and rest my forehead against his. "You did that. You gave me that. In only a few words. No one else matters. Just you."

Seb's eyes close for a moment, and when he opens them again they shine and he whispers;

"I fucking love you, Arlene."

CHAPTER TWENTY

"Yes, we're fine… No Gus, don't worry, I'm not getting out on the road. I will stay put… Dad."

Arlene snickers as she hangs up her phone.

Interrupted by phone. Go fucking figure. Mind you, it was probably for the best. From the slightly panicked look in Arlene's eyes when I was dumb enough to lay it all out, I'm thinking she needs some time. I disappear into the bathroom to clean up a bit and just catch the end of her conversation when I return to the bedroom.

"I'm just gonna heat up that chili now, if you're hungry?" A hint of uncertainty shows in her eyes as she quickly starts putting on her discarded clothes.

"Sounds great, babe. I'm starving. I'll just grab a quick shower and then ice my knee while we eat."

"Okay."

I'm just about to step out of the shower when the bathroom door slams open.

"Seb, I smell smoke. Calling 911. Get the fuck out."

Before I can even answer she's gone. Scrambling for a towel, I quickly tie it around my waist and walk into the bedroom where I can already detect the acrid smell of burning. Without pausing to dress, I grab what I can and drag myself out the door and down the stairs, calling Arlene's name all the way. Fucking woman. Smoke is billowing from the back of the building where the trash bins are. I wish I had slipped on shoes, my feet are sliding on the slick snow and I am literally freezing my balls off, but I don't stop.

Fumbling in the pocket of my jeans I manage to pull out my cell and speed dial Gus.

"Get your ass over here. Fire. Arlene is out here somewhere." Without listening to what he is saying, I put the phone on speaker and head around the corner where I see both trash bins pushed up against the building, flames licking up the wooden siding. But no Arlene.

"Arlene!! Where the fuck are you!!"

The wind and snow feel like little razors on my bare skin. Nevertheless, I drop the pile of clothes and the phone on the ground, except a shirt, which I rip in two and wrap around my hands. I pull at the bins to try and move them away from the siding, but they are hotter than Hades. Even through the wraps on my hands, I can feel the blisters forming. No way will I be able to move these suckers. Cold is no longer an issue, though, but where the fuck is Arlene? I need to update Gus and grab my phone.

"You still there?"

"On my way. Five minutes. Status"

"Trash bins were moved, on fire, siding is lit. It was set. Still outside looking for Arlene."

"Keep the line open. 911 is called."

Working my way around the other side of the diner, the opposite end of the building from the stairs to my apartment, I can see the glow of flames coming from the front. Fucking hell.

"Arlene!!"

This time I hear her.

"Seb. Don't you fucking come out here. This illiterate ingrate is too much of a coward to handle himself without a gun. Stay where you are!"

Like hell. When I round the corner I am only half-surprised to see the fucker whose reminders I am still wearing, with a gun pointed at Arlene's head. The idiot is wearing a stupid grin. He has no idea holding a gun to that woman's head has just painted a giant bullseye on his sorry ass, and not just for me to aim at.

"Geeze, Seb. We've gotta work on your listening skills!" Arlene throws up her hands and rolls her eyes. Her antics fill me with pride. My girl's got some brass balls.

Quickly finding and holding the cocksucker's gaze, I try to ignore the crackling of the flames and the pungent smell of smoke, focusing on the immediate threat in front of me. Kinda hard to do buck-naked. Only one way… bluff.

"Kind of you to come all this way to give me an opportunity to reciprocate in kind."

At the slightly confused look in his eyes, I add, "Sorry. I used too many big words, I see. Shall I translate to a preferred language? Ape, perhaps, *Matt?*" At the use of his name, he does what I had hoped. The barrel of the gun lifts up to cover me instead of Arlene, who doesn't notice and chuckles at my words, which earns her a backhand from the ape. Clenching my fists at my side, I am willing myself not to lose eye contact with him, but instead keep his attention, and the gun, drawn away from her.

"Fucking get your ass over here. Should've finished the job the other day." He forces out between clenched teeth.

As slow as I can I move in his general direction, but angle myself slightly away from Arlene, forcing him to turn away from her. Smart girl. From the corner of my eye I can tell that although one hand is clutching her cheek, with the other one she is carefully pulling herself in the opposite direction. Their positions are now almost reversed, with the goon intensely focused on me, he inadvertently turned his back on Arlene. Something even I know you should be careful with!

When I am almost close enough to reach out and make a grab for his gun, I try for distraction again.

"Why set fire to the diner? You got a thing for matches?"

"Shut the fuck up, you freak. Sit your ass down."

I sit, my ass clenching in protest at the chilly encounter with the ground. Gonna have numb cheeks at best.

"What do you want, Matt? What do you get out of this?"

I'm trying with everything to keep him talking, hoping Gus is catching it all and will approach carefully and hopefully in time.

"You know the fire department is on the way, right?"

He laughs at that. "Why do you think I picked tonight? Gonna take 'em forever. There won't be much left."

"True." I can't resist. "Except for two witnesses."

A loud crash from one of the diner windows bursting with the heat of the fire, momentarily draws his attention. Not hesitating a second, Arlene hauls out hard and kicks his legs right out from under him. Greatly assisted by the surface of the parking lot now covered in a slick layer of snow, he goes down swiftly. A shot goes off, but veers wide and with a sickening smack his head meets the unforgiving asphalt.

"Think he'll make it?"

I hear Gus ask the EMT looking after Seb when the first ambulance drives off with the guy I knocked out. To be honest, I'm more concerned right now with the state of my diner. The fire department showed up a few minutes after Gus did but had made good time taking the fire down. Right now there are no flames visible anymore, but still a lot of smoke and smoldering. I wouldn't know the extent of the damage until I had a chance to go inside and have a look - that is, if the Fire Marshall will let me.

Gus is walking toward his truck and tries to motion me over.

"Arlene, get out of the damn weather! Get in here."

But I shake my head. I don't want to be stuck in a confined space right now, at least not with Gus.

Looking back at where Seb is being checked over, I meet his eyes and see the concern in them. I'm fully aware I left him hanging with his declaration of love earlier, but I'm terrified of saying those words again. Only once before have I uttered those words to a man and look where that left me. It's not that I think Seb would ever hurt me willingly, not like Geoffrey did, but isn't saying you love a man the same as handing yourself over completely? I did that tonight already; at least as much as I could give him.

He waves me over to the ambulance where he sits sheltered from the weather and I can't resist his pull, bruised and battered as he is with a blanket draped around him until he can get some clothes from his apartment. That is, if there still is enough of an apartment to get into. Oh God - my diner. I have to call Beth.

"Come here, babe." He is calling me now and I walk faster. When I climb into the rig and am within arm's reach he hauls me in his arms and presses my head in his neck. He smells like smoke, leftover shower and Seb and it surrounds me like a safe blanket. Sliding my arms under the blanket against his naked back, I press myself to him - needing to melt myself to him. My safety. Since he came eight months ago he has been right there to pick me up or hold me up, and most of the time I haven't even noticed. It doesn't matter what brought him here. It only matters that he stays. Time and time again. Fuck, I love this man.

"You ok?" His deep voice rumbles against my hair.

"I know I shouldn't be, but I am in a way."

Pushing me slightly away from him, he studies my face carefully with one corner of his mouth lifted and a question in his eyes. "Yeah?"

I nod in response and he runs his index finger from my forehead down to the tip of my nose before grabbing my chin and kissing me sweetly.

"Whatever the damage to the diner, we'll fix it. Together." He says with determination in his eyes, making me swallow a few times before I can respond.

"Together. I like that."

He rubs his nose against my cheek and says, "I want you to have the EMT check you out real quick."

Immediately I start protesting. "But I'm fine - "

He shuts me up by pressing his finger on my lips and leans his head against mine.

"Please, Spot. For me?"

Obviously the EMT checks me out and finds there is nothing broken, but suggests a cold pack might come in handy.

A Montezuma Sheriff's Department car pulls in and Joe gets out, making his way over to us.

"You guys are keeping me busy."

"We aim to please, Joe." I try to joke, but it falls rather flat when all of us turn around and look at the diner with almost all of it's windows blown or smashed out and dark soot running up the side of the building.

"Damn, girl. That ain't looking too good. Have you been inside yet?"

"No, we're waiting for the Fire Marshall to do a walk through first."

"Okay. Mind if I get in and ask some questions?"

Joe climbs in the ambulance and we try to tell him what

225

happened, starting earlier tonight when I closed the diner and heard some noise, then Joe turns to Seb and gives him the third degree and an ear-full about heading off on his fact-finding excursion last night, which brings me to an awful realization.

"Oh my God! Julie... What if he doesn't make it? He is the only connection we have to her."

"Already on it, Arlene. We have an officer waiting at the hospital and as soon as anything about his condition is known we'll be all over it. Besides, Gus and Caleb are working on tracking down the sister."

"Sister?"

"Matt has a sister who was bartending at the bar two nights ago. She's the one I was talking to before this happened." Seb filled me in.

I run my hands through my sticky hair. I'm a drenched cat and I feel like the whole damn world has gone ballistic, but I do want to keep my priorities straight.

"Make sure you give Julie and her baby priority, Joe. That's more important than anything."

Seb gives my waist a little squeeze and Joe says, "Of course we will, girl, but you've gotta understand that all this is connected somehow and you seem to be at the center of it all. Too much of a coincidence for it to be anything else."

It took another hour for the Fire Marshall to arrive and do his walk-through and then we were allowed in. Seb had not been allowed upstairs, but someone brought out some of his clothes, so he was warm and decent again.

I gasp in shock when I walk in and see the damage. Holy fuck. Parts of the ceiling are gone and toward the kitchen and the back wall, everything is black and scorched. I don't know whether it is actually all burned or whether they are layers of soot, but it looks awful.

The Fire Marshall turns to me. "I have good news and bad news. What do you want first?"

"Bad news, please. Then when you give me the good news it'll be the start of a new trend," I tell him far more optimistically than I feel.

He smiles at that. "Very well. The damage is pretty extensive. The back area, kitchen, cold storage and office are pretty much unsalvageable, as is the apartment above. There are areas of the ceiling where the fire found its way in between the floors and smoldered quietly while the fire was being contained in other areas which is why you see the hole here. The main dining room is in order, other than the ceiling and the windows."

I've been holding Seb's hands in front of me. He slides in behind me and doesn't say a thing, just slides his arms around my waist. Hearing the scale of the damage the fire has done has me squeezing his hands hard.

"And the good news?"

"It is an obvious arson, but one to which you are victim and between my report and the one you will undoubtedly receive from the Sheriff's Office, you should have no problem whatsoever with your insurance claim. Let me know when the adjuster will be here and give me a call. I will make myself available."

He hands over his business card and with a nod of his head is off to speak with Joe.

"Still doing okay?" Seb asks as he turns me around.

"I guess. A bit stunned to be honest. Not sure how I feel anymore, just really tired now. I think I could sleep for days, I'm so exhausted."

"Let's go home. I'm just going to see how long Joe and his boys are going to be. Check in with Gus before we go. You sit in the truck, I'll be right there."

CHAPTER TWENTY-ONE

It has been three days since the fire at the diner and I'm going out of my mind from boredom. Seb has stayed with me. What stuff was salvaged from his apartment has been moved into my spare bedroom, but he has insisted on folding himself around me every night. Not that I'm complaining, it's the best way to sleep. What am I saying? It's the only way to sleep. I haven't had any nightmares since Seb has started sleeping with me and I am getting more rest than ever before, but it's the days that are driving me nuts. We haven't been able to get back into the diner to clean. Both the Fire Marshall and the Sheriff's Office have been keeping the place locked down for their ongoing investigation, but the word is that we'll be able to start cleaning today. First I have to meet with the claims adjuster and the Fire Marshall at the diner. If everything goes well, we can start cleaning right away. It's possible the insurance will pay for a company to do that, but we figure we can save some money by doing as much work as possible ourselves. Nothing better to do while the diner is closed anyway.

When I try to roll out of bed to get some coffee going, a heavy arm snakes around my waist and pulls me back down.

"Where you goin'?" Seb's gruff sleepy voice is muffled by the pillow, which is half covering his head.

"Coffee." I say, still trying to get out of bed but his stubborn arm keeps me pinned.

We've kissed, we've curled up together in bed, but other than some petting, we've behaved... too well. I've been careful of Seb's injuries and he doesn't seem to be in a hurry either, but it's starting to make me a little unsure.

"Not yet. Lie here with me." Pushing himself up on one elbow, the pillow slips off his head and his hair is sticking every which way, but the sleepy slits his eyes form have a sparkle in them, and the smile he throws me is at full wattage. Hard to resist the man. All hard looks and gruffness on the outside, but it belies the gentle and kind intelligence he harbors inside. I lean over and use my upper body to push him back onto the mattress on his back and rub my cheek against his days' old scruff. When my mouth finds his I explore with my lips and tongue.

"Mmmmm, much better than coffee." He mumbles against my lips. He pulls my body up on his and spreads his legs so mine slide in between. His hands skim down my body and grasp my ass and hold me in place while he rocks his morning erection along my closed thighs. The head of his cock slightly teases the juncture of my legs and in no time I'm squirming, trying to open my legs to give him access but his muscular thighs keep me trapped, and his mouth keeps me distracted. One hand slides along the seam of my butt cheek and finds the edge of my panties; wet already. He groans his approval in my mouth and the vibrations only fuel my own hunger for him. I want to open my legs and ride him – slide myself over his length, teasing myself on his hardness – but I still can't move. Seb's fingers have found my slit and are spreading the moisture over my lips making me undulate my hips, eager for something to fill me.

"Easy, baby... " He mumbles, nibbling his way down my neck.

With both his hands he makes my panties disappear with one fast rip. Seb lifts my hips slightly off him and slides his cock in the tight space between my thighs and my pussy where he just created a slippery channel with my juices. One of his hands spreads my cheeks a little while the other seems to press his length along my slit. Rocking his hips, creating a delicious tight, slow friction that has me moaning out his name.

"Please Seb…"

"What do you want, love. Tell me."

"I feel like I'm coming out of my skin. Please…"

"Need you to tell me." The combination of the barely restrained control in his voice and the lust that burns in his eyes is overwhelming.

"Fuck me. Please, Seb. Hard."

Before I even finish speaking he has me on my back, is ripping my top off and sucks my tight nipple in his mouth. He grabs a pillow, shoves it under my butt, lifts one of my legs over his arm and slams his length home as he pulls hard on my breast. All breath has left me and I feel like I am plunged in a vacuum until he releases my nipple with a plop and invades my mouth with his tongue. Then hunger strikes and I find my hands clawing at his back and ass, trying to pull him deeper inside me. The long deep passes of his tongue mimic the strong rhythmic thrusts of his hips. But I need more.

"Harder."

He stops and looks me in the eyes. "I can hardly control myself…"

"Don't want control. Want you to let go. Fuck me like you *need* to fuck me." I bite out, more eager for his surrender than for my relief.

"Grab onto the headboard." I do as he says and he releases my leg and slides his arms under my shoulders and holds on. "Look at me, Spot. Even when I fuck you I want you to know I'm loving you."

His eyes tell me everything I need to know and I hope mine will tell him what I can't express in words. A careful slide in and out of me quickly increases to a furious pounding with Seb's mouth spouting incoherent grunts and sounds, while his hands hold my body in place against the onslaught. My mouth opens, gasping for air, so close to blissing out as the sound of his balls slapping against my flesh almost sends me over the edge. What finally does is the instant dilation in Seb's eyes when I feel his cock start pulsing inside me, and just like that my body seizes into a massive orgasm that contracts every muscle in my body before releasing into the purest satisfaction. My eyes never leave his.

I let go of the headboard and wrap myself around my man.

"My man." I whisper and a small smile tugs at Seb's mouth.

"Yeah?" He wants to know. My answer is to pull him down and kiss him. I'm no good with those words.

"Arlene!"

"Coming! Hold your friggin' horses, I'll be right there…"

I'm in a mood. This morning's bliss bubble with Seb was rudely interrupted by my fucking alarm clock. Time for the harsh realities of the day; A burned out diner to contend with. Ugh. Having lived in PJ's for most of this week, I find myself suddenly drawing a blank when faced with my closet, which is what has Seb hollering up the stairs about. I've been standing here a good ten minutes, none the wiser. Did I mention I hate clothes? Seriously, I can see the purpose of them - even the attraction, but must they be so complicated? It's one of the things I love about the diner. I never have to question what to wear; jeans and a work shirt. Simple. Now, I don't have a fucking clue.

When I come down ten minutes later, Seb hands me a mug of coffee and leans in for a kiss.

"Coffee is cold, but you look nice." He says with a wink.

Smartass. I'm wearing jeans and a work shirt. I figure I'm going to the diner so it would be fitting.

"Shut up, Seb."

"You're cute, Spot. Let's go." He grabs my hand and pulls me to the door.

I throw him a dirty look but have to fight the little smile that wants to break through. Can't encourage the man.

Good thing I've put on work clothes too. It takes all of ten minutes for the Fire Marshall to sign off on the diner and he's gone, leaving a report with Joe, the insurance company and one for me. To be honest, I had blown this meeting out of proportion a bit, probably from being cooped up inside too long. By the time 11:00 am comes along, I have buckets of soapy water going and I'm rinsing down cutlery, plates and glasses while Seb is pulling out whatever is in one piece and salvageable. The plan is to at least get the soot off, pack the loose stuff up and store it in a container unit in Cortez. Once we have the place emptied out, we're gonna start with the big clean.

An hour and a half later, it's hard to tell what the hell it is I'm wearing at all. When Gus' Yukon pulls in the parking lot, I'm glad for the distraction but disappointed to find Emma isn't with him.

"Where'd you leave my girl?"

"Don't want her to break her neck, Arlene. She's been cooking up a storm though, making sure there's enough to feed an army for lunch and threatening to leave me if I don't bring you back for dinner later, so you better come. She's pissed enough at me already for making her stay home, but she slipped yesterday and fell on her hip which is all kinds of purple today. Last thing she needs is something broken. Stubborn woman won't stay put though."

"No problem, I'll come see the brat. So where's the food? I'm hungry."

"Don't I get a *Hello Gus, and how are you?* Even a hug maybe?" The big lug just stands there guarding the trunk of his SUV while I try to peek in.

"Fine. Come here." Wrapping my soot covered body around his, I whisper, none too softly, "Needy men…"

"Uhm, what was that, Arlene?" Seb's voice sounds from behind me.

Oops.

"Mind unhanding my girl, Gus?"

I step back to see Gus with a big grin on his face, looking at Seb but not letting me go. Boys. Snapping my fingers in front of his face is my gentle reminder that there is a hungry woman standing in front of him, one who is about to get violent if not fed promptly.

"One of you feed me please? Before I disappear?"

Eyebrows raised, the two men look at me and then each other before they burst out laughing. I am not amused.

"That is not funny. Hey! Jesus, you two give me a headache." I stomp off inside to what is left of my bathroom to wash up a little. Good thing the water was kept on.

By the time I get out, Gus has brought in sandwiches, a thermos of hot coffee, some kind of noodle salad, fruit and muffins. Seb catches me around the neck and pulls me in for a short but mighty intense kiss. Okay then, apology accepted.

"This looks enough food to feed an orphanage, Gus. There is at least enough for ten."

"I know, but Caleb will be over shortly and he's picking up Beth. Also, Joe is going to be back soon to fill us in on some progress he has made with respect to Julie's disappearance. He found out about half an hour after he left here this morning."

I feel so guilty. With everything that has been happening Julie has been on my mind, and I've been worried about her, but I haven't been focused on it, and that just seems awful. Seb seems to clue in to where my thoughts are going.

"Don't Arlene. The best thing you did for her was take down that son of a bitch and give Joe a chance to question him. You can't be responsible for everything, worry about everything. Not *all* the time. We do it collectively, and we have not let her down. Not as a group."

My eyes flit over to Gus who has listened in and he nods his agreement.

"He's right. You are not solely responsible for the concern over others, we all are. No worries. No recriminations, okay?"

Yes. Strangely I am okay with that. Something comes to mind that my ever-so-wise friend Emma will toss at me on occasion; 'You are no good to others if you don't take care of yourself first'.

Lunch is delicious, of course, and by the time I have scarfed down yet another muffin, which is undoubtedly going to make a re-appearance on my ass somewhere later, Caleb and Beth have arrived reporting for cleanup duty. I have awesome friends.

CHAPTER TWENTY-TWO

"Sorry I couldn't get back earlier. We had some more developments I wanted to check out before I drove back here."

Joe just walked in at Emma and Gus' place where we all have ended up at after a full afternoon of dirty work. Caleb and I got up in what used to be my apartment, but is now a burned out shell, to try and cover off as much of the hole in the ceiling to the diner as possible with sheets of plywood and tarps to keep the weather out as much as we can. With two contractors coming in from Cortez tomorrow and a third from Durango on Wednesday, we should have the three quotes the insurance company requested by the end of this week and hopefully can get work started as soon as the next.

The small stuff we were able to rescue has been cleaned off

and packed up and tomorrow we'll make a few runs to the storage unit to get it out of the way. Once the dumpster gets there in the afternoon we'll be hauling trash. That ought to be fun. As much as I loved hanging around with Arlene, it feels good to be doing something productive. For some reason sitting at her house for three days felt like waiting for the other shoe to drop, and I am pretty damn sure there is another shoe that is gonna drop. Hopefully Joe has some news.

"First grab a chair and pull it up, Joe. You probably haven't eaten yet either and these guys have been at it all day, too. Eat." Emma waves her wooden spoon in the direction of the dining table that is already pretty crowded, but we all huddle together and Joe manages to squeeze in with a smile for Emma. No one messes with her when she is in nurture mode, especially not when she's been made to wait all day before she could unleash on us. Looks like she hasn't been out of the kitchen all day; dish after dish of salads, vegetables and rolls come out, and finally she calls Gus to help her bring out the roast. When he lifts the thing out of the oven, my mouth drops open and Arlene bursts out laughing beside me.

"Christ, Ems. The entire population of Cedar Tree coming for dinner? We better make room."

The thing is huge. Big enough to feed four families at Christmas. Gus chuckles and Emma whacks him with her elbow, blushing slightly.

"Bite me, Arlene."

"I'd rather bite that, but I'm afraid there is no more room on the table for that monstrosity. What is it? A buffalo?"

"Just beef and you're a pain in my ass. Just put it on the counter, Gus. We'll have to cut it here. Unfortunately, our resident smartass is right. It won't fit on the table." Emma admits grudgingly.

"That looks fucking amazing!" Joe says. "It's been forever since I've had a good home-cooked meal, let alone one that looks and smells like this."

Arlene gets up and starts taking drink orders. When she passes Emma, she throws her arm around her shoulders and kisses her head. "This is why I love ya." She says quietly.

"Yeah, yeah. Whatever." But Emma is smiling as she murmurs her response.

The food is amazing.

"We've been trying to track down the sister of the owner of Koko's. His full name is Matt Collins and his sister's name is Tanya Lopes. I got a call this morning from Monticello that they found a car registered in her name, sitting by the side of the road – abandoned, apparently with a flat tire. She's crossed state lines which makes this much more complicated on one hand, but on the other, it gives us a whole new set of resources. Since the car was found just north of town, the assumption is she was headed for Moab, where it's relatively easy to get lost with all the tourist rentals they have out there."

Arlene is sitting beside me on the couch and has been twitching in her seat since Joe mentioned Matt Collins' name. I know what's bothering her.

"Joe." I interrupt. "Sorry to jump in but can you quickly tell us the condition of the guy? Has he regained consciousness?"

Arlene's hand tightens on my leg and I see Joe notice it as well. His eyes soften as he looks at Arlene and then at me.

"Should have started there, huh? Yes. Got that call when I was about to meet up with you at the diner. He woke up and was responsive and seemed lucid, so I wanted to see if there was anything he was willing to tell me."

A shudder runs through Arlene's body as it finally relaxes, leaning in against mine and I tighten my arm around her and tuck her in closer. She turns her face in my shoulder.

"I wasn't able to get a whole lot out of him before the doctor put an end to it. He's been diagnosed with a severe concussion so whatever he comes out with at this point should be considered questionable - according to *her*." He emphasized with some bitterness.

"*Her,* Joe? What doctor would that be, someone we know?" Gus probes what we all sensed is a sore spot with Joe. Dr. Naomi Waters. No one knows why, but there was some serious chemistry there and a bunch of sore feelings, that was obvious. Other than a scathing glare in Gus' direction, Joe doesn't react.

"Here is what we do know; Mr. Collins' establishment was in some serious financial trouble until about four months ago. A sudden influx of money from an unknown source solved his immediate problems and has kept him afloat since. What we also know is that about two months ago, Mr. Collins started dating Julie."

"What?" Arlene exclaimed. "I don't understand. What do you mean, he dated Julie? She told me she had no one but her aunt."

"I'm not sure what exactly is going on, Arlene, but I aim to find out. The one thing to keep in mind though is that if Julie was his girlfriend, maybe she didn't disappear, but left willingly?"

Just like Arlene, I'm confused. I talked with the girl and she hadn't seemed like she was lying. She appeared to truly be distraught and upset about the problems she was having with her little one. Then again, desperation can make people do stupid things. She may have genuinely felt all those things, except not for the reasons she indicated. Who knows?

It's late by the time we get home and have a chance to shower off the remaining grime of the day. I suggest Arlene go first, but only because I want to walk in on her. I'm sneaky that way. She still gets a little self-conscious with her body from time to time and I want her to know how irresistible she is to me. Funny thing is, it doesn't just have to do with her body - well, that's a lie, it does - but it's the whole thing. Her taste, her smell, her spirit, humor and yes, her fantastic skin with the endless freckles, the awesome overflowing hands full of ass and her fucking endless legs. Never thought I'd fall for someone so unlike me in many ways, at least on the surface. Wasn't looking and *bam*.

Her head whips around when I slip through the shower curtain and settle in behind her slippery wet body. Rock hard already, my cock slips between her butt cheeks and instantly she freezes. I don't stop stroking her body, but slowly create some distance and angle my hips so when I pull her back against me, my cock is positioned against one cheek. I lean my chin on her shoulder and whisper, "Relax, love. Never fear me."

She turns and wraps her arms around my neck, nuzzling and kissing.

"Not you, just ass play."

Stroking my hand down to where I have a good hold of one of her ass cheeks while the other slides up her spine to her neck, I hold her gaze.

"You have a luscious ass that I love, that's all. I'll cop a feel, have a taste, get an eye full - but I will never violate that boundary unless you bring it down. Got it?"

She nods, but I'm not convinced.

"Arlene?"

"Sorry..." She is hiding her face now. "I'm pretty fucked up, right?"

Not wanting to stand in a shower that is slowly getting colder, I quickly wash and rinse us both, help her out of the shower and towel her off. A quick wipe down for myself and I take her by the hand to the bedroom and lift up the covers on the bed for her to crawl under. When she turns her back as I settle in beside her, I roll her right back and see tears brimming in her eyes. Fuck.

"What you give to me, Arlene is more than I ever thought was possible. The feelings you bring out are unlike anything… Well, anything. I already feel blessed beyond my wildest dreams. There is nothing to miss - there is too much to take in. Do you realize how unique it is to find what we have? With our backgrounds, both of our fucked up histories? We were a hundred to one odds. Who could have imagined that you and I would hit it off, let alone fall in love. I don't want perfection… you don't want perfection, we both want real and this is as real as it gets. Wrinkles, blemishes, nose hair and hang-ups… All of it."

"Love you, Seb." She smiles.

Fucking A. She did it.

"Know you do, Spot. Love you back." I lean down to kiss her when suddenly she pushes me off her.

"Wait a fucking minute! I don't have nose hair, do I?" She tries to get up out of the bed, I assume to get to a mirror and I can barely hang onto her as I'm about to piss myself laughing.

"Not you. Me." I manage to get out before she seriously injures me with her flailing limbs.

She immediately stills and ducks her head down to examine my nostrils. Great.

"I don't see anything."

"I trim them, Arlene. Now can we drop the nose hair?"

She climbs back in bed and right on my lap, pushing me back against the headboard.

"I love you *and* your nose hair, Seb. It's quite normal for a middle-aged guy, you know."

Brat. I smack her butt, grab a good hold of her in case she tries to take off and then I get her back good.

"I'm sure, love, except I'm only forty-two, not quite middle-aged yet."

Her mouth falls open and I can't stop my chuckle.

"Wha…You…Forty-two? I'm three years older than you?"

Gotcha.

CHAPTER TWENTY - THREE

"Fan-fucking-tastic…"

I've been sent into Cortez for some work-gloves and there are at least ten different kinds to pick from. How the hell am I supposed to know what they want? Bunch of asswipes, telling me I'm being a pain in their ass and to go 'cool off' in Cortez. All of them snickering too. Men. They thought it was funny I never knew Seb was younger, that I was pissed at him for never telling me. Well now I'm pissed at all of them since apparently everyone had been aware. *ASSWIPES*!

And Caleb is no use at all He is sent to babysit me and instead stays in the car yapping on his phone, so now I have ten different pairs of gloves and not a clue what to get. Fine. I'll get them all. Three pairs of each; small, medium and large and if anyone has anything to say, I'm gonna flip even harder.

Caleb is still on the phone when I get to the truck and barely spares me a glance as he turns the key in the ignition and pulls out of the ACE Hardware store parking lot, then he checks back again and gives the three bulging plastic bags I have at my feet a cursory look.

"Do some Christmas shopping while you were in there?"

"Yes, as a matter of fact. Got every one of my *friends* exactly what they deserve this year." I tell him with a snarky tone.

The "Ouch" from his mouth is far less satisfying when accompanied by the single raised eyebrow and that irritating self-assured smile on his face. *Argh!*

For the rest of the trip I keep my eyes directed out the window and try to figure out why exactly it is that I am so pissed. Do I really care that much about a three-year age difference? No, not particularly. Not either way. It makes me feel a bit more insecure maybe. What makes me mad is that I didn't know. Of all people, I should have been the one to know and I had no clue. I hate that I didn't know. Really, really hate it but that is really no one's issue but mine. Dammit, it's annoying when I find out I've behaved like an ass. Groveling is so not my style.

"Better?" Seb opens the door to the diner, takes the bags from my hands and pulls me close. For the first time since the night before, I look him in the eye. "There you are." In an instant his mouth is on mine and he is making up for lost time. That is, until Gus interrupts us.

"What the fuck? Arlene, were they having a sale or something?" He empties out the ACE bags on the table and we all stare at the mountain of gloves. "How many pairs did you buy?"

"Ehh, thirty? Maybe?"

Four pairs of eyes turn to me and I start to chuckle.

"What? I didn't know which ones so I got them all."

"We're stocked up now." Caleb throws out, cracking everyone up.

With the tension relieved and my hissy fit over, we can start pulling some of the damaged stuff into the parking lot, which is where the container should be dropped off sometime today. Beth and I handle the smaller things and the guys head straight for the kitchen, pulling out the appliances. Seb insists on checking them all first, even though the insurance company has written them all off. He has pulled one of the grill/oven combinations out first. He wants to try and salvage it for personal use he says. Okay then. Don't know where he'd put a big appliance like that, but I'm all for not throwing away what can be saved.

Thank God we haven't had any real precipitation since the storm the night of the fire. The ground is fairly dry and with the sun out it's pretty nice, despite the frosty temperatures. I had held hopes that maybe we would be able to re-open before Christmas, but Seb was quick to point out that with temperatures hovering around freezing and the amount of work that needed to be done, not to mention the speeds at which insurance companies tend to part with their money, it was less than likely we would actually be able to accomplish that. It also gave me an idea. Once we have the quotes in and sent off to my insurer, I am taking Seb on a little surprise trip. I may not be good with words, but I know how to listen. He has done a lot for me, even without me realizing it, and this is a perfect opportunity for me to take care of him for a change.

The buzzing in my pocket drags me out of my thoughts and I don't recognize the number on the screen of my phone when I pull it out.

"Hello?"

"Arlene?"

"Julie? Is that you? Are you ok? Where are you? Is Liam with you?"

Beth, who is working side by side with me in the dining room must have heard the conversation because she disappeared and within seconds is back with Seb and the rest of the guys at her side. Gus mouths *'speaker'* at me and I fumble with my phone to find the right button, just in time to hear Julie's voice again.

"They have Liam. I'm so sorry, Arlene. I don't know what to do, they have my baby!" The fear in her voice is enough to bring tears to my eyes.

"Hold on, honey. Are you alone?" I'm trying to follow the instructions that Gus is mouthing at me.

"Yes, I got away from her but I don't know where they are keeping Liam. Please help me!"

"Julie. It's Gus here. We're going to help you. Where are you right now?"

"A drugstore just inside Moab. She was holding me in an adobe bungalow outside of town but I managed to get away last night after she got a phone call, tied me to the bathroom sink and took off. I used a rusted side of the drainpipe and part of a chipped tile from the floor to get through the zip ties. I ran all night. I'm so scared. I didn't know who else to call… She said the guy they work for has more power than the cops."

"You did good, honey. Is there anywhere you can hide out for a little while? I will make sure you get picked up as soon as possible, but I need you to keep out of sight. A storage room perhaps? Bathroom?"

"Yeah, I can."

Caleb already has Joe on the phone and he is listening in to Gus exchanging information with Julie. After I jot down the number of the drugstore for Gus, he reluctantly lets her hang up and turns to us.

"When you guys are done with the contractors here, would you mind heading over and staying with Emma or picking her up? I'd feel better if she wasn't alone, and I have a feeling Caleb and I will be busy."

"No problem. First contractor won't be here for another half hour, I can easily run and bring her here. She may have some good ideas for us anyway." I offer, but Seb is quick to grab the keys from my hand with a kiss and a whispered, "I'll do it", is off and running.

"Even better."

"How are you gonna get someone there so fast?" I ask Gus.

"They crossed state lines, Arlene. Federal involvement means better resources. Joe probably already has a helicopter on the way. She won't have to wait long, but we are not waiting for that; we have to find that little boy."

Just like that the atmosphere has changed and is now laced with a sense of urgency. Beth is standing off to the side, looking a little pale and I go over to check on her.

"You okay, hun?"

Shaking her head slightly and focusing her eyes on me, she appears to collect herself.

"Yes. I'm fine. Just… You know… Here we were, joking around all morning and even yesterday, so wrapped up in the diner and actually enjoying the prospect of getting a good start in when all this time poor Julie -" She's obviously feeling the same guilt I was… I am.

"I know. I feel the same way, but so much is happening all the time that maximizing on some good moments shouldn't make us feel guilty. Let's use our time wisely here and once the contractors are gone, we'll head over to Emma's. You come with us. We'll all do some thinking and figure out where we are going to put Julie and Liam when they bring him home."

"God, that poor little boy."

Caleb overhears. "Likelihood is that he's alright. If they were using him to keep her in check, they won't want to do anything to the one bit of leverage they have. We have some decent leads, an area to check out. Gus is talking to the FBI agent in charge and with his record for tracking people, you know the best people are on it. As soon as Seb is here with Emma, Gus and I will take off, but I promise one of us will stay in touch with you. Beth, I would feel a whole lot better if you hung around as well. Don't think it's smart for anyone to stay alone right now."

"I'd rather stick close anyway." Is Beth's response.

Just a few minutes later, Seb is back with Emma in tow. She must have been ready and waiting by the door when he got there.

"Hey Ems." I give her a big hug when she makes her way over. "How'd you get here so fast?"

"Gus called and told me to be ready. Gave me two sentences of explanation before telling me he had to go, so fill me in, girls. What's this about Liam and Julie?"

We fill her in as best we can, given that we really don't know that much either, but it seems to satisfy Emma. By this time Gus and Caleb have finished a little powwow they held with Seb just outside the doors and Gus came in to quickly kiss his woman.

"Stay together, okay? Neil is in the office in Grand Junction and Dana is going to run central post from there. You need anything and can't reach me, call Dana. Okay, Peach?" With a kiss to her forehead and a wave to the rest of us, he is out the door, Caleb on his heels who lifts his chin in our direction before he closes the door.

Well. With Emma and Beth walking into what is left of the kitchen, chattering, that leaves Seb and I in the diner. Without thinking I walk into his arms to find a little comfort and he wraps them around me instantly.

"Hurry up and wait for us again. I hate this," I say, the sound muffled by the hoodie Seb is wearing because my face is buried in his neck.

"I hate it too, but they are best at what they do and we have things to do here. Make sure everyone has a place to work when this is all over." Seb's little pep talk helps… a bit.

I lift up on my toes and whisper in his ear. "Sorry I was a crankpot earlier. Love you." A squeeze of his arms indicates he has heard me.

It isn't until close to three that afternoon that the second contractor leaves. Boy. The first one was a bit of a tool. Never had done anything in the food industry but was willing to *learn*. Learn? Hello, we are not an apprentice program here. We are in need of some serious expertise. Both Seb and I nixed him right off the bat when we found out he had no clue about food industry code when it came to the kitchen. Sorry, no time to do your research for ya, bud.

The second guy was better... marginally. At least he had some experience and appeared to be able to start at the drop of a hat, but whenever we asked for a written quote, he kept pushing for a non-written agreement that would be cheaper for us and more beneficial to him. Yeah right, I need that paperwork for the insurance company, smartass!

Given the record so far, I didn't have much hope for the Durango guy tomorrow, but we would wait and see.

By 3:30 pm, we've closed up the diner and pile into Seb's truck, whose extended cab barely fits Beth and me in the back. Tired and a bit punchy, the lot of us make our way to Emma's place. She assures us she has plenty of food and Seb volunteers to cook so he can 'stay in shape'. None of us complain, not even Emma. By now we are all filthy and smell like the inside of a fireplace, but given that Seb promises to feed us we give him first dibs on the shower, despite his protests.

"Share a shower with me." Seb says in a low voice, when he slings his arm around my shoulders as we walk up Emma's porch.

"Not here!" I'm not about to have wild monkey sex in the shower with Beth and Emma sitting 10 feet away in the living room!

Seb chuckles. "You have a one-track mind, you know that? Nothing I'd like better than where your thoughts are at right now, Spot, but I was thinking we could save time and water if we showered together. Besides, I just want to feel you close."

Well, damn if that doesn't turn me into a puddle. A little one.

The snow starts falling just after we finish our dinner and are trying to kill time waiting for some news. Nothing yet. Emma is jumping out of her skin wanting to call Gus but trying to be 'good'. We've figured out sleeping arrangements, which didn't go without some disagreements. Staying here is a bit tight but it is a bit easier for Seb and I to adjust than it would be for Emma at ours, especially now that Beth had called her son in Durango and he was on his way to pick her up to stay with him for a few days. When I mentioned that of course Emma was pissed off good and it took no time at all for her to point out that I had been hiding pain all day long. That had Seb glaring at me.

"You were in pain and hiding it? Why?"

"Oh geeze, Seb. Maybe because it's an everyday occurrence and there is little I can do about it?"

"I know, babe, but I also know if you pace yourself, you last longer. I'm surprised you haven't gone into a full on flare yet."

"Since when are you an expert on my health?"

Seb now looks a bit sheepishly from me to Beth and Emma who are observing our interaction with a little too much amusement.

"Read up on it." He mumbles.

"You what?"

"I overheard you talking to Emma when she first came to Cedar Tree, about specialists in the area and you mentioned someone you were seeing for your Fibromyalgia. Didn't know what it was so I looked it up. Found the information was a little vague so I did some research. Just to keep up on things."

I am stunned. Without words. No one has ever gone to these lengths for me. Hell, what am I saying; I can't recall anyone simply accepting the fact I have this invisible chronic disease. I look over at Emma and I can see she understands my amazement. If I didn't already love this man, he would have sealed himself into my heart permanently now. Fuck me sideways.

Obviously uneasy with the stunned silence, Seb disappears into the kitchen announcing he has some 'cleanup' to do.

"You better frickin' go to that man, Arlene, if you know what's good for you!" Emma whispers, emotion drawn across her face. Even Beth looks affected.

"Hey." Is my brilliant opening when I walk up behind him in the kitchen.

"Hi." Seb doesn't turn around, simply continues to do dishes. He's embarrassed, maybe? Angry? One way to find out. I sidle up behind him and slide my arms around his waist, resting my cheek between his shoulders.

"You once said to me that I amazed you. But I have to tell

you, Seb; if I could write a list of the things I would most value in a mate, you would fit the bill perfectly. You are incredible and I can't believe I was afraid to let myself see it for so long. Thank you for loving me so well, it's the best…the safest feeling I have ever had."

He stills in my arms and slowly turns around, soap and water dripping off his hands when he takes my face between them.

"You make it worth it, Spot."

CHAPTER TWENTY-FOUR

Thank God the couch is huge. I've been restless all night without Arlene. She's still sleeping with Emma in the bedroom and there has been no sign or sound of Gus yet. We stayed up until near midnight before calling it. When I wander into the kitchen to get a pot of coffee going, I peek out into the misty morning light and am surprised to find a decent pack of snow on the ground. Fuck. That's going to make work at the diner a bit more complicated.

A slight rustling behind me has me turning around to find Emma shuffling into the kitchen.

"Morning." She mumbles, stifling a yawn behind her hand. "I can't believe I fell asleep after all. Any word from the guys?"

"Nothing. Maybe we can give Dana a call in a bit and see if

she knows something." I suggest.

"Yeah, good idea. It's not so much that I'm worried about Gus, although I am, but I find it odd they haven't let us know Julie is alright. You'd think they'd have called." She pulls up on a stool at the counter.

"I know. Drives me nuts to sit and wait. I'll get some breakfast going, I need to do something, and besides, we have to be back at the diner in a couple of hours to meet up with the final contractor. Hope he turns out better than the other two." I pull open the fridge and start pulling breakfast ingredients out. "Arlene still sleeping?"

"She is. But she was tossing and turning most of the night. I think she missed you in bed." Emma chuckles.

"Feeling is mutual." I smile back.

"She seems stronger. With you, I mean. Of course she was always a rock, but the attack was so hard on her and I thought for sure the fire would do her in, but instead she just seems to be able to take it in stride. It surprises me. You're better for her than the shrink we took her to that one time."

"I don't think Arlene is ever one to sit down and spill her guts on command. She's more likely to share bits and pieces when she feels she needs to. When it comes down to it, she has a survivor's instinct and knows what is best for her and when. She just forgot to trust herself for a bit there."

Emma tilts her head, contemplating me. The scrutiny makes me slightly uncomfortable.

"You really do get her. I'm glad. You're both lucky."

"I know it." I lean over and kiss Emma on the forehead.

"Should I come back later?" Arlene walks in, all sleep-rumpled and cute. Just the sight of her after a long night alone perks me up like nothing else could, even morning-grumpy as she is.

"Nah-" Emma says, deadpan. "There's room for one more."

"Kiss my ass, Ems." She grumbles, plopping down on a stool next to her.

"Wash it first and I'll consider it." Emma grins.

Arlene throws up her hands. "Gross and too much perky, so dial it down. I need caffeine and my man. You done with him yet?"

"Have at it, you cantankerous cow."

These two crack me up with the constant bickering. I pour mugs of coffee for all of us and hand-deliver Arlene's to the other side of the counter, where I can plant a good-morning kiss on her pouty lips.

"Did I get the order right? Caffeine first, your man after?"

"Mmmmmm" Is all I get from the warm snuggly woman in my arms.

Emma almost leaps off her stool for the phone before it finishes its first ring.

"Gus?"

"A little worried... That's okay, I did sleep some. How is Julie?... What do you mean?... I'm worried now.... Seb? Yes he's here... No, Beth went to Durango with her son for a few days...I agree. Yes, I'll let them know. Love you too. Careful." A little white-faced, Emma turns to us.

"Julie was gone."

Arlene's sharp intake of breath illustrates the shock I feel to my system. Fuck.

"From what I understand, someone came asking for someone with her description at the drugstore, when the owner told her, she got scared and took off. They spent the night trying to track her movements but lost her trace at the side of the highway, where they think she was either picked up or hitched a ride. Problem is, she may not trust anyone anymore, thinking her call to you sent whomever was looking for her."

"Ah, Christ. What a clusterfuck." Arlene is wiping her hands over her face.

My mind is going a mile a minute, trying to think where Julie would go. Who would she think she could trust?

"So now what?" Arlene wants to know.

"He wants me to tag along with you guys today, if that's okay. Told me to stick close because he doesn't have a good feeling about this whole set up. Joe is going to pop in here or at the diner later. He is checking out connections and may want to pick our brains."

"Wasn't thinking of leaving you by yourself anyway, Emma." I assure her.

Joe drops by a little after nine and Emma busies herself in the kitchen with another pot of coffee while he fills us in.

"Gus and Caleb tracked Julie as far as Monticello. She managed to catch a ride with a truck driver who dropped her off at the first gas station in town. The FBI is letting the guys take the lead on this, at least visibly, since she knows them and is more likely to come out of hiding for them than someone she doesn't know. As soon as we can ask her some questions we can hopefully put on a more focused search for her little boy, although I have a feeling they wouldn't have kept him too far from her. I've been trying to find any connections between Mr. Collins and you, Arlene, and I may have come up with something. Have you ever heard the name Bob Armetidge?"

I can feel Arlene shifting in her seat. "Yes. He was the slime bucket for a lawyer my ex had handle our divorce. What does he have to do with all this?"

"Apparently, Mr. Armetidge became a silent partner in Koko's only a few months ago, but that isn't all. One of the partners in his firm is part of Will Flemming's defense team."

A dead silence falls while we all try to digest and process that tidbit of information. Emma comes in from the kitchen and sits down on Arlene's other side, grabbing her hand.

"It's like waking up in the middle of one of my nightmares to find it still going on around me. Geoffrey and Will Flemming in one sentence is almost too much to take in." Arlene whispers. "The idea of the two of them connected, however distantly is terrifying."

I need to swallow a big lump. Truth be told, I am both terrified for her and enraged.

"We have to be careful with conjecture at this point, but I think it's safe to say that the odds of those two violators from your past this closely connected are too rare to call coincidental. Will has quite a network behind him and might easily try and use any and all information he can get his hands on to delay or derail his upcoming trial. Especially the raping and sodomizing, Arlene."

I feel her flinch at the mention and can hear a sharp intake of breath from Emma. I look up sharply at Joe while bringing my mouth close to her ear.

"Just us here, love. You're safe here."

When I feel her relax slightly into my side, I nod at Joe to continue.

"Sorry, girl, but those charges are the harshest ones, and will be difficult for him to defend away. Everything else, even the murder charge, can be painted or slanted a certain way to make him less culpable, but those, especially with your testimony, will throw all of his defense into the pile of 'unbelievable'. He is pulling out all the stops it would seem and somehow fate has placed him on the path of your ex. Also, there is one other thing you should know."

I don't like Joe's tone of voice. It implies more bad news.

"Because the DA has not been able to finalize the depositions, he has had to request a trial delay, which the judge granted. The catch however is that the judge also allowed for bail and house arrest this time, while he awaits trial. Arlene, Will is fitted with an ankle bracelet and restricted in his movements. Any move he does make is traced. He is monitored 24/7."

"I don't understand... Are you telling me he is out? Free?" Arlene casts him an incredulous glare.

"I swear to you I am keeping tabs on you. He won't come near you. Hell, he *can't* come near you. He is stuck in New Mexico with no breathing space. I promise."

As I show Joe out the door I can hear sniffles and the low murmur of Arlene and Emma's voices. I'm thinking Emma may not have realized the brutality of the attack on Arlene, and knowing my girl, she would've softened the edges when she told her best friend. Giving them some space, I head for the kitchen to get some breakfast going.

The truck from Mason Brothers Construction shows up right on the dot at 11 am at the diner as scheduled, which is a damn good sign. The big burly guy who gets out of the cab introduces himself as Clint Mason. I can tell he is already pissing Arlene off since he seems to insist on addressing me and dismisses her and Emma outright. Not a good idea, given the disturbing morning she's had. When he tells them to have a seat while us 'men' discuss business, she blows and I cross my arms, stand back and watch the fireworks.

"Excuse me, Cliff... is that right?" She pokes his upper arm, trying to get his attention.

"Clint, ma'am. I'm just finishing up some business with your husband here and then I'll be out of your hair."

"Ok, *Clint.* I can see we need to get a few things straight. Why don't you have a seat, this may take a while." With a little shove against his shoulder she has him taking a step back and he almost falls in the chair right behind him, then she turns to me with a saccharine sweet smile on her face. Evil Arlene has come out to play. "Seb, honey. Can you see if there is some more coffee left in the thermos for Mr. Clint here?"

Deciding to play along with her game, I pull a Styrofoam cup out of Emma's picnic basket and grab the thermos from Emma, who is almost bursting with contained laughter. She knows it's coming too.

"There you go, *Clint*, honey... Now. Where were we? Ah yes, I was going to enlighten you on a few things. Namely the way things are run around here. You see, *Clint,* this place here? It's mine. My name on the deed, my money in the bank, my check that was gonna pay your ass. And that man over there? He's fine, I'll admit, but he's not my husband, he's my cook. And just because he has a fine set of tools dangling between his legs doesn't put him in charge, you hear me? Now, if you are too big of a pussy to deal with the likes of me, I can't really blame you - I can be a harsh task master - but if you want the job, you had better start off by showing some goddamn respect to everybody here! To my friend Emma over there, who will be here a shitload and has a large amount of input; to our friend Seb here, who aside from his impressive equipment is an equal partner in everything and last but let us be very clear - not least; to me, the person who will have final say in whether you stay or go." Planting her hands on her hips, color high on her cheeks she looks down on her by now rather wilty looking victim who has little beads of sweat breaking out on his forehead despite the frigid temperatures. "Now. If that is something you think you can manage, I suggest we try and start this again."

Without a word, Clint gets up out of the chair, throws back his coffee and stalks out the door. Leaving us to look after him.

"Well damn. A pussy after all." Arlene mutters, sending Emma into a giggling fit.

I stalk over to Arlene and release all my pent up lust on her mouth. Fuck, she turns me on.

"Fierce, babe. That was fucking hot."

"Hellooo, in the room!" Emma squeaks. "And by the way, he's coming back."

When I turn around, Clint is marching back up to the door, pulls it open, puts his hands down at his sides and says, "Mornin' folks, I'm here to look at some fire damage. Who should I speak to?"

At Emma's barely contained snicker, Arlene and I both burst out laughing. A little ruddy in the face, Clint has a little smile pulling at the side of his mouth. "Damn woman, last time I was raked over the coals like that I was eleven and my mom was tanning my hide after she found the cigars I'd stolen from gramps. She was a formidable woman, my mom. I reckon, so are you."

Sticking out his hand he walks over to Arlene who takes it, smiles up at him and slaps him on the shoulder. "Let's get to work, big guy. I can see we'll get along fine."

A month and a half is what it's going to take. Arlene is a little down, probably still clinging to the vague hopes of being open for Christmas, but we're looking at the new year for sure. Clint knows what he's doing, that much is clear. A great relief after the two morons we had here yesterday. His crew is coming in as soon as we can get the quote approved by the insurance company and in the meantime he is going to look for temporary accommodation for them locally. Commuting from Durango here every day gets a bit much, so he figures four consecutive twelve to fourteen hour days and three off will be most productive all around and his guys will like the three days in a row home with their families.

New year, new beginnings. Let's hope it will be enough to untangle this mess.

CHAPTER TWENTY-FIVE

Julie is back!

It's my first thought again this morning and still I'm so relieved. I had started to feel like I was stuck in a centrifuge, sucking me further down with every new piece of bad news that found me. Last night Gus called Emma to say they were on their way home and wouldn't be too long. Apparently they picked Julie up in Dove Creek, only an hour or so from here, so she was definitely on her way home.

The poor girl was frightened out of her wits and agonizing over her missing little boy. Emma and I got her settled in a warm bath with something hot to drink and seeing that Emma is a lot better at the nurturing bit than I am, I left her to keep Julie company and went to see what I could pick up from the guys.

Always an imposing sight, to have these three fine examples of the male species gathered in one small space, I sat next to my favorite one and listened in just as Gus explained the benefits of having friends among all levels of law enforcement. Apparently state patrol had checked in with the various gas stations and had been able to help him track her moves.

"I want to keep her here tonight. I already talked to Joe, who is clearing it with the feds' field office. They want to talk to her but she's exhausted and not up to any intense questioning, so we'll do what we can here and pass on anything she can give us now and let her rest until tomorrow. I'm sure there won't be a lot of sleep involved for her anyway with the little one still gone. So far she mentioned the name Tanya-"

"That's Collins' sister, the one who was tending bar at Koko's." Seb clarified.

"Right. She said Matt had gotten angry with her when she told him she couldn't be involved with this anymore. He targeted her when he found out she was working for you, Arlene. She found this out when trying to break it off with him, right after the incident with the cat. Very early on he had charmed her and promised to take care of her and Liam before using the kid to pull her strings. She didn't feel she had anyone to turn to for help, so she went along. Told to text him when you were most likely alone or by the phone, she kept telling herself it was nothing but a prank, but when he killed the cat right in front of her, she knew she was in way over her head and couldn't go through with it. Instead of coming to us or going to the Sheriff's Office or the police, she confronted him. That's when he took control over her by grabbing Liam from her. Tanya was going to take her to Moab where Matt would bring Liam later, but when Matt didn't show and Julie started asking questions about her son, Tanya got agitated and tied her up. I figure the night Julie got away was when Tanya found out her brother had been in the hospital all this time. She took off in a panic and left Julie tied in the bathroom."

"Holy crap. It explains a few things but nothing to do with me. Does she have any idea why?" I want to know.

"All she knows is that Matt seems to get instructions as well. He's not working by himself, but maybe later we can find out a little more from her. For now, we'll let her have a rest."

When Seb and I finally go back to my place. Caleb is staying, helping keep watch over Julie. Frankly I'm glad to have Seb to myself for a bit. However much I want an end to this, I need the odd stolen moment where I can stop thinking and worrying and simply be and feel. That's what Seb allows me.

When I roll over looking for the man on my mind, I find his side of the bed empty. Damn. Shoe's on the other foot now. A peek at the clock tells me it's only 5:30 am, and I throw on my old ratty robe to hold off the worst of the morning chill. I find him in the kitchen on the phone, talking in soothing tones and I know his sister has had one of her nightmares. This is a pattern I have become familiar with in very short order and I can see how much it kills him not to be near her, which is why I can't wait for the right time to let him in on my plans, but not yet. Not until I'm sure it's safe.

I snuggle up on his back and it pleases me when he doesn't even flinch, but instead grabs one of my hands that have snuck around to spread on his stomach and kisses the palm before placing it back. Damn, he feels so good in my space. I never thought I'd say that about anybody. Even Emma, although I love her to distraction, will get on my nerves after too much time together. I always figured I'd end up living by myself, but with Seb, I feel peaceful. He never seems to get in my way, he just fits.

I hear him telling his sister, Faith, he loves her before hanging up and turning to me.

"Bad dreams?" I ask, when he runs his hands through his hair before placing them on my hips and pulling me between his legs.

"Hmmmm. I need to go see her, Arlene. I've put it off for so long, not wanting to disrupt her routine until I was ready to make a real change, but I miss her. And she misses me."

"I know. We'll make it happen. Soon."

I'm starting to think I should reconsider my original plan. Making him wait any longer just seems cruel. Indecision and guilt overwhelm me when his arms go around my waist and he lays his head on my stomach. I mindlessly stroke his hair, lost in thought.

With Seb in the shower after coffee and toast, I make a quick call to Emma to see how Julie made it through the night and for any further news.

"Morning, girl." Gus answers the phone.

"Hey big guy. Get any sleep?"

"A bit. We're waiting for Joe to come over and take Julie in to meet up with the Feds."

"How's she doing?"

"Terrified, but she was able to give us a few leads to run down. Poor girl is riddled by guilt and Emma has her hands full ensuring her that no one faults her for doing what she needed to do to protect her son. Right now she feels like she's failed everyone, including Liam."

"Anything we can do?"

"Not right now, girl. Just hang tight and stick together. Once we hand Julie off to Joe, I'll maybe drive Ems over to your place. I'll see if Joe can spare a guy to keep an eye out while Caleb and I follow up on those leads. We'll be faster than any investigation the Bureau puts out there."

"I feel pretty damn useless, I have to say."

"Hang in there. We know much more now than we did twenty-four hours ago. Who knows where we'll be by the end of today."

I barely end the call before the phone in my hand starts ringing. No caller ID. Fuck.

"Hello?"

Nothing.

"Unless you have something to say to me, I'm gonna hang up." I throw out there, ballsier than I feel.

"… *want mommy…*" The little voice can be heard in the background and bile starts creeping up into my throat.

"Where is he? He's just a little boy, let him go." I plead, clutching the phone to my ear, hoping to keep the connection to the little frightened guy.

This morning's conversation with Faith is weighing heavily on my mind. I'm letting the hot water of the shower pound down on my tense shoulders, hoping for some relief. I'm impatient to get her over here, but it would be selfish to have her make that transition before things have settled down again. Goddammit. It breaks my heart every time I hear the tears in her voice, still trembling from the after-effects of her nightmares. I'm so torn between needing to see Faith and staying here to make sure Arlene is alright.

Through the pounding of the water in the shower, I can hear the front door close and I wonder who would come by this early. Suddenly uneasy, I turn off the shower, step out and wipe myself down quickly before pulling on some jeans and calling for Arlene as I walk down the stairs.

The house is empty. A piece of paper, ripped from a notebook is on the kitchen table.

"So sorry. Call Gus. Baby at diner. No choice. All my love....."

I can't think but my body responds immediately by grabbing the phone and dialing.

"Be there shortly, girl." Gus' voice breaks through to my brain.

"She's gone."

"Seb? That you? What... I just fucking talked to her not ten minutes ago!"

Emma's cry in the background barely registers as I try to form the words.

"A note... she left a note. Fucking hell, Gus! She left a note! A fucking note!" Panic suddenly hits me and I run to the front door and pull it open to find only my truck sitting in the drive.

"Seb! Information, man. I need information. Get it together." Gus admonishes me.

Right. I can do this. "It says; So sorry. Call Gus. Baby at diner, and then 'no choice'. What the fuck is she doing?"

"Stay put, Seb. We're heading over."

"Like fucking hell I will! You outta your ever-loving mind? That's my Arlene out there… My woman, Gus. Mine."

Slamming down the phone I run to grab my boots and a sweater from the bedroom, pound down the stairs and out the front door. Three times. Three times I have failed to protect what is mine. Three chances I've had and I have blown them all. First time got Arlene raped and almost killed, the second time she almost lost her business and now… God I can't even think about that.

I fly through the streets on my way to the diner, blowing through every stop sign I encounter, barely able to keep my truck on the slick roads, and then on the last turn off to the diner, I see it; Arlene's rusty old truck sitting in a ditch at the side of the road with the driver's side door wide open. I pull in right behind it, jump out and call her name, stalking around her truck for any signs of her. There is nothing. Not a sign and not a sound.

The other side of the ditch has some woodland that runs partially behind the diner and borders onto the Ute reservation.

Something drives me to head in there, leaving my truck and following my gut. The brush is fairly thick and because the sun doesn't reach all the way in, some frost and patches of our early snow remained on the ground. I'm not a tracker, but I can tell the difference between an animal print and a shoe print, and I can also distinguish a man's size from a woman's. The footprint I'm looking at looks to be a woman's size and appears to be alone. I manage to follow the tracks to where I'm pretty sure the back parking lot of the diner borders.

I am frozen, wearing nothing but my idiotic threadbare robe and some boots I grabbed while running out the door, but nothing is going to stop me from going after that poor little boy. Fucking killed my truck going in the ditch when I slid around the corner. I'm furious at my own stupidity for not grabbing anything I could use as a weapon when I left the house. I wasn't even thinking, I just ran. The voice that haunted my nightmares, Will's voice, was telling me I had a choice; me or Liam. Seriously? That's not a choice. Almost pissing myself in fear, I managed to scribble something for Seb before taking off.

The thought of what a sick motherfucker like Will could do to that baby had me almost puking up my guts. It scared me more than what was undoubtedly waiting for me, but it isn't until I crawl out of my disabled truck that I start thinking I shouldn't give in so easily. So instead of walking the rest of the way along the road, I pick the woods instead, hoping for some element of surprise, although I'm not quite sure what I would do with it.

The cold is crawling into my body and making me stiff and sore all over. I reach the back parking lot to the diner and can hear some rustling coming from the direction of the burned out dumpsters. Could be animals, although what they would want with a bunch of ashes I don't know. Looking around for any sign of life, I find none - other than the slight rustle I hear again. I make my way over to the container closest to the back of the diner and try to peek in. When my head clears the upper edge, I can see Julie's little boy sitting in a corner, his little back against the side of the dumpster. His eyes are closed, his lips almost blue and one of his little hands is moving restlessly through the burnt debris at the bottom. Not good. This is not good. With another quick look around, I start hoisting myself up over the edge when out of nowhere, I hear Seb from behind me.

"Arlene!!"

A slightly cooler head on my shoulders, I ease my way up to the tree line to take a look. Wearing only her ratty robe and some snow boots, I can see Arlene trying to climb in to one of the burned out dumpsters in the back. What the fuck is she doing? What freezes the blood in my veins though is the man and woman coming up the side of the building from the front, a gun clutched in the man's hand, edging toward the container that has Arlene half-dangling out of it. I am pretty sure I've just found Tanya, Matt Collins' sister. And as for the man, his build is very familiar but his features are hidden by the hood pulled low over his head.

I blindly grope for my phone, only to remember I ran out of the house with my keys, boots and a sweater in hand - nothing else. Fuck! Seeing the man sidle around the edge of the wall, sighting his gun on Arlene's back has me yell out her name in warning, realizing at the same time I am now in full view against the edge of the trees. I can feel the whiz of the bullet before I hear the shot go off. Slivers of wood and bark explode away from the tree trunk right beside me with the impact of the slug, stinging my cheek. I drop down to my stomach and try to crawl backwards into the cover of the trees, keeping my eyes on the dumpster that holds Arlene. Armed or unarmed, any indication they lose interest in me and go after her, I am going in; arms waving. No way are they harming a hair on her body.

My only thoughts are to draw them away from her and slowly pulling up into a crouch, I start making my way along the tree line, trying to stay under cover but making enough noise to keep their attention. The guy with the hood keeps firing off shots each time I move, but so far the only damage is done by flying debris. When I notice both of them edging away from the building and towards the woodlot, my hopes rise, but when the man stops and calls to Tanya to keep an eye on the container, they deflate instantly. I know that voice. I know it really fucking well.

Realizing Arlene won't be able to get away unnoticed, my next choice is to simply keep the cocksucker occupied until the cavalry arrives, which should be any time now.

Unfortunately when the first support troops pull in, Gus' Yukon, the man changes his tactics quickly and with a single shot kills Tanya. I'm so fucking confused, 'cause that was the last thing I was expecting, but when the next thing he does is fire a round into the dumpster where Arlene has found refuge, only to walk around it and fire once more, but from a different side. I crawl up and storm out of the trees, bellowing her name loudly, uncaring that the barrel of the gun is swinging in my direction.

I hear two shots but can't feel a thing after the first one hits. The impact takes me down and when I try to catch myself, my arms can't seem to break my fall and I slam to the pavement. Then all there is darkness.

The panic in his voice has me throw myself headfirst into the dumpster, where I land head over ass right next to the little guy who hasn't moved an inch. The only thing moving is his little hand that seems to be searching for something. I grab him and try to wrap my robe around him, hoping my body heat - or what's left of it - will keep him warm, just as I hear a shot going off. Jesus! Seb... How did he get behind me? Is he shot? I am so cold, I can barely move, especially with the frozen little guy in my arms. I hear Will shouting at someone to keep an eye out. Burning to know if Seb is alright I crawl to the side of the dumpster, and am about to heave myself up to take a look over the edge when another shot goes off and then another. This last one bores a hole in the side of the container, right opposite of us. With Liam braced in my arms, I throw myself down on the bottom, trying to cover his little body with my own. Holy fuck!! Another shot ricochets off the inside of the dumpster and suddenly I hear Seb's voice again, yelling my name. Two more shots sound and as suddenly as Seb's yelling started, it gets cut off. Silence follows and I find myself unable to move, unable to look at what I know will be Seb's lifeless body. I can't. So I hold the little boy and wait.

Gus finds me and lifts me up, baby and all.

"He's hurt but will be fine, girl. He'll be fine, I promise. Ambulance is on the way."

A relieved sob bursts from my chest as Gus tries to lift me over the edge of my burned out sanctuary.

"Wait. Lift him out first." I let my robe fall open and find two little eyes staring up at me. Little blue eyes that were firmly shut just moments ago, and when I try to hand him to Gus to lift him over, his little arms and legs wrap around me like a monkey. Holding on for dear life.

Gus chuckles. "Looks like you're stuck with him. He isn't about to let go."

Struck with a moment of clarity I ask, "Will?" I can see Gus swallowing and steeling his face.

"Dead. He won't ever get to hurt you again, Arlene."

"I'm so sorry."

"Don't be, I'm not. I grieved the loss of my brother a long time ago; I didn't even know this man."

Seb sustained a bullet to his shoulder. He was lucky. Only a few inches could have had a much different outcome. Of course, Seb being Seb, he didn't like the ride in the ambulance, complaining all the way to the hospital, but I wasn't going to take any chances and insisted he go. He reluctantly agreed, but only because he didn't want me upset, which I was getting having just lived through another trauma.

When he notices my eyes tearing up, he sits up on the stretcher and pulls me beside him, ignoring the EMT's protests.

"We're okay, babe. We both got through this in one piece and the little guy will be okay too – Thanks to you."

CHAPTER TWENTY-SIX

"He doesn't like me."

"Does too. Look, he's smiling." Emma tries to point out.

"That's a smile? Thought he had gas. Look at me, he's gotten me all wet. I'm a mess!"

"Shouldn't have let him play with your beads. He likes gumming them. Poor guy must be in pain."

Emma has a dreamy smile on her face. I just try my best not to shove the guy off my lap.

Just then Seb walks in from the bedroom.

"What is this? I'm told to go have a rest and the next thing I know you have another man drooling all over you?"

"I know..." Emma says, "don't they look good together?"

"Very cute." Seb observes as he bends to give me a sweet kiss and blow a raspberry on Liam's little belly, making the chubby toddler giggle.

"You stealing my woman, little man? You know she likes to be slobbered all over, don't you? And getting her shirt all wet; smart little fella."

In love with Seb's colorful tattoos, Liam abandons my lap for Seb's as soon as he sits down beside me. When the little guy accidentally bumps Seb's shoulder, he winces, still sore from the bullet that luckily tore straight through. It missed anything vital and cleaned out, stitched up and supplied with painkillers, Seb was sent home to rest, which he doesn't like doing, but he won't give up little Liam, no matter how often the little bruiser bumps him where it hurts.

It's an absolute shame he is not a father. He takes to it as if it's the most natural thing in the world, when I feel all arms and legs around little kids. I can't give him that. Won't ever be able to give him that. It doesn't feel good to know you might be the one thing standing in the way of something that looks like it was meant to be.

A tug on my shirt shocks me out of my maudlin thoughts and

two sticky hands and a wet slobber kiss from a two foot tall little charmer manages to put a smile back on my face. I can see Seb looking on with a satisfied grin. That man is far too observant.

It's been four days since we got Liam back and Emma and I volunteered... Well, Emma volunteered herself and me, to look after him while Julie has her first counseling session. Guilt is eating at her and she has a long road to go, but she won't have to go it alone. No one blames her for what she did. Under the circumstances, each of us would likely have done the same. Her biggest hurdle will be to forgive herself and that takes time. I know that all too well.

Today Clint is starting at the diner and I am beyond excited about that. We received word from the insurance company on Saturday that the quote was approved and I called him immediately with the good news. I have to remember to drop off some food tonight at the motel, which is where his crew will stay until we've found them better lodging, but by my calculations, four nights out of each week with the guys doubling up on the rooms, it looked like the motel might end up cheaper than a short term rental. Although not having a kitchen and living space would start wearing thin after a while, I'm sure. For now it'll do.

Gus is going to meet with Clint at the diner this morning and we'll go have a look this afternoon. Hopefully once work is on the way, and with Seb forced to rest until at least next week, I can finally put my plan into action. I have decided to let Emma and Gus in on my secret and they were all over it like white on rice, doing their part in making phone calls and ensuring the facility is up to par, not to mention enabling me to finalize everything before making promises I might not be able to fulfill. If all works out, we leave on Wednesday, and he won't know until we get to the airport in Durango. I can't wait to see his face.

"Weird, isn't it?"

"What, love?"

Seb is lying with his head on my lap on the couch. It's the only way I can get him to stay still for more than five minutes at a time. We're supposed to be taking a nap now that Liam and Emma have left before checking in on Clint at the diner.

"Just like that the air is out of the balloon. Feels strange all this constant tension and then nothing."

Seb sits up and pulls a hand through his hair.

"Not exactly nothing, Arlene. Two people are dead and Caleb is still being grilled by a very pissed off Federal Bureau of Investigation. They will likely want to talk to us again too before we see the end of this."

Feeling put in my place, I have to tamp down the instinct to become defensive. He's right. We may be in the clear but the trouble isn't over for everyone. Gus and Caleb are being hauled over the coal for Will's death and not waiting for official law enforcement before 'acting'. No one bothered to question how it came to be that Will showed up in Cedar Tree. Over state lines, without his ankle bracelet, or that if it hadn't been for Gus and Caleb, or Seb for that matter, both that little boy and I would be dead by now. No. They were too busy covering their asses.

"You're right, and I didn't mean it like that. It's just that we don't have be so vigilant anymore. I should feel more relieved than I do, but the air still feels heavy."

"It does, doesn't it." Seb leans back against the couch and uses his good arm to pull me toward him. "Come here. Let's see if we can find you some relief. I've been sporting blue balls for days now not being able to get inside you."

The combination of his low rumbling voice and the hot intent in his eyes, dark with lust, is enough to have heat pooling between my legs. Even injured and in pain, his instant command over my body seems inevitable. Gingerly settling myself on his lap, I voice my concern. "But your shoulder-"

"More worried about my dick than my shoulder right now, Spot. Quit talking and kiss me. I'll let you do all the work."

Firmly settled on his lap with the feel of his need for me firmly nestled against my pussy, I lean forward with my hands on either side of his head against the backrest. I slowly kiss his eyes, his jaw and ease my way over to his lips when he loses patience; grabbing me by the back of my neck and holding me still. Without hesitation, his mouth takes control over mine and hunger takes over. God that man can kiss. Wet, warm, strong and invasive, I am swept away in sensations that have me rocking on his lap.

"Shirt off." He mumbles between kisses and I comply without question, breaking away from his mouth to whip it over my head. Another two seconds has me divested of my bra and his hand is kneading my breast.

"Love your tits, Spot. Soft, tasty…" He finishes, his lips already wrapped around my nipple and pulling hard. "Ahhhh… Fuck, Seb. So good."

I have only one fucking hand to work with and all I can think about is how to get her naked right now. Days I've been in pain, but it never seems to stop my body from craving her when she's around. Fuck, but she tastes good. The little sounds she makes are such a turn on. Being able to reduce this strong woman to moans makes me feel on top of the fucking world. So much more than I had imagined.

"Babe, I need you naked. Let me taste all of you."

Heavy-lidded and with the high flush of arousal on her face, Arlene doesn't hesitate to climb off and pull down her jeans and underwear at once. Standing in front of me in all her glory she looks like a warrior woman; a true amazon. So fucking gorgeous.

Fumbling one-handedly with the buttons on my jeans, I manage to get my fly half open before she swats my hand away and quickly undoes the rest, sliding my cock free from its confinement. When she immediately bends down to suck on the tip, a shiver runs from the base of my skull down to my toes.

"Fuck, baby. Hold on. I need a taste of you first."

I slide down on my back on the couch and pull her over. She immediately lifts her leg to climb over my mid-section but with one hand on her butt, I urge her up to where my mouth can reach her.

"Love your smell…" I grab her by the hips and hold her as I run the flat of my tongue along her folds. "Love your taste…" Encouraged by her low moan, I spread her lips with my tongue and find her entrance. When I plunge into her I can feel her pussy twitching around my tongue and I know it won't take much to make her come. Nudging her clit with my nose has her grinding her pussy down on my face, riding me. I grab hold of her ass with both hands and slide my lips around her button and suck in deep pulses, her hands wound in my hair tightening to the point of pain. Screaming my name, she shudders her release and I almost come myself from the sight alone.

"Beautiful…"

When Arlene starts clambering off me, I try to hold her back. "Hey. Where are you off to?"

She looks at me with a half-grin. "I just had the ride of my life. It's time for yours. Sit up."

Good lord have mercy If a sexy, slightly submissive Arlene gets me hot, a take-charge vixen Arlene gets my blood boiling over. I don't waste time and carefully pull myself up, my cock sticking out of my jeans almost purple with anticipation. Looking up at her, I can tell from the glint in her eyes that she noticed the state of my pride and joy as well, but instead of sitting down on my lap, she bends to lick and kiss my lips.

"Mmmm, I taste good on you."

I grab my dick and squeeze the base. "Jesus, woman. Keep it up and we're done here."

With a little chuckle, the evil minx turns around presenting me with a close view of her gorgeous ass. More than two hands full, it fits her tall body perfectly and feels amazing to hold on to. She backs up and with her legs framing mine, she slowly lowers herself on my almost painful erection. Soaking wet from her orgasm, the feeling of her tight channel and the slick grasp of her vaginal muscles is indescribable and again, I have to exert almost inhuman control not to blow like a teenage boy.

With her hands on my knees and her ass in my face, Arlene rides me reverse cowgirl style, and with gusto. It doesn't take much before I have to grab her hip and adjust the pace or we won't get to enjoy the ride. The slight jiggle of her ass each time she slams down on my cock is the sexiest fucking thing I've ever seen. All woman and all real. God I love how unbridled she can be. I love her.

Arlene's panting is matching my own labored breathing, and I want her to come again with me. I'm close. Slipping one hand around her to find her clit, and my thumb of the other to rub her perineum, right behind our connection, all it takes is some slight pressure to send both of us over the edge. Bucking my hips under her with the aftershocks, I wrap my good arm around her and pull her body back onto mine.

"You floor me." Is about as much as I can voice, depleted as I am.

Gus raises his eyebrow when we show up half an hour later than we were supposed to.

"Sorry we're a bit late. Something came up." Seb says with a big smile on his face. Gus bursts out laughing when I elbow Seb in the ribs.

"Holy shit, Seb. Hang a sign around my neck, why don't you, 'Just fucked'! Couldn't be more clear than that." I grumble, but inside I'm a bit smug to have brought out this light-hearted side of him.

Slinging his arm around my neck he pulls me in for a kiss. "Sorry, Spot. Couldn't resist."

"Yeah, whatever. Throw me under the bus." But I have to smile when I say it.

"Everything okay here?" I want to know from Gus.

"No problem. If you want to talk to Clint, he's in the back working on the demo of the old apartment and back wall. Says he wanted to talk to you about rebuilding the apartment above 'cause he has some ideas. I'm gonna take off, check in with Emma and probably be at the mercy of some investigator again this afternoon. Be glad when this is finally over."

I walk over to Gus and give him a big hug. "Me too, big guy, me too."

CHAPTER TWENTY-SEVEN

"Explain to me why I need new furniture again?"

Arlene and I are on our way to Durango for some kind of shopping trip. The stuff of nightmares. After talking to Clint the other day she agreed with him to make the apartment a two-bedroom instead of a one-bedroom. I already told her I didn't need two bedrooms, but she totally ignored me. Fine. It's her building, never mind that I thought we might just keep living together. At Arlene's house, or somewhere new. Guess I shouldn't jump to conclusions and now she wants to get new furniture for the place too. Totally infuriating. I don't even care as long as I have a place to put my head, if I can't be with her all the time.

"I want the place to be furnished, Seb. Insurance covered it so why wouldn't we buy back what was lost?"

"Yeah, but why can't we order online? Does it really require going from store to store? Seems a waste of time to me."

Arlene chuckles next to me. "You are adorable when you're grumpy, you know that?"

"Did you say adorable?" I growl, tossing her the best angry glare I can muster up, but she isn't falling for it.

"Yup. Frickin' adorable. Your eyebrows all scrunched up and your lips get pouty. It's cute."

That's it. First turn we get to, I pull off and put the truck in park. First she fought me about who would drive this morning, claiming I couldn't drive one-armed. The hell I couldn't. I have never needed two hands to drive, ask anyone! And now this…

I turn to her and take her mouth, kissing the sass right out of her.

"Whoa! Not that I mind but what was that all about?"

"Adorable, Arlene? Cute? Do you see anything cute on me?" I wave my hand over my body and she promptly starts laughing so hard, tears start rolling over her cheeks.

"Oh my God. Seb… You should see your face. You are so

easy."

I am. I admit it. Out of commission for days now, unable to do what I want to do and now being forced to go *shopping* and listening to Arlene call me adorable. Hell yes, I'm easily riled. I've had it up to my eyeballs. I'm frustrated and I feel absolutely useless. But I also feel ridiculously happy hearing Arlene's full-bodied, rolling laugh. Damn that is a good sound. One I've heard more in the past few days than in all of the eight months before.

With another punishing kiss and a stern look, I start the truck up again and turn to head back on the highway to Durango. Shopping.

In all honesty, spending any kind of time with Arlene was fine by me, even shopping, and it was nice getting out of the house and Cedar Tree for a while for that matter. The drive on the 160 is a nice one, especially once you hit the foothills. Scenery changes quite suddenly and before you know it you're driving through lush foliage and grey rock. Much different from the drier mesa.

When Arlene prompts me to continue on the 160 instead of taking the turn off into Durango, I'm trying to figure out what stores would be out here. Only thing I can remember this way is the airport.

"What store are we going to?" I ask her.

"Hmmmm, forget the name, but it's somewhere near the airport. Just follow the signs there, I know I'll recognize it when I see it."

I'm about to pass the entrance to La Plata airport when Arlene grabs my arm.

"Pull in here, I think we've gone too far."

"Seriously? Arlene, there is nothing out here? Are you sure that…" I forget what I was going to say for a moment when I look to the front of the terminal. "What is Caleb doing here? What is this?" I'm confused as hell when I see Gus and Emma walk out of the terminal and stand beside him. What the fuck?

"Park the truck, honey." Arlene says. I look at the slight smile on her lips, still trying to make sense of this. Pulling into the first spot I see, I turn off the engine and turn to her.

"What is going on, Arlene. Why are we here? And hell, what are *they* doing here?"

She puts her hands on my face. "You know how much I love you, right?"

I nod, because I do, even if she isn't the most demonstrative of people.

"Trust me?" She wants to know.

"Of course."

"*We* are going to get Faith."

I'm not entirely clear I'm hearing this right. "Sorry?"

"You and me, we are flying to see Faith and maybe bring her home with us."

I can't think. I can't seem to process all the logistics, but before I can formulate a question, Arlene is already answering it.

"She misses you, you miss her, and I want you happy. It's simple."

I shake my head, it isn't as simple as she thinks.

"Arlene, you're amazing to want this, but it isn't that easy."

She leans in and presses her lips to mine, never losing contact with her eyes.

"Trust me." She whispers. "Just get out of the truck, come with me and trust me."

I do what she asks, but I am overwhelmed and frankly scared to be hopeful.

Stopping in front of Emma and the guys, Caleb hands me a

suitcase.

"Your stuff. Well, I guess yours and Arlene's."

I grab the handle, and mumble a subdued *'Thank you'* to a smiling Caleb. Gus hands me an envelope, slaps me on the back and says, "Just go with the flow."

And finally Emma hands over a bag of food. Of course. She grabs me in a big hug and gives Arlene the same treatment before almost shoving us into the terminal.

"Better get your asses on that plane or you'll miss it!"

Poor guy. He looks as stunned now as he did half an hour ago when I dropped the bomb on him. Only shakes his head every now and then, makes to say something and each time changes his mind. My objective was simple; get him to the airport with as little warning as possible and the guys would help me get him on the plane before he had time to think too hard or protest, but I didn't expect for him to literally be struck dumb. Eager to find out what he is thinking, I ask him, "Do you have any questions?"

He barks out a laugh. "Questions? I may have a few. As soon as I figure out how to ask them."

"Why don't I tell you from the start what we've been up to."

"We?"

"Yes. We. Found out I couldn't do this alone so I called in some help."

I watch in amusement as his eyebrows disappear up into his hairline.

"Help? You asked for help? Pigs must be flying."

"Haha, smartass." I smile at him a little nervously, not quite so sure now he would welcome my interference.

"If I had to be away from you for any stretch of time, it would be hard. When I hear you talking to Faith on the phone I can hear the pain in your voice and I hate it. So I wanted to help, but I wasn't sure how and I couldn't do anything as long as things weren't settled here at home."

When the flight attendant comes by with drinks on offer, Seb waves her away impatiently, urging me to go on.

"I talked to Janet a few times." I confessed, waiting for his reaction.

"Janet? Faith's caregiver? How… "

"Got the number from your phone. I told her I wanted to find a way to make your reunion with your sister happen sooner than later and she was ecstatic. Said that it would be the best thing for Faith, since her nightmares had just been getting worse and she thought being away from you for so long seems to make things harder and not easier as time goes by. We talked a bit about Faith's needs and what kinds of facilities you had looked at here. We made some phone calls to see about placement."

Having two seats all to ourselves, with no one next to us, Seb flips up the armrest between us and pulls me on his lap.

"I love you for wanting to do this for me, Spot. So much it almost hurts, but the placements here are more costly, I already looked into that. I'm saving up, which is why I haven't been to see her much and I've been told it would be another six months at least, before they might have a spot for her."

It kills me to see the dejected look on his face.

"I know. I've been told, but here's the thing… The money? What you were paying me for rent, you no longer owe me." I have to put my hand on his mouth to stop him from interrupting me. "Hear me out, please. You can stay with me. Janet wants to come and see Faith settled in. Plans to stay for a month at least to make transition easier, maybe longer. Says she wants a change of scenery. Gus and

Emma are offering their guesthouse for them to stay or just Janet, if Faith would prefer to stay with us. It's being finished this weekend for them. It's all one level and has easy access; all done for Emma's benefit, but it would work for Faith as well. Are you still with me?"

Swallowing hard, he nods. "Just processing here... Where will Caleb and the other guys stay when they're in town?"

"That's the beauty of it. Caleb has an out of town job as of Monday and he will spend the last night here at the motel, but after that the apartment over the diner should be ready. With two bedrooms." I smile triumphantly.

"You have really been working this to the bone, haven't you?" His arms tighten around me and he looks at me with amazement written on his face.

"We will all help out and when Janet decides to move on, if a spot hasn't opened up for Faith yet by then, we've got it figured out, but we can do this - as the big messy family that we are. Don't you think?"

His jaw clenches and I am losing my steam. I still don't know if I've done good, or overstepped. He wraps me up tightly in his arms and buries his face in my neck, holding on for dear life. Stroking his back I feel a shudder run through him and in a breaking voice he says, "You are the light at the end of my tunnel, Spot."

And I cling to him and smile. Big.

CHAPTER TWENTY-EIGHT

The state facility in Billings, Montana, where Faith has been living the last five years or so, has the look of an old penitentiary. Steel bars cover every visible window and the old brick facade is a testimony to harsher times. Hard to believe this is a place where people are being cared for, but I hope looks are deceiving.

Seb's hand in mine is tensing as we walk up the wide steps to the front doors.

"You okay?" I ask, squeezing his hand lightly.

"Anxious to see her, is all," is his gruff reply.

He hasn't said much the entire way from the airport here, and I haven't pushed him. I understand the need to process things at your own pace when you are thrown in the deep end so to speak, especially when it deals with things that are close to the heart. I know I've probably breached his comfort zone in terms of involvement, but I want him to know that as much as I accept him as part of my life, my future, he can and should do the same with me. Still, a man who has probably talked and shared more in the past few weeks than I imagine he ever has deserves some time to catch his breath.

A friendly brunette with big horn-rimmed glasses and a huge smile opens the door only moments after we ring the bell.

"You're here! I'm so excited." Throwing her arms around Seb she gives him a resounding kiss on the cheek. I reluctantly let go of his hand and step to the side. "And you... You must be Arlene. I can't tell you how good it is to meet you face to face." She promptly envelops me into a big hug as well.

This must be Janet I realize, and recalling the frequent friendly phone calls we've shared over the past weeks, I give the woman a firm hug back. "So glad to meet you."

"Janet." Seb smiles at her, and then me, with a little wink thrown in.

The bubbly woman pulls us inside while chattering on about

how excited Faith has been since finding out this morning that her big brother was coming. Janet had chosen not to tell her before, since length of time was a difficult concept for Faith and having her wait too long would take the fun out of the anticipation.

"She's been making drawings all morning, Seb. Happy ones this time. You'd better get an extra suitcase to take those all back with you." She looks at Seb with a questioning glance.

"Hoping to take the artist back too, Janet. And a certain someone who needs a holiday?"

"Woot! You told him!" She grins at me. "I wasn't sure how you were going to play this and I didn't want to get my hopes up but; Yay!"

Almost skipping down the huge gloomy hallway, the short bouncy woman looks way too happy for a place like this.

"My bags are packed. I did it just in case and I have a potential sub-let on my apartment all lined up. I am so ready for an adventure, you have no idea." Janet waves her arms around as she talks, using her entire body to emphasize her words. She is one bundle of energy.

"Go on, go in. She's expecting you." Janet opens the door and urges us inside, but I stop on the threshold.

"I think I'm going to give them some time." I look at Seb

taking three big strides into the room, covered wall to wall with brightly colored pictures almost all depicting a large man, holding the hand of a little girl. There sitting in the wheelchair by the barred window is a gorgeous woman with long braids in her hair and a happy smile on her face, so far from the little girl in the drawings. Without hesitation, Seb lifts his sister out of her chair and swings her around, making her squeal.

"Are you okay, love?" Janet asks when she sees the wetness on my cheeks. "Come on, let's get a coffee." Not bothering to wait for my answer, she hooks her arm in mine and leads me to a little office at the end of the hall.

God I've missed her. The way she clings to me like a monkey and laughs her little girl laugh.

"Sebastian!"

I bury my nose in her braids and inhale deeply as I swing her around. She always smells of lavender, her favorite scent. Janet always massages her useless muscles with some lotion that smells like that.

"Hey, pumpkin. I'm so happy to see you."

"Me too! I've waited so long." That sets Faith off babbling about her drawings and the friends she's made with a squirrel in the vegetable garden out back and all I can do is smile until my face starts hurting.

"How come you're crying, Sebastian? Are you sad?"

Startled, I put my fingers to my cheek and bring them away wet.

"No honey, I'm happy. Very happy. Do you want to know why?"

Sitting in her wheelchair, a gorgeous woman with the mind of a little girl nods her head enthusiastically.

"I have a friend, a really good friend I would like you to meet."

"Yeah? Where?" Faith looks at the door suspiciously.

"She's just gone with Janet for a minute but she'll be right back."

"Will she like me?"

Fuck, the girl breaks my heart when she looks at me like I have all the answers in the world. I will never be able to live up to that. I stroke my hand over her cheek. "She will love you, just like I do."

Arlene comes into the room half an hour later, a little tentatively and with eyes that look like she's been crying. I get up and pull her against me.

"You ok, Spot?"

"Yup. Want to introduce me to this beautiful young lady here?" She smiles at Faith, but I can feel the tension coming off her. She's nervous about this.

"Honey, remember the friend I told you about? This is Arlene, my girlfriend."

Faith's eyes cautiously take in Arlene and then the arm I have around Arlene's shoulders.

"Hi." She says quietly.

"Hi Faith. You're even prettier than your brother told me."

This earns Arlene a little smile, but Faith will need some time to warm up to someone new. I haven't told her about coming home to Colorado with me yet, wanting to take it one step at a time. She'll probably need to adjust to the idea.

When Arlene asks to be shown the vegetable garden I had mentioned to her, I can see Faith's reservations slip a little more. Excited to show off her favorite pastime, she calls Janet to take us down to the garden. Point two for Arlene.

In stark contrast with the forbidding front of the building, the gardens in the back are surprisingly spacious and beautiful even in winter. Discovering Faith's interest in growing things, Janet had asked to have a vegetable patch put in as part of Faith's therapy and it worked. It had given Faith a very positive self-image and ironically, a better ability to communicate her feelings, something she had not been able to do for many years, resulting in self-destructive tantrums that were difficult to control without medication. The garden is something she will miss more than anything and I am concerned how she will respond to leaving it.

Again, Arlene seems to have picked up on everything, because she carefully begins questioning Faith on how one should start a vegetable garden. Telling her she has a small restaurant and she would love to grow some of her own.

"You know, it would be wonderful if one day you could come and maybe help me build my garden. Help me grow the vegetables until they are big enough for us to pick, then Sebastian can prepare them and the people that visit the diner can taste the wonderful veggies we've grown."

Having Arlene use my full name fills me with an immense sense of well-being. Having her chatting away with Faith about the garden and the restaurant exposes the remnants of dreams I had many years ago, ones I thought were long buried. Dreams I put to rest, but that suddenly doesn't seem that unattainable anymore.

"You were great with her. I had a hard time keeping my hands off you." Seb whispers in my ear while he pushes me up against the wall in our hotel room.

We had both been exhausted when we left Faith for the night, but somewhere Seb must have found his second wind because the moment we are through the door of our hotel room, his mouth crashes down on mine and he devours me. Wild and hungry, his restless hands are squeezing and kneading my flesh, sliding over my curves, while I have tangled my fingers in his hair, pulling and tugging. Any fatigue I may have felt is gone, replaced by a humming just under my skin, a need to taste and feel and fuck. Goosebumps rise all over my body and I can actually feel my nipples and my clit engorge with blood. I feel ravenous.

With my back against the wall, Seb rubs his hard body against mine, scraping over my sensitive nipples and against my pussy. So instantly hot.

"Your smell drives me crazy and I don't want to control myself." He growls in my neck.

"Don't. Just let go. Let go of everything. Give it to me, I can take everything you've got."

"Wrap your legs around me, I only have one arm to carry you and I'm not putting you down."

Doing as he asks, my arms are tight around his neck and my legs around his waist. With one big hand on my ass, he walks me right into the large hotel bathroom, where he lets me slide to the floor and turns me to face the mirror behind the counter. Putting his chin on my shoulder and sliding his hands under my shirt, he locks his eyes with mine.

"Gonna undress you, right here. Gonna touch and taste you and then I'm gonna fuck you. And you're gonna watch me do it."

Ohmygod... I almost go down, my knees buckling. I arch back, curving my ass against his hot, hard length and leaning my head back on his shoulder. I've never been so turned on. So fucking horny I could come on the spot. My mouth falls open against the full body sensations that have me whimper like an animal. I don't lose eye contact with him in the mirror. His eyes are mesmerizing, glowing with dark intent. His lips are wet and slightly opened, his breath panting out in bursts, beside my ear. His hands... Fuck me, his big rough, working hands are stroking my skin into a frenzied heat. When they slip under the edge of my bra and find my nipples, I can't stop the full-bodied *'Yessss'* that hisses from my mouth. Impatient now, Seb whips my shirt over my head and uses one hand to release the catch on my bra in the back, the other holding it to keep my breasts covered in view of the mirror. Christ, the view of his big tattooed arm crossing my chest, covering my breasts is beautiful.

"You see what I see, Spot? You and me. We are amazing together."

"Mmmmmm." Is my intelligent contribution, all cognition concentrating on more important things, like the hand that was just at my back, slowly sliding to the front of my pants and undoing the button and zipper. He works my pants down while still holding my breasts covered.

"Love the anticipation of your fucking luscious breasts, babe. Gonna love even more, watching them bounce when I pound into you."

The contrast of the private, gentle and sweet Seb, with this raw, dirty and rough-edged Seb is the biggest turn-on.

Slowly, he lets my bra fall away and without his arm to hold them in place, my gravity challenged breasts swing free. I go to cover them with my hands, feeling a little exposed under his intense glare via the mirror, but he stops me and holds my hands down on the counter.

"Don't. Most glorious sight I've seen."

Looking up, I see myself, but on fire. My hair is messed up, my eyes shine, my face and chest are flushed and when he pulls me up straight in his arms, I can see a ripe body. A soft, eager, and aroused, ripe body. The look in Seb's eyes tells me he believes me beautiful. So I am. His eyes are the only ones that matter.

"You. Are. Breath-taking." He says, and I smile.

"Bend over."

Without hesitation or any remaining self-conscious feelings, I stretch my arms over the counter, spread my legs and grant him full access. I wasn't expecting the long lazy lick, from my clit all the way up my crack. But I don't budge, I allow myself to feel, just to concentrate on the sensations he is creating. His hands on the globes of my ass, he plays me with his tongue from front to back, making me tremble on my legs. One long hard pull on the super center of nerves between my legs, and I am on the verge of coming.

"Not yet." He cautions, pulling away and lining his large

cock up with my opening. He grabs the base and plays with the head of his dick through my folds, lubricating around my pussy.

"Look at me."

I lift my head slightly and find him standing behind me in all his colorful glory, hands on my hips. Then he slams home, making me lose my breath.

"Unnhhh…"

At a furious pace, Seb fucks me so hard, the sweat is dripping off his body on my back. I barely have time to take a breath, before the mother of orgasms has my eyes rolling to the back of my head. But Seb squeezes my neck and bites out; "Watch."

I watch. I watch as the intensity slides out of his eyes, replaced with a look of wonder. I watch as his clenched jaw suddenly falls open in utter submission. And I watch when his lips form *"Love you",* just before his seed fills me in hot spurts.

CHAPTER TWENTY-NINE

By Friday we had edged on to the subject of Colorado several times and Faith seemed to feel more at ease, talking about herself in Cedar Tree; what she would do, where she would stay when she visits. Still all in distant terms, but enough to encourage Seb to broach the possibility of Faith coming with us to find a home close by. All four of us; Faith, Janet, Seb and I are bundled up against the cold, sitting at a picnic table in the garden just after breakfast on Saturday enjoying the morning sun, when he brings it up.

"But what about my garden? Who will take care of it?"

Anticipating that concern, Janet has come up with a plan. "Well, you know Mr. Hoyden, the gardener? He says he will be happy to look after your garden, if it's alright with you that he sometimes brings some of the vegetables home for his family. What do you think? All the plants are gone for the winter anyway, and he will make sure new plants will come in for the spring."

When Faith still looks a little subdued, I add; "And remember I have that new garden that needs to be started in the spring in Cedar Tree. I could really use your help."

With the promise of a new garden to put in, she moves on to her next concern. Leaving Janet behind. But when she finds out that Janet is coming with us for a while, she gets excited.

It takes us most of Saturday to pack all of Faith's things. Not always an easy task, especially since some of it has to be shipped separately; we can only carry so much with us on the plane. But with Janet's help and her brother's promise that she can come along to bring the extra boxes to the UPS store for shipping, she is fairly easily appeased

I still find her staring at me from time to time, trying to gauge me. Not quite sure how I fit into this little world of hers that has existed of only Seb and Janet for as long as she is able to remember. I myself am still confused half the time, talking to someone who looks like an adult for all intents and purposes, but can only think and reason like an eight-year old. It takes a little practice. But the love between Faith and her brother, is something to behold. The adoration in her face when she looks at Seb is enough to make me fall as hard for the sister as I did for the brother. I may not be the world's most nurturing figure, or all warm and cuddly like Emma or bubbly and cheerful like Janet, something people gravitate towards automatically, but I have a feeling Faith and I will find our way.

The rental loaded up with Seb and my small bags and several suitcases with as many of Faith and Janet's belongings as we can carry, we pull up to the curb at the airport. Seb's dropping us off with the luggage before quickly dropping off the rental and meeting us at the baggage check-in. While Seb and Janet get Faith into her wheelchair, I take off in search of a cart. Those fucking things are never around when you need them, but you trip over them any other time. A security guy directs me into the terminal where he says I can find more. I scan the large hall in front of me in search of the carts, when my eyes catch on something. Something that has the blood turn to ice in my veins. A movement, a gait, that seemed all too familiar, but when I turn back in the direction I think I saw it, I can't find it.

After a minute to scold myself for being an idiot, I finally spot a row of carts by the set of outside doors and head over to grab one for our bags.

The cart piled high, Seb deposits us right inside the doors and tells us to wait while he returns the car.

"I have to pee." Faith is squirming in her chair and is obviously uncomfortable.

"I'll take her," Janet says. " Are you going to be okay here with the stuff? I have to find a disabled washroom."

"Of course. Go. Better now than on the plane."

With those two off to find the washrooms, I wheel the cart over to a row of seats and sit down. I'm amusing myself by watching people go by, when I can feel the hair on my neck stand up and goosebumps rise on my skin and I stand up, feeling suddenly very vulnerable sitting. An uneasy tingle along my spine has me scanning the terminal from side to intently trying to spot what it is that has me on edge. Is someone watching? I am so focused on the faces and the bodies in front of me, I don't register the soft footsteps approaching me from behind. When a hand falls on my shoulder, the breath stalls in my throat.

"Hey you, what are you looking at?" A familiar rumble sounds from behind me and I whip around.

"Holy Christ, Seb! You scared the shit out of me!" Bending over, I lean my hands on my knees and try to catch my breath.

"Whoa, babe. What is that all about? You almost jumped out of your skin? Something happen?" Concern evident on his face, he pulls me upright by my arms.

Don't I feel like a fool now. So I'm not going to expand on that and decide to say nothing. "Nope, just tired and jumpy I guess. Eager to get home."

"Me too. I miss the diner. Miss cooking. Miss our bed."

He makes me smile, despite the residual shakes. "Our bed, huh? You didn't like the bed in the hotel?" I ask, eyebrow raised.

Wrapping his arms around me he comes close enough to touch my nose with his.

"Love the bed in the hotel, and the shower, and the tub and the counter… oh, and the wall." He chuckles. "But there is something about the bed at home that just feels… right."

Putting my hand on his chest, I push him back a little and

look in his eyes. "Are you sure you are okay with all of this?"

"Of course. It's amazing. Why? I don't seem happy?"

"It's just that... you never said anything one way or another about moving in on a more... permanent basis." Fuck. This is why I don't like emotional stuff. I suck at being careful or sensitive. I just need to know things, even when I am terrified I'm the one who will get hurt.

"Permanent? You want me around, permanently? Arlene, are you asking me what I think you're asking me?" Seb's face is a blank, I can't get any read of him, so I panic.

"No! No... of course not. I'm just- just..." My mouth slams shut when Seb bursts out laughing and I shove his chest hard, trying to get out of his arms. The bastard won't let me, though. He has me pinned tight.

"Let me go, you ass!"

"Nope. I'm just having some fun with you, Spot. Relax. Hey!" I give Arlene a little shake when she won't stop trying to wrestle out of my arms and force her to look me in the eye. "Listen to me. I couldn't imagine not being able to wrap myself around you every night. Not having your freckled face to wake up to every morning. There is nothing I want more than permanency with you, Arlene. And let's get this straight, even if you wanted me to leave, you'd have a hell of a fight on your hands, 'cause I wasn't planning on going anywhere."

I can feel the fight going out of her and her forehead comes to rest on my collarbone.

"We good?"

"Yeah... we're good." She says in a soft voice, nodding her head against my shoulder.

"Perfect. Now where have my sister and Janet gone off to?"

"Bathroom, they must have a hard time finding a suitable one for Faith. It's been a while."

"Let's go find them and get this load checked in." Pushing the cart with one hand and grabbing Arlene's with the other, we start walking.

We've checked three washrooms and still no sign of Janet and Faith. Arlene is starting to fidget at my side and I'd feel a whole lot better knowing where they are too.

"Let's walk back to the entrance." Arlene suggests. "Maybe we've just missed them."

Walking briskly, we make our way back to the seats where I found Arlene earlier. Nothing. Fuck.

"Try calling Janet's phone."

Berating myself for not thinking of something so simple earlier, I pull out my phone and dial her number, which goes straight to voicemail. I shake my head at Arlene who is watching me closely.

Just as I am about to walk over to an information desk to have a call put out over the sound system, I hear my name.

"Sebastian!"

From the other side of the check-in counters I can see Janet pushing a waving Faith in her chair, coming toward us and the tight feeling that had started building in my chest deflates like a balloon.

"Sorry it took a while." Janet apologizes when they reach us. "The only washroom large enough to allow me to help her was downstairs at the Arrivals level."

"No problem. We were just worried when we couldn't find you. Oh, and your phone is off." I point out.

"Turned it off already. I always forget on the plane." Janet explains.

"Okay. Well, let's get this show on the road."

Janet and Faith lead the way with Faith chattering on about the nice man from the elevator, while Arlene and I follow behind.

Forty-five minutes later, we are boarded and ready for take-off.

CHAPTER THIRTY

"Can we go out in the snow?"

It's been a little over a week since we've been back from Montana and it's been snowing off and on for a few days. Faith and Janet are getting settled in at Gus and Emma's in the guest house, getting spoiled rotten by Emma of course. I have to admit I was a little disappointed when Faith wanted to stay with Janet, but Arlene pointed out that with all of the changes in her life, Janet was the one constant right now and it made sense for Faith to want to hang on to that for a bit. I get it. But it still stings.

I look outside where the snow has just stopped falling, leaving behind a pristine white blanket Faith is eager to explore. With little else other than occasionally checking in on the construction progress at the diner, and trying out some new recipes, I keep myself busy finding ways to keep Faith occupied. Finding out she loves the snow had me run out and get the biggest, old-fashioned wooden sled I could find and rig it up with a heavy-duty stadium seat and a harness. It holds her in snug while I pull her through the snow, and I love hearing her laugh and having fun again. Next week she would enter the outpatient recreation program at the Vista Mesa in Cortez, a long-term care facility we hope she will like. The waiting period for a room for her will give us a chance to get her familiar with the facility, the people and the routine through this outpatient program. By the time a room becomes available, she will be quite comfortable there already and it won't be as much of a transition. In the meantime, Janet is here and doesn't appear to be in a hurry to go anywhere soon. I have a feeling there is something going on with her, but I don't know her well enough to dig.

"Okay, pumpkin. Let's get you bundled up and outside for some fresh air."

I watch Arlene as I slide myself in and out of her. Her beautiful green eyes are heavy-lidded and her body is arching off the bed every time my hard cock hits the right spot inside her. I'm on my knees and have pulled her up on my legs, using my hands to spread her wide. My favorite position. Watching every part of her come apart under me, being able to touch her as I can see myself fucking into her. Phenomenal. My balls pull tight against my body as I can feel the surge of release starting at the base of my spine. Not wanting to go over alone, I lick my thumb and rub in tight circles over her engorged clit, causing her to shiver at each pass. When I can't hold back anymore, I press down with my thumb and I can feel the walls of her pussy clamping down on my cock.

"Fuck baby, every time is better." I manage, lifting her up by the hips and pumping into her until my own orgasm fills her. I pull her up and roll on my back, Arlene on top with me still inside her. I love to feel the weight of her on me.

Sated and lazy, we stay like that for a while.

"Good morning to you too." She says finally, a smile in her

voice making me chuckle.

"Damn right it is. Only way to start a day off right."

"Mmmmm. But now I need a shower. I want to be at the diner for ten, that's when the new bathroom fixtures are being delivered and I want to make sure they sent the right ones this time, before the driver takes off again."

Arlene has been supervising the construction and renovations at the diner in quite the 'hands-on' manner. Taking on tasks like accepting and checking deliveries to the site, helping out with the scheduling and making sure the guys are all stocked with food and drink, she doesn't want anything to stand in the way of the diner opening as soon as possible. Clint has been quite good-natured about her involvement and after their initial run-in, those two actually get along quite well now.

She lifts up and rests her chin on her hands on my chest. "What are your plans for the day?"

"I need to drive into Durango. There are a few kitchen supply places I want to check out and I can make a stop at the Home Depot to pick up those tiles we ordered for the backsplash behind the counter. With all the structural work almost done and Clint starting on the re-finish of the dining and bathrooms, next on his list will be the kitchen. I want to make sure we know what we want and can get it on time, so there is no lag in the schedule. But I might be a little late to pick up Faith, can I call you?"

"Of course, why don't you just let me pick her up. That way you don't have to rush at all. Oh and by the way, you know Home Depot delivers, right?"

"Yes I do, wise-ass. But why pay extra for delivery when I'm going to be in Durango anyway? I'll drop Faith off at Vista Mesa and drive right through. Anything you need?"

"Nope. I have all I need right here." She says as she snuggles in to my chest again.

"Thought you were having a shower, Spot?" I chuckle into her hair.

"Shut up, Cookie. You talk too much."

I lie back and laugh harder than I have in a very long time. Life is fucking good. Finally.

"Ems!"

"Yo, girlfriend! How's it hangin'?" Emma goofs when I pop in on her on my way to the diner.

Gus is sitting at the counter, just shaking his head at our antics.

"Morning, big guy. How does it feel to live in something other than a doll house?"

"Much better now that the last of the hammering and drilling is done." He says.

My eyes flick to Emma, and I burst out laughing when I see her pout at him.

"Jesus, you two. You feed off each other, I swear." One more shake of the head and Gus dives back into whatever computer file he's working on, doing his best to ignore our cackling.

The expansions on their house finally done, Emma has been busy trying to clean the layers of dust that have settled on everything - only to reappear a day after.

"So. You wanna come see some shiny new bathroom fixtures?" I ask Emma who nods eagerly.

"Anything to escape the dust." She says.

"Not so sure coming with me to a full on construction site is gonna help you do that, sweet cheeks." I point out.

"Okay. Anything to escape *my* dust. That better?"

"Whatever you say. Well, get dressed already. It's fucking freezing outside and I gotta get there before the driver takes off again."

"Sergeant-Major, Sir!" Emma toddles off with a jaunty salute to get her coat. Brat.

We pull in just as the delivery truck is trying to leave. Oh hell no. I turn the wheel of my old F-150 and park it right across the entrance to the diner's parking lot.

"What the hell are you doing, Arlene?" Emma demands.

"The bastard is about to drive off again. Last time he did, he left us with the wrong supplies. I'm not letting him go until I've checked the delivery. You stay put."

I get out and walk over to the delivery truck, where the driver is already dropping down from the cab, swearing up a storm.

"Are you nuts, lady? I got a schedule to keep. What the heck do you think you're doing, blocking like that?"

I walk up to him, crowding in his space. "Listen here. Last time you delivered, you high-tailed it out of here as well. I didn't even have a chance to sign off on it. Not that I would've; it was the wrong stuff! If you think I'm gonna let you go, without checking and signing off on those fixtures, you've got another thing coming!"

The driver's face is turning an unhealthy shade of red. "I don't have time for this. Get outta my way."

I'm about to give him a crushed scrotum for Christmas as he grabs my arms to manhandle me out of the way, when someone pulls him off me and slams his back into the side of the truck.

"Tell me you weren't putting your hands on the lady now, were you?" Clint has to bend his big frame down to get in the face of the driver, who visibly shrinks at the sight of the burly contractor and simply shakes his head. "Good thing too. Why don't you back the truck right up and come on in, so she can check the delivery first. The way it's supposed to be done."

Stepping back, Clint lets the guy climb back in the truck and back up. When he turns to me and gives me a wink, I can't resist.

"I had him, you know." I put my fists in my sides for emphasis, but it only makes Clint smile bigger.

"Oh yeah?" He says, eyebrows raised.

"Would've served him crushed nuts for Christmas." I say, turning around to get my truck parked, leaving a deep booming laugh from Clint behind me.

"Shut up." I say to Emma, who is chuckling beside me, which only serves to make her laugh harder.

"Sorry." She says, not sorry at all.

The next ten minutes are spent opening and looking over every one of the boxes that were dropped off. Finding all but one of them correct. One had a wrong model faucet, which oddly pleased me. I walked over to the driver and waved it under his nose. "See? Still not right. This is the wrong one, I'll sign off on the rest but not this. And I'm gonna need it within twenty-four hours."

"Call the office," is all he'll say. So I make him wait while I contact the supplier, taking great pleasure in pointing out their incompetency. They promise to send someone else out by the end of day. Just in time I remember having to pick up Faith, so I give them my home address, telling them to drop it off there after five.

With a great flourish I sign off on the correct boxes and hand the papers to the driver, who takes off, swearing all the way.

"You are one heck of a lady." Clint says, leaning against the wall to the new kitchen with a big smile on his face. "Too bad someone got in there before me." And with a wink he turns around and walks away.

"Wow." From Emma, who sidles up beside me and is staring at where Clint disappeared.

"No shit, wow." I agree, a little baffled, especially given the initial treatment I got when we first met. Nice man he turned out to be. Fine-looking big man too, and I have to admit, feels good to be looked at that way again, but the only man I want is already mine.

Emma sticks her finger in her mouth and pushes it to my arm. "Psshhhhh, hawt!" She giggles.

I whack her hand away and wipe the spit off my arm. "You're weird and oh gross, woman!"

CHAPTER THIRTY-ONE

It's not easy, getting Faith up in the cab of my truck, but with her hanging on to the door opening and me trying to lift her by the legs so I can slide her butt on the seat, we are both giggling. That, of course, is not helping matters. We finally manage and I am relieved that getting out will be a shitload easier, when she can just slide out.

Faith doesn't seem at all fazed that I came to pick her up and is quickly telling me all about her activities of the day and the new friends she is making.

"...and you know what? They will even let us make a garden in the spring. Kim told us we could." She says, her contagious smile beaming up at me.

Kim is the therapist who is working with the group that Faith is assigned to. She was quickly taken with Kim, who seems to have the patience of a saint. Me? I'd be hanging off the chandelier by now! Faith is one of only two outpatients in the group and the rest live at Vista Mesa full time. They range anywhere from eighteen to eighty-three, but no one seems to care about the differences in age. Nor do they seem to notice each other's limitations, whether physical, developmental or both.

"That's great, sweetie." I say, glad for the simple things we can do to make her life a happy one. Makes you take a really hard look at your own perceived crosses to bear. Sobering, really. Between Faith and Seb, they are teaching me a lot about happiness. About finding it. Everywhere. And very little is needed, I'm discovering. Once you open yourself to the possibility, it seems to be there for the taking.

Once home, and very grateful for the temporary ramp Seb put up last week, I get Faith inside and ask her what she would like to do.

"Can we bake something?"

"Sure, honey. What were you thinking?" I mentally go through my the fridge and pantry, knowing that Seb probably has kept it well-stocked. I've hardly been in my own kitchen in the last few weeks since Seb has been with me. I certainly can't compete with his cooking skills, but I'm sure I can whip up something to bake with Faith.

"Can we make pancakes for dinner?"

"Pancakes for dinner? Isn't that a breakfast food?" I tease her.

"Well, someone told me that today was 'breakfast for dinner' day at the Vista, and that made me think of pancakes, 'cause they are my favorites."

"Let me see what we have, but I'm sure we can fix up some 'breakfast for dinner' for us. Maybe we'll make an omelet and some bacon too? For your brother, when he gets back?"

"Mmmm'kay."

"First I have to clean up a bit. I'm still dusty and dirty from working at the diner. Do you want to watch a show, while I have a quick shower?"

I have her installed in front of some Full House re-runs she seems to love and take my tired ass up the stairs, pulling clothes off as I go. I feel gross, having spent the day hauling stuff back and forth, yanking open boxes and digging through them, helping sand down some patchwork on the walls. There is an entire mold of the inside of my nose forming in my nostrils. Yuck.

Checking at the top of the stairs one last time while the shower is heating up, I can hear her laughing along with the canned laughter from the show. Quickly I hop under the hot stream and let the water pound the fatigue from my muscles and the dirt from my hair and skin.

Lots cleaner and feeling much better, I dry off as I walk into the bedroom and pull some underwear and sweats on. Comfort clothing and warm. It's chilly out.

I stop at the top of the stairs to listen, but can't hear a thing.

"Faith?"

No answer. I hear nothing, even the television is quiet. The hair on my skin stands on end as I make my way down the stairs.

It's been a frustrating day, going in and out of a number of kitchen supply stores, very few of which have the type of industrial-sized equipment that I am in need of. Almost resigned to the idea of having to drive all the way to Grand Junction to find the right appliances, or concede and buy everything online, I hit the final store on my list. Bingo. This place seems to have an entire warehouse in the back with restaurant supplies.

It's almost four and even though Arlene had said she was going to pick up Faith, I still don't want to be home too late, I want to spend some time with her over dinner, before I return her to Janet.

When I walk in, a young man walks up.

"Hi, is there anything I can help you with, or would you prefer looking around."

Normally I'd prefer to do things on my own, but given the time, I chose to go for help. "Sure. I am looking to outfit a new kitchen for a diner. Two restaurant sized grills, one large range, two convection ovens, refrigeration, stainless steel work tables; the lot."

"Wow. New venture?" The kid asks, looking interested.

"No, fire burned out the kitchen. It's an existing diner, going through some renovations."

"Sorry to hear that. I'm sure we can help you. Come on back."

An hour later, Eric, the helpful sales guy who turns out to be a new graduate from the Culinary Institute, has me set up with just about everything we need, including his phone number, should we want an extra hand in the kitchen. He is eager to garner some experience, and who knows, we might be able to find some use for him. I tell him thanks and that I'll take his information to my boss. What I don't tell him is that I am shacked up with said boss. He doesn't need to know.

After picking up the tiles at Home Depot, I am halfway home when my phone vibrates in my pocket.

"Hello?"

"Where are you?"

"Joe? What's up. I'm on my way home from Durango. Why?"

"Arlene with you?" Joe wants to know, inserting a small needle of fear under my skin.

"She should be home with Faith. She was going to pick her up in Cortez. Why, Joe? What the fuck is going on?"

"Just found out Geoffrey Williams has been out for over a week and as of yesterday missed his scheduled parole meeting."

"What the fuck? I thought you guys were keeping tabs on him? How come we didn't know he was out?"

"FUBAR, Seb. Feds shut down every trace GFI had running, pending the outcome of their investigation of their own fuck up with Will Flemming. Everything they connected to that case was confiscated, from GFI and from my office. We dropped the ball, big time, never followed up and I'm thinking neither did GFI, otherwise we would've found out. I gotta try and get a hold of Gus, see if he has anyone close. He is down in Grand Junction with Emma."

"Jesus! Yes, I know, they were on their way out this morning when I picked Faith up. I gotta go. I have to call Arlene."

Joe's next words have the fear spreading like wildfire through my veins.

"No answer. I already tried, buddy. I'm on my way now."

Keeping half an eye on the road, I hang up and immediately start dialing the house phone. No answer. When it goes to voicemail I leave a brief message.

"Babe, you get this, give me a call when you can, right away. Love you."

I'm hoping if something has happened and she can hear me, she'll know I'm coming, but I don't want to alert anyone else who might be there. I have the same result calling her cell phone and leave her a similar message. The possibilities of where she could be run through my head. She would have been long home by now after picking up Faith. Did she even make it home? Were they out somewhere? I'm trying to focus on all possibilities that don't involve a worst-case scenario, but none of them seem plausible.

The thought of that bastard getting his hands on her again has me seeing red. I'm going to rip him apart. But when the realization that Faith might be in danger as well, has the contents of my stomach boiling up. I pull off on the shoulder and just manage to wrench open the door and hang out before I throw up the entire contents of my stomach. Not taking any time to clean up, I simply yank the door shut, wipe my mouth on my sleeve and take off driving again, fuelled by fear and adrenaline, praying that my girls are okay.

Because I don't think I could survive if they aren't.

CHAPTER THIRTY-TWO

I am holding my breath as I carefully walk down the stairs. Something is not right. It's almost pitch-black downstairs and I am sure I left the light in the hallway on. The only visible light is coming from outside.

"Faith?" I call out tentatively, my hand sliding along the wall as I take another step down. No response.

Automatically my hand goes for my pocket in search of my phone, but I remember leaving it on the kitchen counter before heading upstairs to shower.

As I take the last step down I almost jump out of my skin when I hear the house phone ring. I immediately turn in its direction, but before I can even move one step, a hand clamps on my mouth from behind. I'm not fast enough to avoid being pulled back against a hard body. A familiar fear settles over me when I recognize the smell of cigar smoke. And when I hear his voice in my ear, I realize I'm in big trouble.

"Waited for this moment a long time, sweetheart." He says, sarcasm dripping from his voice. "Better not answer that call. Wouldn't want to have anyone interrupt our little reunion."

His hand still over my mouth, and his other arm holding me securely around my waist, I can't do anything but shuffle where he directs me. First I need to know where Faith is.

As my ex-husband moves me over to the windows, he instructs me to pull the drapes. Once all of the windows are covered, he flips on a light beside the couch and shoves me down on it. That's when I spot Faith tied down in her wheelchair with duct tape covering her mouth. Her eyes are wide with fear.

"Let her go, Geoffrey. You have me, do what you want but let the girl go." Looking at the man who already took so much from me now holding a gun pointed at me, I barely recognize him. Sure, the face is the same, but he has bulked up quite a bit while in prison. I do recognize the evil sneer on his face. It's one he liked to use on me to make me beg to be left alone. Then he slowly shakes his head 'no'.

"She's a fine piece of pussy, Arlene. Gonna take care of her after I'm done with you. At least that one won't fight back." He has to laugh at his own joke. Sick bastard.

"Geoff. Please let her go, she has the understanding of a child, don't do this." I try, but my attempt only earns me a backhand across my face.

"Enough of the whining, you bitch! I'm-"

Just then, the phone rings again. Instinctively I try to get up, but Geoffrey yanks me back by the hair, putting the gun right against my temple. I can hear Faith whimpering. I lock my eyes with hers and try to reassure her with a little wink. But then I hear Seb's voice leaving a message.

"Babe, you get this, give me a call when you can, right away. Love you."

Hope floods through me as I consider the implications. He knows - I can hear it in his voice, and if he knows something is up, he would be calling in the troops. My mind starts to imagine how close to home he might be. Geoffrey doesn't give me an opportunity to consider long, though. Enraged by the message, he pulls my head back by the hair he still has a firm grip on and brings his face so close I can smell the remnants of cigar and alcohol coming off his skin and rancid breath.

"You whore! You fucking him? Huh? Tell me, bitch!"

I try to keep my mouth shut while he shakes me by the head like a rag doll. I can feel clumps of hair pulling free of my scalp.

"You put me in that hell hole to rot and now you're fucking him?"

Not able to hold back anymore, I let loose. "You put me in the hospital, you miserable bastard! You killed my baby... almost killed me! What did you expect? A fucking medal?"

"I told you I was coming back, didn't I? I will always come for you. You belong to me!"

"I belong to *no one*!!"

All my rage and pain collected over years seems to surge through me at this moment and all I can see is blood. His blood. I don't even think, I simply rip my hair from between his fingers and slam my forehead into his face as hard as I can.

Geoffrey's hands fly up to his face, where his nose is pouring down blood. In the next instant I have my hands fisted together and I haul out as hard as I can between his legs. His knees buckle and with another swipe of my hands, I have the gun flying out of his hand. His turn to whimper.

I don't waste any time to scramble after the gun before he gets his wits about him. Ducking under the coffee table where I saw it disappear, I feel around for it. The tips of my fingers touch the cold steel and as I'm closing my hand around it, a firm yank on my legs almost pulls me out from under the table. Fuck.

Pulling into our street I can see a hand-full of patrol cars half-way up the road to Arlene's house, blocking the road. I stop at the roadblock and see Joe running up to my truck.

"No further, Seb. Looks like he's in the house and I don't want to take any chances."

Sliding out of the truck, I push past him to head up the road to my girls, but Joe pulls me back.

"Buddy, you go marching up, you might as well sign their death warrant." That stops me in my tracks. I lean over, hands on my knees and try to calm down my breathing and my thoughts. Joe's hand never leaves my back.

"We're gonna approach with caution, but you have to stay here."

I am up like a flash and in Joe's face. "Like fuck! You're gonna have to shoot me to keep me behind." I growl, poised for a fight and at this point I don't give a flying fuck who gets hurt in the process. No one stands between me and my woman, or my sister. Like hell.

"I can't have you running off half-cocked, man. I have to be able to trust you stay behind me and listen. You got me?"

"Yeah, yeah. I've got ya, now let's fucking get going."

With one last pointed glare at me, Joe turns around and starts heading into the front yard of the closest house. I stick close behind as we make our way as close to the houses as we can, to avoid being spotted from Arlene's place. Joe in front, and a deputy behind me, we don't come in with a lot of gun-power. We don't need it, I would take the guy apart by hand if need be.

When we reach the corner of Arlene's house, I notice that other than Arlene's truck there are no other vehicles on this side. I poke Joe in the back.

"If he's in there, where's his car?"

"My guess? Planning for a quiet getaway after doing what he came here to do." Concern is evident on his face as it sinks in that killing must have been all that had been on Geoffrey's mind.

"We'll try around the back, see if anything is open there for easy access."

We are just making our way into the backyard when two loud shots ring out and my stomach drops. But then I take off, ignoring Joe's shouts behind me, with one thought on my mind. Getting inside.

From the back deck, I find the sliding door unlocked and step into the kitchen, Joe right behind me.

Sitting on the floor in the middle of the kitchen is Arlene, rocking Faith in her lap. For a second I fear the worst until I hear the little whimpers coming from her. Dropping down on the floor I pull both of them between my legs and fold myself around them, while Joe continues further into the house.

"You hurt?" My voice cracks when I whisper the words in Arlene's ear.

"We're good. Better now." She says, holding on to my sister and leaning back in my arms.

Furiously scrambling to get a good grip on the gun as I'm being pulled out from under the table, I manage a solid kick that meets resistance. Instantly the grip on my leg is released and I pull myself out on the other side of the table, gun in hand, shaking like mad. I look back and see him curled over on the floor. Good, must've hit his balls again. I hope they rot and fall off. The fanatic glint in his eyes as he glares at me is unmistakable. He intends to make me pay.

I back up into the kitchen, keeping the gun pointed in his direction. Once there I slide behind Faith's chair and whisper in her ear. "You just sit tight. I'm gonna get us out of here, okay? Going to untie you now, but you stay still. Can you do that?"

At the slight nod of Faith's head, I hold the gun with one hand while the other frantically works to get the tape off her wrists and the chair's armrests. I freeze when I hear movement in the other room, I can't see him anymore but my ears are attuned to every little sound. Frantically pulling at the strip of tape on the other side, I just manage to pull it off when Geoffrey appears in the door opening, a sneer on his face.

"You won't shoot me. You're too big a coward, Arlene. Always were, always will be."

Before he finishes the first step in the kitchen, I pull the trigger. I will never forget the look of surprise on his face when he is stopped in his tracks by the bullet entering his stomach. But he is still standing. Without stopping to think, I pull the trigger again. This one takes him down. I drop the gun, sink to my knees and sit on the floor when I feel Faith's hand stroke my hair. When I look up, she has her arms out and I pull her out of her chair into my arms, where she cries.

Next thing I know the safety of Seb's smell and body surround me. Exhausted, yet feeling stronger than ever, I lean back into the comfort of his body.

CHAPTER THIRTY-THREE

"Can we open presents now?"

Faith is perched in her chair by the Christmas tree, clapping her hands with all the excitement of finding presents littering the floor underneath the sparkly lights.

Even though it has only been a hand-full of days since our ordeal, Faith has recovered amazingly well. She wasn't hurt, we made sure of that when the EMT's arrived and we had her checked out, but we were sure the events of that night would scar her more emotionally than she already had been. Boy, did his sister surprise him. The past few days he had taken her to Vista Mesa for private counseling sessions, to ensure she had help processing the events.

But if anything, it seemed that Faith in all her innocence, had found a way to translate the experience into something positive. Sure, she still would have some negative reminders from time to time, but for the most part she had seen Arlene fight off her abuser and it had given her a sense of her own power. Not to mention that Arlene was the subject of Faith's adoration now. Even if Arlene herself wasn't quite sure what to do with it yet, Faith seemed to have awoken some dormant, nurturing part of her.

I'm just proud. Proud of my sister, for her naive resilience, but most of all I'm proud of my Spot. Fuck if she didn't slay her own damn demon. Something I would've done for her. Hell, something I wanted to do for her, but I have to put that aside when I look at the change it has brought about in her. Always a strong woman, now she doesn't seem to feel the need to prove it with her attitude all the time anymore. I even suspect she might be proud of herself. And this time, she didn't resist at all when some therapy was suggested for her to deal with the fact that she had killed a man.

"Let me just pour us something to drink, and then we'll start with one present, okay?" Arlene suggests. "Janet, Gus and Emma are coming over soon and we'll all open presents together."

As she tries to walk past me into the kitchen, still wearing the sweats she pulled on this morning after rolling out of bed all rumpled and sexy after a very merry Christmas wake-up session, I grab her and pull her on my lap.

"Coffee won't get itself, you know." She feels the need to point out. My smartass.

"Mmmmm, but you taste better than any caffeine this early in the morning." I mumble against her lips.

"Guy-ys. No more kissing."

Both of us turn to Faith, who rolls her eyes right on cue, making us chuckle.

"Fine." I say, "but you better get used to it."

"Whatever." Comes out of my sweet little sister's mouth stunning me and sending Arlene into fits of laughter.

Grabbing her around the waist before she gets up off my lap, I growl. "Wonder where she got that from, Spot?"

Arlene is still laughing when she pushes off and heads into the kitchen. I look at Faith who sits there with a triumphant little smile on her lips. Great. Two women with attitude.

The first present we pull out from under the tree is for Faith. She stayed over last night and has been waiting so patiently for this moment. She attacks the paper with fervor and squeals in delight when she sees the Easy Bake Oven we have bought her. She loves hanging in the kitchen with me and always wants to help. After motioning us each over for hugs and kisses, Faith points at a gift for Arlene I was going to give to her when alone, but I guess now is as good a time as any.

"Wait." I tell her, getting up to sit between my girls on the floor. "Okay, you can give it to her now." I tell Faith, who hands the package over to Arlene beaming ear to ear, knowing full well what it is.

"You guys keeping secrets from me?" Arlene teases as she slides her fingers between the ends of the wrapping. Faith nods enthusiastically and I am keeping my fingers crossed she will keep it together long enough. Slowly wrapping back the paper, Arlene's eyebrows rise when she sees the box on her lap.

"Kellogg's Corn Flakes, huh? Just what I always wanted."

"Noooo, silly. Open it up more." Faith blurts out, having been the one to wrap this thing up.

Carefully Arlene slips open the taped up ends of the cereal box and pulls out a wad of crumpled up newspapers, 'causing Faith to burst out giggling.

Digging deeper, Arlene pulls out a rolled up piece of paper. Faith's contribution. When she unrolls the picture with Faith's favorite subject, but this time with a slight variety, I can see the tears forming in her eyes. I have to swallow myself, remember almost bawling like a pussy yesterday when Faith showed me the picture she had drawn of the familiar little girl holding hands with the man beside her. This time she had added a woman with short blond hair holding on to her other hand, and I almost lost it right there.

"It's beautiful, honey. So beautiful." Arlene smiles at Faith through her tears.

"There's more!"

"More?"

Nerves are twisting in my stomach when I see Arlene's hand disappear into the Kellogg's box once more. Her eyes grow as big as saucers when her hand encounters the little box hidden in a far corner. Her eyes flick to mine, instantly recognizing the moment. So I turn on my knees to face her.

"Pull the box out, babe. I've got something to ask you."

One hand still in the cereal box, the other clamped over her mouth, Arlene shakes her head, making me laugh. Not changed that much after all.

"My love... are you going to pull out the box?"

At an agonizingly slow pace, her hand pulls free of the

cereal, holding a little velvet flipbox. I take it from her and flip it open so she can see inside.

"I had every intention of always being your rock. Always protecting you. Even before I loved you. I don't know what drove me here to Cedar Tree and to you, but I'm so grateful I wound up here. You didn't need a rock, though. Didn't need any protection. You were an immovable force to be reckoned with, right from the start. So fierce and strong, you were able to slay your own dragons. Didn't need me for that. And I found more joy in watching you stand up for yourself than I could have, had I slain those dragons for you."

I take the ring out of the box. A ring made of the prettiest river rock I could find, polished, buffed and fitted into a wide silver ring as unique, robust and strong as the woman whose finger it belongs on.

Grabbing her hand in mine, I hold out the ring in the other.

"Will you be my rock? Our rock?" I nod at Faith. "Will you let me hold on to you so you don't wash away? Marry me?"

The slightest nod of her head and I have the ring on her finger. Then she bursts out laughing. Okay. So not the response I was hoping for.

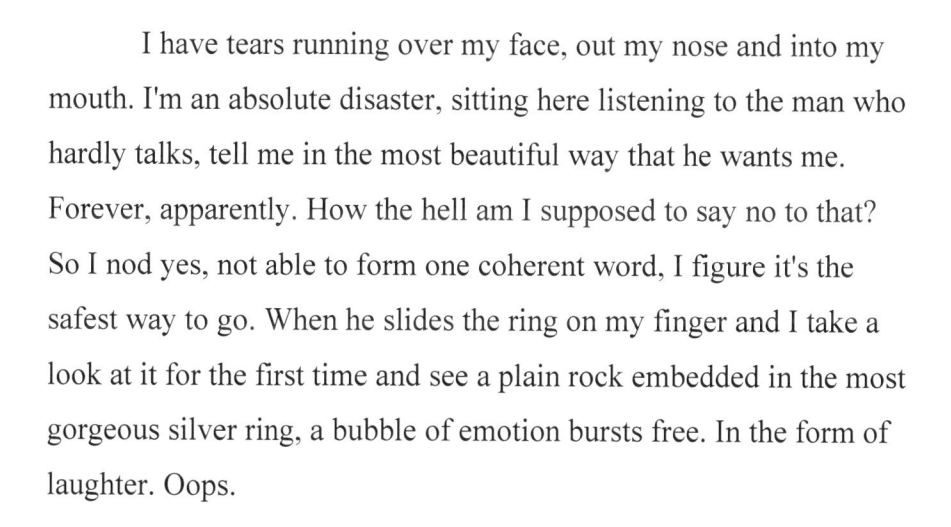

I have tears running over my face, out my nose and into my mouth. I'm an absolute disaster, sitting here listening to the man who hardly talks, tell me in the most beautiful way that he wants me. Forever, apparently. How the hell am I supposed to say no to that? So I nod yes, not able to form one coherent word, I figure it's the safest way to go. When he slides the ring on my finger and I take a look at it for the first time and see a plain rock embedded in the most gorgeous silver ring, a bubble of emotion bursts free. In the form of laughter. Oops.

"Seb, honey." I put my hands on his face and lean in close. "This is perfect. So perfectly me, it's scary you know me so well. I never have and never will be a diamonds and pearls kinda girl, but this…" I stick my hand out displaying my gorgeous ring prominently. "This is uniquely me."

The slight worry on Seb's face disappears and I wrap my arms around his neck and sink onto his lap on the floor. "Love you so much." I whisper in his neck.

"Ditto, Spot. Always."

"They're here!!" Faith's loud announcement cuts through our little moment, bringing back the reality of the day. Right. Christmas and I'm still in my sweats. Tough, they'll have to deal.

"I have something for you too, but I'll give it to you later."

I have to laugh at the wiggling of Seb's eyebrows. One-track mind.

The house fills with the smell of fresh baked goods, courtesy of Emma, of course, coffee and the sounds of laughter. Congratulations are flying when Emma sees the 'rock' on my finger and although Gus sends Seb questioning looks, my Ems seems to get the significance of the ring right away.

We exchange gifts, mostly for Faith's sake and have a relaxing day. I even have a chance to grab a shower and change at some point, although my selection in clothes is not much better; yoga pants and sweater. One of the things I love so much about Emma and Gus is that they don't fuss either. Emma told me she was ready to come over in her PJ's but Gus made her put some pants on. Pants for Emma simply means pulling on another pair of sweats or yoga pants.

Seb and Emma disappear into the kitchen and the four of us remaining decide to go for a walk while they do their cooking.

"Happy?" Gus wants to know, as we follow Janet pushing Faith's chair along the trails behind our house.

Sliding my arm in his, I put my head on his shoulder.

"Yeah. Never thought it was possible, but yes. Pretty damn blessed, big guy." I tell him.

Gus clears his throat a few times, before launching in. "Look. I owe you a big apology. I dropped the ball on your ex. Never should've happened. I...-"

I pull him around by his arm, stopping him mid-stride.

"Stop right there, Gus. I don't want to hear it. I don't want to hear your or Joe's apologies about what happened."

When he tries to speak up again, I cut him off. "No. I'm serious, my friend. We, Faith and I, are fine. In fact, we are better than fine. In some sick way I needed to face him; needed the opportunity to assert myself. Do you know I haven't had a single nightmare since that night? Not one. Where I had dreams almost nightly before. I never thought I would be able to kill someone,

Gus."

"Nor should you have had to, if only…" He tries again.

"Stop it and hear me out. I don't regret it for one moment. Get that through your thick skull. Not one second do I have any feelings of regret or remorse for stopping that son of a bitch getting to Faith or to me. You understand? I would pull the trigger again, every time. No hesitation. Sadness, yes. I feel sad it had to come to that, but mostly for the years I've spent loving that man first and fearing him after. There would have been no stopping him, I see that now. And the only person who could was me. And I did. I did, Gus - I stood up for myself and my family and I'm still standing. Don't beat yourself up over stuff you had nor have any control over. Look at me and just be happy for me. I'm better for what happened. I promise."

"God, you are one hell of a woman, Arlene." His voice is gruff as he folds me against his big frame.

"If this is my Christmas present, I want Christmas every day." I tell Arlene as I smooth her hair back from her face so I can see my cock sliding between her lips.

A full day ending with full stomachs and a tired Faith who is whisked off home by Janet. Gus and Emma leave shortly after and leaving clean up for tomorrow, I don't delay pulling Arlene upstairs to our bedroom, where she immediately starts stripping down. I barely have my shirt off before she's on her knees in front of me, freeing my already rock hard erection from my pants.

"Fuck, babe. Your mouth on me is the best fucking feeling." I groan as she takes me deep and swallows on the tip.

With one hand at the base of my cock, her other hand disappears between her legs and I see her working her clit furiously as she sucks me off. Hell no.

"Enough, Spot" I growl as I try to pull back from her mouth. Pulling her up under her arms, I grab the hand that was just between her legs and suck her fingers in my mouth.

"Mmmmm so wet for me."

Pushing her down on the bed I crawl in between her legs and lick my way up her body. All the way from her pussy, over her mound and belly, circling and sucking her nipples before finally licking my way into her mouth. Her legs fall open to make room for me and my hands run from her breasts to the underside of her arms, pushing them up over her head and linking my fingers with hers. Our mouths fused, I slide myself into her slick passage, absorbing the moans from her lips. Ahhh yes. This.

"Best gift ever." I manage to get out, laying back with Arlene in my arms. Both still trying to catch our breath.

"Another gift in your bedside drawer." She mumbles from the vicinity of my armpit.

I fling out my arm and manage to pull open the drawer and pull out the envelope I feel in there.

"What's this?"

Arlene pops her head on her elbow as she rolls to her side. "Open it and find out," she says with a little smile.

Ripping open the envelope, I pull out a wad of papers, looking very official. All I can see is the name of the diner and not only Arlene's, but my name as well.

"Explain."

"Simple really. Before we went to pick up Faith, I had this part already planned. I was hoping you would share your life here with me in Cedar Tree, and I want to share mine with you."

"But this is your diner."

"Our diner as of December 23rd, when I put my signature on the papers, signing half of it over to you."

"I can't accept this." I don't know what to feel. Part of me is honored and excited, but another part nags at me, telling me I have to make my own way, take care of my own family.

"Yes you can. If you truly believed everything you told me this morning when you asked me to marry you, you would. You told me in so many words that you loved the strength in me, the independence. To me, that translates into equality. This is where it starts. You have put as much blood, sweat and tears in that diner since you've been here as I have. You have kept it running when I couldn't. We complement each other in every way. Evenly. We share a life together, we need to share our business. Equal partnership, all across the board."

Damn that woman, using my own sentiments against me.

I don't think long. There really is no choice. She is right. We are equals in every way and I won't let old hang ups and principles get in the way of our joint future. So I roll her over on her back and kiss her senseless.

"Does that mean I get to boss you around from time to time now too?" I tease her.

"Like you haven't from the start." She huffs.

EPILOGUE

"Cut some more parsley for me, will you?"

"Right away, Boss." She winks at me, pulling out another bunch from the fridge and setting it on the cutting board.

Today the doors officially open to the new and improved Arlene's Diner. We had a little tiff over the name, which Arlene wanted to change to include mine, but I put my foot down on that one. It's been a bit longer than anticipated, the renovations that is, but Clint and his crew have done a fantastic job getting the diner ready for business.

I walk out into the dining room, to find Faith finishing up folding napkins in pretty shapes.

"How are you doing, pumpkin?" I ask her, leaning down to give her a quick hug and kiss.

She smiles up at me the way she does these days, completely open and unguarded. Happy to be surrounded by friends and family.

Janet is getting ready to move on now that an early spot has opened up at Vista Mesa. The next two weeks we're going to transition Faith into her new home and Janet is going to stick around for that, after which she is off to a new job on the west coast. It's been two months since Faith and Janet came back to Cedar Tree with us and money will never repay what that woman has done for Faith and us.

"Ya'll ready for a stampede?" Beth yells out from the front door, snickering as she points her thumb over her shoulder, indicating the substantial crowd that has gathered in the parking lot. Holy shit.

"Ready!" Faith calls out, holding up a hand-full of folded napkins.

"Good to go!" Julie smiles as she waves her kitchen towel over her head.

"Yup!" This is Janet who is putting the last of the sugar containers and creamers on the tables.

I simply shrug my shoulders as I make my way back to the kitchen, where Arlene stands in the door opening.

"Open the fucking door already!" she yells out, making Faith gasp behind me.

"Arlene! A dollar for the swear jar!"

All of us burst out laughing as the first ones through the door Beth pulls open are Gus and Emma. Of course.

"That kid is gonna send me to the poor house." I say to no one in particular as I turn back into the kitchen to make sure everything is in order, before I go out and mingle. Give Beth and Julie a chance to seat them first.

"That kid is gonna make you watch your dirty mouth." Seb grumbles, slipping his arms around me from behind.

"Pffff, I thought you liked my dirty mouth."

"Mmmmm, yes, that's true. In fact, I have some fond memories of the cold storage. Want to go christen the new one?"

I turn in his arms and slap his shoulder. "Behave, will ya? We have a diner full of hungry people that need feeding."

"What about my needs?" Seb's low rumble has my knees going weak. Cheeky bastard knows exactly the effect he has on me too.

"Customers first, Seb." I try.

"Seriously?" Beth stands just outside the cold storage room with her arms crossed. "Now, you figure is a good time?"

Seb is snickering behind me as I scramble to straighten my clothes and curse the flush that I can feel creeping up my cheeks. That only gets worse when I see the group assembled in the kitchen. Emma and Gus, of course; Clint, Julie, Mrs. Evans and just coming in are Caleb with Katie in a wheelchair. I cover my face with my hands, mortified at the collective smiles and smirks.

Seb pulls me against his body. "Come on, Spot. We've got people to feed."

THE END

ABOUT THE AUTHOR

I love being creative. From an early age on I danced and sang, doodled, created, cooked, baked, quilted and crafted. My latests creative outlets have been influenced by my ever present love for reading. First it was blogging, then cover art and design and lastly writing.

I was born and raised in the Netherlands, had my children there and moved to Canada with two toddlers and eight suitcases, mostly filled with toys. I'm not a stranger to new beginnings. I thrive on them.

With my kids grown and out in the world, I am at the prime of my life - the "Ripe" part of the fruit!! The body might be a bit ramshackle, but the spirit is high and as adventurous as ever. Something you may see reflected here and there in some of my heroines.... none of who will likely be wilting flowers.

I craved reading about 'real' people, those who are perhaps less than perfect, but just as deserving of romance, hot monkey sex and some thrills and chills in their lives, but found too few of them. So I decided to write about them myself. Hope you enjoy them too!!

Freya

https://www.freyabarker.com
https://www.goodreads.com/FreyaBarker
https://www.facebook.com/FreyaBarkerWrites
https://tsu.co/FreyaB
https://twitter.com/freya_barker
or mailto:freyabarker.writes@gmail.com

Made in the USA
Charleston, SC
24 January 2015